EXPANDED EDITI
—ALTERNATIVE ENDINGS!
(ORIGINAL WAS TITLED: *FLUTE SONG*)

~ ~ ~ ~ ~ ~ ~ ~ ~ ~

WHAT THE REVIEWS SAY
ABOUT THE FIRST EDITION:

"It is a fascinating story...."
—The ROSWELL DAILY RECORD

"...well written and suspenseful...."
—SCIENCE FICTION CHRONICLE

"It would make a superb film....
deft plotting, rich characterisation, and
grace of style....a thoroughly satisfying read."
—S.T. Joshi, in NECROFILE

"However you feel about the controversy,
you are almost sure to enjoy Burleson's novel...."
—NEW MEXICO MAGAZINE

"Burleson has done a marvellous job of fictionalizing
the 'Roswell Incident' to the point that one must
wonder just how close to the truth he may be."
—AMERICA ONLINE WRITERS CLUB

"The chase is on in true thriller fashion."
—UFO MAGAZINE

The
Roswell
Crewman

DONALD R. BURLESON

BLACK MESA PRESS
Roswell, New Mexico
————— 1997 —————

REVISED/RETITLED/EXPANDED EDITION. Original edition was
published by Black Mesa Press (1996) under the title *Flute Song*. In
this current new edition, Chapter 28 has been added, the Comments
and Acknowledgments section has been partly rewritten, and slight
corrections have been made in the text.

Cover illustration © 1997 by Lisa Dusenberry. All rights reserved.
Cover design © 1997 by Gari Gold Kennedy. All rights reserved.

PUBLISHER'S NOTE: This is a work of fiction. All locales
mentioned in this novel, though geographically real, are used
fictitiously. All the human characters in this novel are fictional, and
any resemblance between them and real persons, living or dead, is
entirely coincidental.

Library of Congress Catalog Card Number: 97-93189
ISBN: 0-9649580-1-5

Printed in the USA by

MORRIS PUBLISHING

3212 East Highway 30 • Kearney, NE 68847 • 1-800-650-7888

Dedicated to

WALTER HAUT

and to the memory of

Major JESSE MARCEL

A tone
Of some world far from ours,
Where music and moonlight and feeling
Are one.

--Percy Bysshe Shelley,
"To Jane: 'The keen stars were twinkling'"

Comments and Acknowledgments

Something extraordinary happened in the New Mexico desert during the Fourth of July weekend of 1947. In the midst of a violent nocturnal thunderstorm, there was an explosion, and something fell out of the sky. What was it? Controversy has raged for years over that question. Whatever it was, it left about fifty acres of metallic and other debris scattered over a remote sheep ranch between Roswell and Corona, New Mexico.

The 509th Bomb Group at Roswell Army Air Field (later Walker Air Force Base) began sending military people out to cordon the area off and pick up the debris. Initially they allowed their information officer, Lieutenant Walter Haut, to issue a press release to the effect that the Army had recovered the wreckage of a flying saucer. Shortly afterward, however, Brigadier General Roger Ramey of Eighth Air Force Command claimed that the whole thing was a mistake--that the debris was from a weather balloon, and that Major Jesse Marcel, the 509th's chief intelligence officer and one of the first people to see the debris field, should have known his job well enough to recognize a weather balloon when he saw one.

With minor variations, the government has stuck to its weather balloon story to this day.

The evidence against this cover story, though, is overwhelming. The interested reader may consult Kevin D. Randle and Donald R. Schmitt's book *The Truth About the UFO Crash at Roswell* (New York: M. Evans and Company, 1994). Randle and Schmitt, perhaps to a greater extent than anyone else who has ever worked in the field of UFO research, have done their work diligently, dispassionately, and with balanced judgment. They have brought forth several hundred witnesses, people whose lives in one way or another were touched, changed, by those strange days in Roswell--people who in many cases have spoken up in defiance of threats to themselves and to their families.

7

I, for one, am convinced, on the basis of the evidence, (1) that an alien spacecraft indeed crashed in New Mexico in 1947, (2) that there was at least one survivor of the crash, and (3) that the United States Government, to conceal the true events, has conducted the most elaborate coverup in the history of humankind. (This coverup must be regarded as outrageous, considering the significance of what was covered up.)

Given these premises, this novel asks what might be happening in some people's lives now, half a century later, because of the Roswell incident.

New Mexico is well known and belovèd to me. I have taken slight license with topographical details in the area of the Three Rivers Petroglyph Site--where indeed one may see rock drawings that look quite a bit like flying disks--but otherwise the setting is essentially real.

In suggesting, fictively, that the survivor of the crash might have been kept hidden in the desert wastes north of Holloman Air Force Base proper, I am again taking fictional liberties. I should mention, on the other hand, that when I was stationed at Holloman in 1965, I was told that a boy in Alamogordo listening to practice bombing runs on shortwave had heard radio chatter suggesting that some sort of UFO had landed. I also heard persistent rumors that a flying saucer was concealed somewhere on the base. (This was many years before the motion pictures *Close Encounters of the Third Kind* and *Hangar 18* dealt with such notions.) I recall that the people who whispered these stories were obviously very frightened.

Still, my novel is a work of fiction. While I have tried to make the events of *Flute Song* not significantly inconsistent with the essential facts of the Roswell occurrence as I understand it, no character in the novel is intended to resemble any real person, living or dead; any imagined resemblance is coincidental.

It may be well to mention that I am not in general an aficionado of UFO lore. Frankly, I think that stories of abduction by aliens, for example, are not likely to have any basis in fact. I suspect that the vast majority of UFO reports are mistaken or untrue.

This in spite of the fact, ironically, that I have seen a UFO myself. When I was five years old my family was visiting my grandparents in Breckenridge, Texas during a holiday weekend--I am fairly certain that this was the Fourth of July, 1947--and I was to sleep outside on a cot on the porch, which was open to the air. I remember seeing a rather large circular object pass silently and very rapidly across the sky. Given the probable timing, this object may well have been related in some way to the Roswell incident. (I am indebted to John Price, director of the UFO Enigma Museum in Roswell, for pointing out to me, when I told him of

8

this childhood experience, that during the weekend in question there were reports of UFO sightings over large portions of Texas.) Let me be very clear: *Roswell really happened.*

I am grateful to Kevin Randle and Donald Schmitt for providing us all with the fruits of their painstaking research; thanks to them, we know a great deal more about what happened at Roswell, and have an enlarged sense of how much there is that, due to government secrecy, we are not allowed to know. Salutations to the Randle and Schmitt research team. (Others have done vital groundbreaking work as well. Stanton Friedman, in particular, is to be congratulated for first persuading Jesse Marcel Sr. to talk about the Roswell incident. Had this not happened, perhaps none of the other witnesses would ever have come forward.)

I am personally indebted to my friends Walter Haut, Glenn Dennis, and others on the staff at the International UFO Museum and Research Center in Roswell, New Mexico for the insights they have provided. Walter Haut, the information officer who released the original news story about retrieval of the fallen craft, has taken time to talk with my wife Mollie and me on a number of occasions, as has Glenn Dennis.

In July 1994 I asked Walter whether he thought it possible that some of the soldiers sent out to clean up the debris field might have smuggled away some of the debris. He said no, those soldiers must have been thoroughly searched. This is no doubt the case, but I have taken the liberty of fictionally differing with this view. I still have the feeling, sometimes, that pieces of debris (other than the ones under government control) exist somewhere: odd foil bookmarks in musty volumes squirreled away in attics, perhaps, or unaccountable scraps of metal lying forgotten in the rusty bottoms of toolboxes--or pieces of debris kept hidden by people who understand very well what they are and why they must be concealed. This may be the fiction writer's wishful thinking at work, and Walter may well be right in saying that there almost certainly is no "private hands" debris floating around. Nevertheless, I would dearly love to see and touch a piece of the stuff.

Profound thanks go to my friend and associate John Brower, without whose support the revised/retitled 50th-anniversary-of-the-crash edition would scarcely have been possible. Thanks for believing, John.

This novel is inspired by a sense that the long-concealed events occurring near Roswell, New Mexico in early July of 1947 were the most significant events in human history. The novel is dedicated, with heartfelt appreciation and thanks, to Walter Haut, and to the memory of the fall guy of the whole Roswell affair: Major Jesse Marcel.

Donald R. Burleson

1

Hap Trujillo and the Debris Field

The voices were vague distant ships of sound cutting through a gray fog of daydream.

"Poor old fellow, I can't help feeling sorry for him."

"Who?"

"Mr. Trujillo. Look at him down there, all alone. Just sits and hums to himself. Nobody ever comes to see him."

"No one but that Mr. Ross, from time to time."

"Yes, Alice, but I don't think Mr. Ross is family."

"Doesn't he have any family?"

"Oh, he says he has a daughter, but she almost never comes to visit. You know how the young people are today. Always busy with their own lives. I wonder if things, well, you know, aren't right between Mr. Trujillo and his daughter."

That was the trouble. Just because you kept to yourself and just sat quietly, people thought you couldn't hear, couldn't understand what they were saying about you. Well, no matter, he had more important things to think about. More important things to remember. Far more important things.

For yet another time--how many times now? a hundred? a thousand? countless times--he let his thoughts slip back to those strange days, half a century gone, when his life had changed forever. He was back there in New Mexico, a healthy young G.I., twenty years old, back at the 509th Bomb Group at Roswell Army Air Field in early July of 1947. . . .

# # # #

The duty sergeant was in the barracks door with a clipboard.

10

"All right, men, the colonel wants a special work detail pronto, so listen up. Sanchez. Parker. Civitelli. Lindquist. Kowalenski. Trujillo. Jackson. Williams. Rosenstein. McDavies. Keating. Get your field gear and fall in in front of the orderly room in ten minutes ready to move out. You'll be going upcountry with Sergeant Fletcher."

They had driven far out into the desert north-northwest of town in three army jeeps, Sergeant Fletcher driving in the lead, the others struggling to keep him in sight through the yellow dust that rose in dense clouds from the unpaved roads. Carlos "Hap" Trujillo was in the second jeep, in back with Jack Parker; Kevin McDavies was driving, with Jim Keating beside him in the front seat. The sun was blistering hot, a typical dry-hot desert day. The land they were driving through was desolate, remote, nearly unpeopled; only an occasional decrepit outbuilding or an ancient windmill broke the sameness of the terrain. Gradually the roads became more primitive and finally vanished altogether; for the last several miles, the vehicles bumped across open chaparral country, slashing through dense growths of sagebrush and yucca, finally coming out on a great desert plain.

"Well, here we are, wherever the hell *here* is," McDavies said, jumping out. The sergeant's vehicle had stopped in front of them, just short of a shallow arroyo. Behind, the other jeep was pulling up and stopping in the drifting dust. All around, there was nothing but sand and sage and turquoise sky.

Well, that wasn't quite true. There was something else.

Hap Trujillo was climbing out of the jeep, trying to make sense out of what he was seeing.

The plain in front of them, as far as his eye could follow it, was littered with--something.

Parker was nudging some of it with his feet, a little nervously, a little as if he thought it might be radioactive or something and he wasn't sure he wanted to touch it. "Hey, Hap, what do you suppose this crap is?"

"Damned if I know," Hap said, absently; for some reason, he couldn't take his eyes off the debris. It gave him a peculiar feeling. Most of it looked like little strips of tin foil, or maybe lead foil, a dull metallic gray in color. The wind stirred slightly, and the foil fluttered and shifted, like something weightless. There were also tan-colored, pencil-size strips of material like little I-beams; Hap picked one up, and it felt like balsa, or maybe one of those new plastics everyone was talking about after the war. And there were gossamer threads of something that looked like a very small-gauge, silky sort of wire.

What in the world had happened here?

11

But there was no more time for woolgathering; Sergeant Fletcher was taking charge of the situation.

"All right, men. This is going to be a cleanup operation. This here land is part of somebody's sheep ranch, and the colonel wants this mess picked up, every last scrap of it."

He motioned behind him, and everyone turned around. For the first time Hap Trujillo noticed now that several Army trucks had pulled up behind the jeeps, and that other jeeps and trucks were arriving from different directions across the desert. Also, out just about at the limits of sight, and in one direction even stretching over the horizon out of sight, a large ring of MP's had begun to encircle the debris field, at intervals of fifteen or twenty feet, standing at parade-rest, their backs to the debris. Christ, Hap had never seen so many military police in his life. And it looked as if there were a few civilians here and there too, government types with dark suits that looked uncomfortable in the July heat. But Sergeant Fletcher was still talking.

"Some troops from other bases will be joining us. We have heavy-duty wheelbarrows. Four-man squads will be formed, and you will be moving across the field, one wheelbarrow to a squad. You will make your first pass and pick up the biggest pieces. You will make your second pass and pick up smaller pieces, and so on, as long as it takes. The last two passes will be shoulder-to-shoulder on hands and knees. If we don't get it all today, gentlemen, the operation will resume tomorrow."

"Sergeant?" It was McDavies.

"What, soldier?"

"Uh, well, ah--what is this stuff?"

The sergeant spat into the sand. "Word from Eighth Air Force Command is, it's a weather balloon. Hit by lightning. Don't matter what it is. I have my orders, and you have yours." He motioned at the crowd of men approaching. "We're going to have a Captain Howard in charge here today, that's him coming up now. Like I said, you'll be working with some other troops, so let's show 'em what kind of stuff the 509th is made of. Ah-teyun-HUT!"

Snapping to attention, Hap Trujillo thought: a weather balloon. Yeah. Right.

Weather balloon, my ass.

They spent the day, a hot day under a relentless desert sun, picking up wheelbarrow-loads of the debris, talking quietly among themselves as they worked. The debris itself was astonishingly light, though obviously metallic; handling it gave Hap the creeps, somehow, especially that wispy foil that seemed to straighten itself back out even when you wadded a piece of it into a tight ball and tossed it into the wheelbarrow. Hap wished he could talk to McDavies or Keating or

12

Parker, but they were in other squads somewhere. The three other guys working with Hap were people he'd never seen before, and from the conversation, he gathered that no two of them were from the same base. Apparently one fellow was from Sandia, up in Albuquerque, and another was from the air base at Alamogordo, and he thought he heard somebody mention that the third man was from Los Alamos.

Hap wondered if it was the same in the other squads, no two men from the same place.

Helping the soldier from Los Alamos arrange some larger pieces of debris in the wheelbarrow, Hap said, "This shit don't look like no weather balloon to me, man. What do you think?"

The man eyed him a little sullenly and kept working. "Soldier ain't paid to think. Bossman says it's a weather balloon, it's a weather balloon."

Right, Hap thought, typical career man, all the right attitudes, hope you enjoy your thirty years, pal; now me, I'm getting out when my hitch is up. Later the man from Sandia Base nudged Hap on the arm. "Could'a been one of them experimental craft people talk about. You know, Russian, maybe. Or maybe one of our own, who knows?"

"Hell," the soldier from Alamogordo chimed in, "buddy of mine back at the base says he heard it's a goddamn flying saucer. This shit's only part of it, there's got to be a lot more somewhere. My buddy said they was tracking the thing on radar before it crashed."

"Oh, yeah?" the Los Alamos soldier cut in, frowning. "Well, maybe your buddy talks too much. Lots of people talk too much, you know that? Good way to get in a lot of trouble."

After that, nobody said very much. At one point when no one was looking, especially not the guy from Los Alamos, Hap deftly fingered a small piece of the foil into his boot, being sure to poke it down far enough so that nobody could see it.

Just one small piece, an irregular strip maybe on average an inch wide, five inches long. A worthless-looking piece of foil like something that would get thrown out with the trash any hour of any day in any kitchen. Yet here he was, going out of his way to steal it.

At the end of the day, most of the debris seemed to be cleared up, but anyone could see that there was still some remaining; the cleanup would surely be continuing the next day. For now, Captain Howard stood everyone in formation and ran an inspection, ordering each man to turn his pockets inside-out to show that they didn't contain any souvenirs of the debris. Hap, with the captain and a number of sergeants looking on, was afraid even to look at his boots, afraid someone could read his guilt on his face. But all they checked was pockets.

13

"Work remains to be done on this cleanup, soldiers," Captain Howard said, "but the troops will be rotated and you men will not be returning here tomorrow. Now listen carefully to this gentleman here."

Captain Howard moved back, and one of the nondescript civilians that Hap had noticed before stepped up in front of them and cleared his throat. "Anything you've seen, or think you've seen, or anything you've heard here today, is classified by the government of the United States of America as top secret. You soldiers were not here today. Neither was I. Neither was the captain here. Neither were any military police. Neither was anybody at all. Nobody was here. Nothing happened. Nothing. If you ever say anything about this operation, I guarantee you you'll be brought up on charges of treason against your country. And gentlemen, I don't have to tell you what could happen to you then. If you love your country, you will keep your mouth shut. If you're a traitor at heart, well then, just go ahead and talk, but don't think we won't find out about it. One word, one word to your mother, to your brother, to your wife, to your best buddy, and I promise you, gentlemen, you will regret it. More than you ever regretted anything in your life. I trust I make myself clear."

He walked away, and the captain stepped back up. He removed his sunglasses and just glowered at them for a moment, his face like a griffin in the setting sun. "Dismissed."

"Damn," McDavies said as soon as he, Hap, Keating, and Parker were back together beside the jeep. He lowered his voice, even though with all the people milling around and all the noise, it would seem unlikely that anybody else could hear him. "Those are some pretty powerful threats, over a fucking weather balloon falling on some old boy's sheep ranch, don't you think?"

"Like the man says," Jack Parker replied, "I ain't even here."

Before anyone else could say anything, Hap noticed that on one of the military trucks a few yards away with its tailgate down, several pieces of debris, big chunks looking something like aluminum, had spilled over the edge onto the ground. Some sergeant from one of the other bases was already bellowing orders. "You men. You, and you. Get this picked up and fasten that tailgate."

Parker and Hap went over and began picking up the pieces. In the process of tossing the last one into the truck, Hap felt a streak of pain in the palm of his left hand, and saw that he had cut himself on the edge of the metal. Blood was trickling between his fingers and dropping in the sand. Sergeant Fletcher, standing nearby, had seen what happened, and was handing Hap a rag to wrap his hand in. "There's a first-aid kit in the jeep. Put a compress on that hand, and you report to the infirmary as soon as we get back to Roswell, get yourself taken care of."

14

It was a long, dusty ride back. Nobody seemed to feel much like talking, so Hap was pretty much alone with his thoughts.

And with a strange, vague strain of music that went running through his head, insistent for a while and then gone.

# # # #

Long ago, long ago. But he remembered the music, all right. From time to time it echoed in his thoughts, even now. Had he been humming it? The ladies down the way must think him odd, a lonely old man, sitting quietly, humming to himself, scarcely ever stirring. Well, he had his thoughts. That hot July day, back in the New Mexico desert half a century ago, had been strange enough, but the night, the night had held things stranger still. . . .

# # # #

It was dark by the time they got back to Roswell and came on through the front gate in their three dusty jeeps. McDavies pulled up under the sodium lamps in the lot near the base hospital to let Hap out. "You take care of that hand, now, Hap. Christ, you may be ugly but you're one of the best friends I've got."

Hap smiled ruefully and shook his head, waving with his good hand as McDavies backed the jeep up and drove off toward the motor pool. "Yeah," he said, if only to himself. "I'd say friends are pretty important, right about now."

He had no way to know that it was the last time he would ever see McDavies.

There was a surprising amount of activity, especially for this time of night, around the hospital. Trucks and jeeps were parked everywhere, military police were moving about, and a number of civilians were present. Hap went up the front steps, in the door, and down the side of the hallway that branched toward the outpatient infirmary.

It turned out that his hand needed a few stitches, and the whole time they were working on him, everyone seemed nervous, distraught, scarcely speaking to him. He wondered what in the world was going on. Did all this fuss and strain have anything to do with whatever it was that had crashed out there in the desert?

"All right, Private Trujillo, you're all done. Keep that bandage on tonight. Come back tomorrow and we'll have another look and change the dressing." Even in saying this, the doctor on duty seemed distracted, preoccupied, and kept glancing toward the door to the hall. Hap nodded his thanks and went out.

"What the hell do you think you're doing in this building?"

It was a large, tough-looking MP, and he had a hand on Hap's arm.

15

"I--I had to come to the infirmary," Hap spluttered, showing him the bandage, "I cut my hand and had to--"

"Well, then, be on your way. Only authorized personnel are supposed to be in here. Exit the building by the front door."

"Yes, okay, I'm going." He rounded the corner and went through the hall doors, angling as if he were going to head for the front door, but once out in the entranceway, where a lot of very agitated people were running around, he ducked through another door on some nameless impulse and headed down a side hallway toward the back door.

In a minute he was out the door, standing on the concrete platform in the rear delivery bay. There was one streetlamp on out here, some distance to the side; there should have been others, but they seemed to have been extinguished, and the illumination from the one working lamp was pale and diffuse. Some Army trucks were backed in and parked just below the platform, and even in the uncertain light he could see, in the back of one of them, bulging from beneath the mottled green camouflage canvas, the edges of what could only be more pieces of debris--not like the tiny to fair-sized pieces they'd been picking up out in the desert, but big chunks, one of them curved like the underside of a canoe. There were a lot of MP's and other military people standing around, a lot of talking and noise, orders being barked, remarks being exchanged, and Hap had stood there in the shadows only a few seconds before another MP was heading straight up the steps for him.

But Hap had stood there long enough to see what he saw.

Walking from an ambulance parked out a little distance, moving up toward the rear of the hospital, still some thirty or forty feet out and walking in the midst of several people, military and civilian, who seemed to be intent on surrounding it, guiding it, was a small figure, like a child.

Something about the figure instantly made Carlos "Hap" Trujillo's hair stand on end. Not because he was afraid of *it*, but because of what he instinctively knew it must imply.

The figure, only about four feet high, thin and frail-looking in a dull gray metallic garb that looked like a little flight suit, had its wispy body surmounted by a disproportionately large head, a sort of pear-shaped head out of which two large, moist-looking almond eyes shone blackly even in the near-dark.

It was walking into the hospital under its own power, its steps bird-like, its large head nodding, nodding.

It was obviously not human.

# # # #

How long must a man remember? It wasn't fair, that he had ever seen what he had seen, because they didn't want him to see, didn't

16

want him to remember, but as God was his judge, he hadn't *meant* to see it, hadn't known it would be there.

"Mr. Trujillo? Mr. Trujillo? It's time for your pills."

Yes, yes, pills. What pills were there that could change things back, make him young again, well again, happy again?

That night, his peace of mind had vanished forever. That dreadful night, at the rear of the base hospital. . . .

# # # #

"Sergeant, I want that soldier detained." He didn't even know, couldn't even see who had said it, but the MP that had started up the stairs was at him now, pinning his arms, dragging him away down the delivery platform. Back where he had been standing, a group of people surged up the steps, and he could only imagine what moved with them, shielded now from view. But he had no leisure to think about it, because he was being interrogated.

"What is your name, private?" one of the MP's asked, fingering a spiral notebook and a pencil. Hap told him.

"All right, soldier, what did you see?" This was a civilian, a beefy-looking, broad-faced man in a dark suit, of which the coat was open wide enough to reveal a shoulder holster. "Talk. What did you see?"

Hap swallowed hard. "I saw--somebody coming from the ambulance. It was--he was a little kid, maybe nine or ten, I suppose, I don't know. I guess he must of been hurt, but he was walking on his own."

Hap's entire field of vision was crammed full of unfriendly faces--the government man, two or three other civilians, a couple of MP's, and some high-ranking military brass he'd never seen before, officers he was sure weren't assigned to the base. A colonel was addressing him now.

"You're almost right, soldier. You saw a child coming out of the ambulance. That's good. That's almost right. It was--a child. It would have been a child, if anybody had been there at all. But you really didn't see anybody."

"Sir?"

"Nobody, soldier. Do you understand?"

"I--yes, sir--I just--"

"Because you do need to understand," one of the civilians said, leaning close to him, "you really do. See, you're never going to breathe one word of this, the rest of your life, or ever even remotely suggest you were here tonight or saw anything. That's the way it's got to be. Now, look, I know how tempting it is sometimes to talk about things that we shouldn't talk about. A lot of time goes by, and you think, well, I could say something to my girlfriend, I could say something to Mom, I could say

17

something to my brother. You have a family, don't you? A mother, a father? Some brothers and sisters, I'll bet." The man's tone of voice was kind, his face pleasant, smiling.

"Yes sir, my folks and my sister and my two brothers live out in Silver City. I'm the youngest."

"I'll bet you love them."

"Yes, sir," Hap said, "we're a very close family."

The scary thing was, when he thought about it afterward, that the man's smile grew even warmer-looking, and the kind tone of voice did not change at all with what he said next.

"Well, you know, son, things can happen to people. Bad things. People have accidents. People disappear. It happens every day. It's a big desert, who knows what ever happens to some of these people? You don't want anything like that to happen to your mama and papa now, do you, Trujillo?"

Hap felt as if a death-hand were at his own windpipe; his throat felt dry when he replied: "No, sir."

"Well, then, you just remember what the colonel said. You MP's take him back to his barracks."

Two military police took him by the arms and hustled him away, without speaking. Even with the rough handling, Hap felt relieved to be returning to the barracks, because he hoped to see some of his friends there. But after his grim escorts left him off, he saw that only a few of the guys were around--and nobody that had been out in the desert picking up debris, nobody except Sanchez.

"Hey, where's McDavies?"

"Gone, man," Sanchez said.

"Gone? Gone where?"

"Who knows, *pendejo*? Gone. His locker's cleaned out. Looks like some of the others are too. I don't know where anybody is. Peterson said McDavies went to the flight line right after you and him got back. I think they flew him out someplace."

Hap was dumfounded. "What do you mean, flew him--they don't just--I mean, even if he was getting reassigned, it takes time to cut a set of orders, man, they don't just tell you--and what about Keating and--"

"Trujillo?" The duty sergeant had come in the door behind him, and was handing him a sheet of paper. "Orders. Get your shit together and be on the flight line in fifteen minutes. Wear what you're wearing. Sanchez, you stick around, they're going to have some orders for you too."

Hap looked at the paper in his hand. "Hey, that's not my serial number."

"It is now," the sergeant said. "C'mon, you better move it."

18

Hap wouldn't think about the little piece of foil inside his boot until later; there was no time. By sunup the next day he had flown all night on a lonely military transport, and was in Montana, where he would spend most of the rest of his military hitch. He would hear no more from any of his Roswell buddies.

Ever.

# # # #

He wondered now, as he had wondered so often over the years, whether any of them, those others, his faraway old friends, had ever seen each other, heard from each other again, scattered as they no doubt all were to remote and obscure places, serial numbers changed, records altered, forwarding addresses missing, to keep them from talking to each other.

He wondered if any of them, besides himself, were even still alive.

All things considered, he supposed there were worse things than being a lonely old remnant of a man, liver rotted away with alcohol, eyes bad, sitting in a nursing home in Wichita Falls, Texas. Sitting and daydreaming, thinking sometimes of--*those* things; a tired old man with a daughter named Lucy who never came to visit.

There were worse things. He *remembered* worse things.

Far worse.

2

Anne Hawk and the Crewman

First, the long jeep ride out across rattlesnake country, where even with the coming on of autumn the desert sands would shimmer with heat by midday; then the grim security gate ("Good morning, Dr. Hawk," from a military cop who smiled but who would kill you, without a moment's hesitation beforehand or a moment's remorse afterward, if you took one step beyond the gate without your badge), then to the silent, efficient elevator, the short ride down, the smooth opening of the door, then the long blank underground corridor, lighted with perfect wan monotony, stretching its seemingly endless way from the elevator bank, past nameless rooms, on through the subterraneous New Mexico desert in the bare northern reaches of Holloman Air Force Base, stretching on through the sand like some strange blind worm, until one reached a dead-end: Room 108. All very different, down here, from what one might think up on top, out in the daylight, looking at a sign over the guard shack reading, innocuously: STATION 7. The vast majority of the Air Force personnel back down at the main base didn't even know this complex existed, let alone what was in it. How many times had she been through this now, this tedious routine?

Yet even after all these years, it never quite became *just* routine. Not when you were going to be with the Crewman.

She went through the ritual of the print-scan, the palm-scan, and the tongue-touch saliva test, inserted the metal edge of her badge into the mechanism on the door, and heard the tumblers click deep down, saw the door glide automatically open, slowly, efficiently. Efficient like the elevators, efficient like the security guards, like everything. Sometimes it seemed wearisome, at moments nearly unbearable, this efficiency, and she wondered what it would have been like to lead a normal life or have a normal career. A job that really *was* routine.

But no, this was never just routine, not any of this, when in a couple of minutes you were going to be sitting with *him*. She had sat with him, talked with him, studied him and studied from him, for twelve years now.

Every time, in some ways, seemed like the first. It was like that old book *Zen Mind, Beginner's Mind* that she had read years ago. No matter how much you learned, you were always a beginner. Always.

The Crewman never chided you about this. It wasn't his way.

She entered the room with the soft blue light, the room she had seen virtually every day for over a decade of her life, and went to the kitchenette in the side alcove and poured herself a cup of coffee, and sat at the conference table and waited.

In a few minutes the other door, the terminus of a corridor leading from other regions in the complex--from the Crewman's living quarters--swung slowly open, letting in a barely noticeable whiff of canned air from the hallway beyond.

And the Crewman came in, wispy, not quite four feet tall, frail-looking but (as was well known by now) stronger than he looked. He slightly inclined his disproportionately large head in that inimitable way, and blinked his large dark eyes once, and sat down across from Dr. Anne Hawk, evidently ready for the morning's session to begin.

And the conversation started, a conversation between a middle-aged linguist from Yale, on one side of the table, and, on the other, a creature from another world.

The latter was of course a guest, these past five decades, of the government of the United States of America, the sole survivor of the crash, from a crew of five. Was he a guest or a prisoner? One would need to know some perhaps unknowable things to be certain. Old friends, these two, in any case, Dr. Anne Hawk and the alien face across the table.

"Did you sleep well?" the Crewman asked, in English this time, rather than in the language Anne had long ago dubbed L-1. His head slowly bobbed in that way which Anne had long since learned to interpret as a kind of concern. It was never easy, characterizing psychological matters like "concern" when one was dealing with the Crewman. "I have been worried about you. You look tired, you know." He spoke, this time, with his mouth, though Anne to this day never quite knew how much of the effect was the sound coming from that shallow, vestigial-looking orifice (which the Crewman would never have used in communicating with his own kind) and how much was mind-transference.

"Oh, you shouldn't be worried," Anne said, feeling her features ease into a smile. She *was* tired, in truth, and knew that he knew. "I did sleep well, yes. But it's good of you to ask. I trust you slept well also." It was an old joke, and the now-familiar humor-vibrations (or so she thought of them) passed between them as always, with a quick subliminal whiff of a song in the mind, a mind-sound like a windy, reedy flute echoing in a desert canyon. Anne knew, every one of those scant few human beings who knew the Crewman knew, that he needed no appreciable amount of anything that a human being would understand as sleep, and indeed that his physiological needs overall were few and simple.

"This morning," Anne said, "I would like to know some more about the quasi-verb form in L-1 that you started to tell me about last time. I'm particularly interested in what you called the semi-endo-resultative aspect of the form. I have to confess I find it a little puzzling. Would you enlighten me?"

The crewman placed his long forearms on the table and flexed his fingers. He had no thumbs, just four spindly fingers on each hand. "What would you like to know about the form?"

"Well," Anne said, "you were mentioning the difference between the connotations of a unitary infix, like the particle *mhlwa* in *p'dhhi-mhlwa-nanr,* and a split infix as in *p'dhhi-mhl'-'nge-wa-nanr.*"

"Yes," the Crewman said, blinking slowly. "Let me try to explain." The explanation, starting in English but rather quickly shading off into L-1, treated of matters, as so often was the case, that were essentially psychological: Crewman psychology. The structure of L-1, Anne had spent the last several years discovering, was inextricably intertwined with matters of alien psychology that defied saying much of anything about them at all in English, or in any human language. Or almost any human language; Anne was very glad, at times, that the list of languages that she spoke fluently included two Native American languages.

The Crewman's explanation, long and (if one could use such purely earthbound terms at all) patient, lead to other questions and answers, and by the time Anne felt that she had pretty well covered the ground she had hoped to cover, it was late morning, and the Crewman as always bid her a quaintly formal-looking adieu and opened his door and went off toward his quarters, leaving Anne thinking about lunch.

And thinking, as these days she seemed so much more often to be thinking, about her years with the project, with the government.

Had she been foolish to choose the life she'd chosen?

She nearly chuckled to herself, to think how that question might sound to most people--had she been able to discuss her work with

22

anybody, which of course she couldn't, since it was all several layers above top secret--how it would sound, to ask that question, when really she was in some important ways a privileged person.

It was nothing to sneeze at, this professional record of hers--a Ph.D. in comparative linguistics from Yale at the age of twenty-two, a history (though was it history, would it ever be, if it was *always* going to be top secret, all of it?), one should perhaps say a would-be history, a history never to be read, of service in secret government projects all over the world, before she was finally assigned to the Crewman. She knew the Crewman better than any other human being alive.

Certainly better than her predecessor George Quintana had known him: Dr. Quintana, whom, oddly, Anne had never had a chance to meet. Not to deny, certainly, that Quintana had broken important ground in his own eight years with the Crewman, as had others in a lesser way before him, all setting the stage for Anne's own thorough-going but still tentative investigations into the incredibly complex mazes of L-1 and the Crewman's mind. Quintana had been the first to scrap the older classification paradigms of linguistics (agglutinative languages, inflectional languages, the standard analytical categories of grammars and so on) for a much more flexible and inclusive system that tried to account for the intricacies and the psychology of L-1. And indeed Dr. Quintana had spoken twelve languages fluently and had enjoyed, earlier in his life before secret government service stopped the practice, a long career in publishing his scholarly researches into pure linguistics; Anne had read all of his early articles in the journals. But Dr. Quintana had not been born at Nambe Pueblo in New Mexico, had not grown up on Indian land; and Dr. Quintana did not speak Navajo or Tewa. Anne spoke those, and seventeen other languages besides--not counting L-1, in which she was gradually gaining some modicum of proficiency--and she had been the ready choice when Dr. Quintana's association with the project had terminated.

For reasons unknown. Anne had never been able to find out what happened to him. She still read all the scholarly books and journals, even if she was forbidden to publish in them herself, and she had never seen or heard any trace of Quintana.

At times, she could even admit to herself that yes, he was dead, must be dead. In all likelihood, he had either burned out and become unstable, or had begun to develop an attitude problem, and in either event--well, one knew how scenarios like those must end, in this line of work.

Anne left the complex, drove back to the main base, traded the military jeep for her own car, and drove toward Alamogordo, hoping for a nice relaxing lunch. She had another session coming up with the Crewman in the afternoon as usual.

Was it so bad a life? They'd bought her a nice house in town, up on the east side nearly in the foothills, a twelve-room adobe with a pool; they paid her a luscious salary, with health benefits and retirement prospects that would make most people writhe with jealousy.

And they watched her constantly.

She had no real friends, nobody she could trust, nobody she could speak her mind to. There was only the Crewman, and though she valued her exchanges with him, one sometimes needed *human* friends.

One needed to be more than just a well-paid, lonely egghead crunched in the middle of the biggest government coverup in human history.

3

The Hunter and the Sky-Child

A cold white moon rose over the desert like a face of bone. From somewhere up on the mesa, faint voices chanted and sang: the elders in the *kiva* praying for rain. Here below, on the valley floor, the lone hunter rested for a moment, stone ax in hand, at the mouth of a dry arroyo, feeling the sand cool and crisp beneath his feet, watching the shadows of piñon branches creep across the arroyo bottom in the pale light of the moon. The hunter remained perfectly still and quiet, listening, long enough to have seen the shadows move, but he heard only the tiny insect sounds of the desert at night. No larger animals were anywhere near; he would have heard them, would have smelled them.

He was nearly ready to move on up the arroyo, hoping in spite of everything to corner some elusive animal in the twists and turns of the sandy arroyo walls. He had turned to take a step, and that was when it happened.

He saw the tufted shadows of small plants jitter before him, as if some flickering light, some fire of dry brush, had been kindled behind him; his own shadow on the sand grew rippled and strange. He turned to see what the source of this light could be, appearing so suddenly in the night.

And when he looked, he did not understand what he was seeing.

A large round silver object was settling into the sand some distance out in front of him, brushing the sage and the chamisa aside like some great fat bird easing itself into its nest. But this was no bird. Whatever it was, it issued a low whirring sound from somewhere deep within itself, and came to rest and was quiet.

It was like nothing the hunter had ever seen before. Something about it, some feeling that it imparted, made him freeze to the spot, hardly daring to breathe.

For the first time since childhood, the hunter knew deep, brooding fear in his chest.

Much time passed. Nothing happened. The hunter was almost beginning to breathe easier.

Then the great silver bird opened up like a cracked egg, and a strange frail child came out.

The child in some ways looked not like a child at all, this visitor from the sky, but rather like a wise old man, with large dark eyes full of deep expression, some expression that the hunter could not comprehend. He wore some sort of bundle or pack on his back, like a hump, and out of this bundle long tubular reeds extended to a sort of mask only partly obscuring the face, leaving the great dark eyes uncovered.

The sky-child took a few steps toward the hunter and stopped, and seemed to be considering what to do. His thin chest moved up and down, breathing like the hot little chest of a sparrow; he put one thin hand--four fingers, no thumb--to his face and pulled the mask down and off, and stood breathing heavily. Blinking his large eyes several times slowly, he let the tubular reeds dangle loose, trailing the mask. He looked at the hunter and raised his spidery hands, palms upward, as if in greeting.

It was then that the hunter, transfixed, noticed that several other wispy little sky-children had come out of the great silver egg and were coming up to stand behind the first, one by one pulling their masks down and off.

One was carrying a long stick-like object, perhaps as long as the upper bone in a man's leg. This object had several holes pierced in it. The hunter involuntarily tightened his grip on his hunting ax, and watched.

But the sky-child only put the end of the object into his thin little mouth and began to blow. A sound came out, then more sounds and more, until the hunter thought his head would break with trying to hear them all, understand and remember them all. The sounds were oddly musical, something like the singing or chanting of the old priests when they went down into the *kiva*--long, lilting, plaintive notes that were somehow so sweet, so enchanting, that the hunter, feeling his face moist, realized he had begun to weep as the lovely music swirled around him in the crisp desert air. He had begun to weep, and there was no shame, for these were tears of joy.

26

The sky-children gathered about him. The one with the music continued making his incredible sounds and swaying in a somehow vaguely mischievous-looking little dance, and one by one the others took the hunter's rough hands in their own frail-looking but strong little hands, and bobbed their heads and looked into his eyes and let him look into theirs--*and made pictures in his head*, incomprehensible scenes of great beauty and peace that gradually gave way to the familiar scene, the desert at night, his homeland, around him. Somehow, expressionless though they seemed, the very faces of the sky-children held a tranquillity unlike anything the hunter had ever known, even in the wizened face of a shaman. Gradually the sky-children left him and moved back toward the great silver egg, and it swallowed them up, and the crack disappeared as the egg became whole again. The egg rose slowly, silently into the air and moved off, across the moonlit desert, away, gone.

For the first time then, drying his eyes on the back of his hand, the hunter saw that a group of his people, the people of his village atop the mesa, had come halfway down the mesa and were standing, looking, gesturing, talking among themselves.

They, too, had seen.

But the hunter had been *touched*.

The people came down to the base of the mesa and talked with the hunter.

"It was the Trickster," one old man said.

"Yes, only the Trickster would come down from the sky. When he is Coyote Brother he is bound to the earth, but he changes and moves, and sometimes he lives in the sky," another said.

"When he lives in the sky, he is the Crow," the hunter said. "This was different."

"It was the Trickster," the first old man said again.

# # # #

None of them could know, could remotely imagine, how many reverberations down the ages this encounter would have. The hunter, feeling deeply, poignantly moved by what he had experienced, went that night halfway up the side of the mesa and chose a large, flat-faced rock and carved the outline of a playful-looking humpbacked figure with a flute held to its mouth in long thin arms.

In time, there would be hundreds of such rock carvings, all over the region for many miles around. There would also be countless carvings of round objects with points of light encircling them, for the great silver eggs would be seen more than once, and their contours would live in more than one rockcarver's mind. But the most striking depictions would always be the wispy roundbacked figures, so common on rock faces

27

throughout the region that they would seem to constitute not an imagined figure of folklore so much as a real historical presence. A thousand years later, scholars would photograph and catalog them, these petroglyphs depicting the humpback-kachina Kokopelli, the fluteplayer, the rain-priest, the rakish fertility figure.

The mythically eternal Trickster.

The abiding remnant of an encounter, one moonlit desert night in what would one day be New Mexico--an early encounter with little people from the sky.

4

Hap Trujillo and Roommate

Memories again. Disturbing ones. Again.

"Good morning, Mr. Trujillo. Your orange juice and your medicine."

My medicine, he thought, wryly. How do you doctor a life like mine?

His left hand, trembling, involuntarily came over to cover his right hand, and the memories of the old days swirled him away once more. . . .

# # # #

He wondered if the rest of the people at Roswell, those involved in the activities at the debris field, had been sent to places as remote and obscure as this. Yeah, this was about as remote and obscure as it could get without falling off the earth altogether, this nameless little radar station in Montana with its half-dozen dinky little buildings widely scattered inside a sprawling security fence. Hap, not being a radar operator or technician, was one of the group fondly known as "support personnel," and in fact was put to work sorting mail in the installation's almost comically tiny post office, really just a dingy room at the rear of a creaky wooden building that also housed the laundry, infirmary, lounge, and base library, this last item a pretty pitiable collection of tattered paperback books. It wasn't an exciting place to be, this station; on your time off you could get on the rattletrap military bus and go twenty-four miles into Mosby, but there was still nothing much to do when you got there. You got into the habit of sticking around, reading a lot, playing cards, shooting pool, listening to the radio; some guys ended up sending away for correspondence courses on how to play the bassoon or speak Icelandic. Some guys got lucky and were transferred out.

But at least the barracks were an improvement over the old open-bay arrangement he had lived in at Roswell; these quarters were two-man rooms, and they tried to put only people with similar work hours in the same room, so that you could get a pretty decent amount of sleep no matter what shifts you worked. When Hap arrived he was billeted into a room with a sandy-haired fellow named Jerry Weller, who was just recently out of basic training and who had been assigned no roommate. Hap almost felt guilty, intruding on the man's recent run of luck with private quarters, but actually Jerry Weller seemed glad to get someone in with him. "You need somebody to talk to sometimes around here. Place is so *damned* quiet, drives a man nuts after a while." Jerry was from eastern Arizona, near Tucson, and knew some of the area around Silver City, New Mexico, where Hap had grown up. They talked about home, and became fast friends.

But there were things to worry about. One night when Jerry was in town and there was no one else around, Hap took steps to protect the little strip of metal foil he had pinched from the debris field in New Mexico, which up to now he had simply hidden by slipping it into a magazine. He had an old Spanish copy of *Don Quixote de la Mancha* that his family had given him in the hope that he would read it, a book which in all truth he felt rather unlikely to struggle through, though he had had it with him ever since enlisting. He found a place in it where facing pages were blank on one side with a rather uninteresting illustration on the other. He slipped the foil between these pages, pressed it completely flat, and ran a very thin line of paste around the inside borders to seal the pages together. The pages were opaque, and the foil itself was so thin and so nearly weightless that the hiding place was very inconspicuous; unless you checked the list of illustrations and noticed that you couldn't find one of them, you would never notice the pasted-together sheets, which turned as easily as flipping a single page. He put the Cervantes volume up on the shelf in his locker among other books. The foil was as well hidden now as he could manage.

And he would tell no one. Not even Jerry Weller. It was better at this point that absolutely no one knew.

He tried then to put the whole Roswell affair out of his mind.

# # # #

But as time went on, the Roswell memories bothered him-- haunted him--more and more. The memories, and their astounding implications.

One memory in particular.

That glimpse, in an uncertain wash of electric light, that glimpse of a thin little figure walking bird-like, unassisted, into the rear of the base hospital at night, surrounded by more military police and big brass than any occasion would have called for.

Any occasion but the presence of a creature from space.

30

Some nights, Hap woke up screaming. And nameless nightmares scuttered back down the holes of his subconscious mind like dark, vile spiders, before he could quite see them in the light. Sometimes his screams would wake Jerry, across the room in the other bunk, and Jerry would ask him in the dark what was wrong, and Hap, very much wanting to tell him just what *was* wrong, would have to mumble something about "just a bad dream" and try to go back to sleep.

He had been more deeply affected than he thought, seeing what he had seen in that traumatic moment in the delivery bay behind the hospital.

He was haunted by it, and he needed to confide in someone.

No question, he desperately needed to confide in someone, threats and regulations be damned. Someone he could make understand the urgency of silence, someone he could trust not to tell anybody else.

He decided to pick the right time and place and tell Jerry Weller. Here among strangers from unfamiliar places, Jerry was a boy from back home, and he liked the feeling of that. He would pick the time and the place carefully, for sure.

# # # #

It turned out to be one night when Hap had been at the station for about two months. He and Jerry were coming across the field from the little base theater after seeing the Bela Lugosi *Dracula* for the third time in two weeks because it was the only film showing; it was late, nearly midnight, and though other soldiers had ambled out of the movie house at the same time, Hap and Jerry had no one within earshot at the moment. Hap stopped in the middle of the field, looked around to be sure that no one else could hear, and motioned for Jerry to stop too.

"There's something I've got to tell you about. Something that happened to me the last place I was stationed."

And he told him, omitting the part about nipping a piece of the debris--someday he might be ready to show that to somebody, but not now--skipping the metal foil but telling all the rest: the debris field, the cleanup, the rumors about the crash of an alien spacecraft, the threats from the government men and from the military brass, the injury to his hand, the trip to the base hospital--the unthinkable, unforgettable thing he had seen when he came out the back door, where he wasn't supposed to be. The alien walking on its thin little legs.

Hap fell silent and gave the story time to sink in. Jerry Weller, running a hand through his hair, looked dumbstruck. "Jesus God."

Hap peered at Jerry's face in the pallid light of distant sodium lamps. "You do believe me? 'Cause I wouldn't blame you if you didn't. I mean, I know how crazy it sounds."

31

Jerry let out a ragged breath. "Well, what can I--you sure as hell didn't imagine it. It's not something I even want to think about, but hell, of course I believe you, I *have* to believe you. What the hell choice do I have?"

"Well, I'm glad I told you," Hap said. "I--I just needed to talk about it. I think maybe it's helped me to talk about it. But Christ, don't even *think* of telling anybody else, man. Ever."

Jerry shook his head. "Phew. Shit no, man, hey, I understand. We'd both be in trouble, right?"

"Promise? Nobody. Not ever."

"You got it. Promise. Just one question, though."

"What is it?"

"Well," Jerry said, looking around now himself to see that nobody else was listening, "you said they read you the riot act about taking anyway any of that--stuff."

"The debris?"

"Yeah."

"Well?"

"Well what?"

"Well, did you?" Jerry's face shaded off into a mischievous grin.

"Take any of it? Are you kidding? After what they said, all those threats? Shit, no." It was the first lie he'd told his new friend, and the only one he'd ever tell him, but it was one he knew he had to tell.

"Too bad," Jerry said. "God, do you know what it would mean to have a piece of that stuff? I think *I* would've grabbed some."

"No, I don't think you would've. Me, I didn't dare. I didn't want anything more to do with the business, especially after all that stuff they said about killing our families and everything. They were serious about that shit, man. And look, I don't think we ought to talk about it any more, even just you and me, now that I've told you. I mean, what if there's microphones or something in the barracks?"

Jerry clapped him on the shoulder. "Okay. You got it. Not a word. You're right, you never know when somebody might be listening." He stood for a while looking down, without speaking, and finally shook his head, as if considering the whole thing over again and finally forcing himself to dismiss it. "I don't know about you, but I could use some shuteye."

"Yeah, me too," Hap said, "and you know, I think I might be able to sleep now and not have nightmares. Thanks for listening. I feel better, I really do."

And he did feel better. And he did sleep the whole night through without nightmares.

# # # #

The next afternoon he had hoped to get Jerry to go into town with him, just to get off the station for a few hours, but Jerry said he had K. P.

"Well, okay," Hap said, shrugging, grinning. "Hey, if you'd rather wash dishes, I can understand that."

"Get out of here," Jerry said, punching his arm. "Catch you later."

Hap went into town and grabbed a hamburger and did a little shopping, and came back on the bus just after nine o'clock. Dropping his things off in his room, he walked over to the lounge, had a beer, chatted with a couple of guys who were there playing pool, and headed back across the field toward the barracks.

And in the middle of the field he stopped, because he suddenly realized someone was following close behind him.

He turned around, and it was Jerry, grinning. "Hold up, man. God, you walk fast."

What was surprising was that Jerry had two other men with him, people Hap hadn't ever seen before.

"Hi, Jer. Didn't know you were here. I thought you'd still be in the chow hall washing pots and pans. Who--"

"Oh," Jerry said, "these are a couple of colleagues of mine."

Colleagues? It struck Hap as a strange choice of words, one that somehow made him nervous.

"There's something we wanted to talk to you about," Jerry said.

Oh, Christ, Hap thought, surely the damned fool hasn't gone and blabbed about it to these people, when I asked him not to--

"See, we have a problem," Jerry said. The other two had moved around to the sides, slipped behind Hap, and grabbed his arms, pinning them back. "We have a serious problem, Hap," Jerry continued. "It has to do with talking about things you shouldn't be talking about."

Suddenly, even in the pale light, Hap noticed that Jerry's face, now close to his own, looked a little different. Had he been wearing makeup or something before? He looked older now.

"Jerry, I--look, I didn't--"

"Oh," Jerry said, patting him gently on the cheek, "yes you did, Hap. You talked about some things you were told not to talk about. See, we're not even going to say what they were, right now, out here, because we're not supposed to talk about them either. But *you* know what they were, don't you?"

"Jerry, please--"

"My name isn't Jerry, but you go ahead and call me that, Hap, since I'd like to think that we can handle this little situation in a friendly

33

and positive way. Now, we're going to be lenient this time. Maybe you didn't understand--when they first told you about not talking, you remember?--maybe you didn't realize how important that was. We thought we'd explain it to you a different way, so you'd understand."

He motioned to his companions, who tightened their grip on Hap's arms. At the same time he fished a pocket knife out of his jacket pocket and opened it, moving it a little back and forth, letting the blade catch and reflect the dim light. He nodded, and the other two men tripped up Hap's legs and sent him sprawling to the ground, where they still held him tight. Jerry, or the man who had called himself Jerry, took Hap's right hand and pressed it down against a flat rock, uncurling the fingers, forcing them to extend. Quickly, deftly, he pressed the blade into the flesh just below the knuckle of the forefinger, slammed the blade on the dull backside with the heel of his hand as if chopping carrots, pushed the blade through to the rock, and took the finger off.

Hap could never have imagined such pain, and scarcely even knew that the screaming in his ears was his own. He reeled, went slack in the grip of the two men holding him from behind, and began to pass out. Immediately a hand was at his face with a little bottle, and the overwhelming pungency of smelling salts filled his nose.

"No you don't, you chili-eating little spic bastard," Jerry said, his voice low and even and unperturbed, while he slipped the severed finger into a jacket pocket. "You're going to be awake to feel every bit of this." By now blood was spurting from the wound, and one of the other men, loosening his grip on Hap's arm, was lighting a cigarette lighter and pressing the flame to the wound to cauterize it. Hap's mind tried once again to retreat from the pain, to retreat into the blessing of unconsciousness, but the bottle with the smelling salts was being prodded into his face until his nose started to bleed. He began to scream, but his throat constricted and went so dry that the scream choked off in the middle. At this point Jerry grabbed him up by the scruff of the neck and held him so that their faces nearly touched. Inconsequentially, some corner of Hap's disordered mind noticed that the man's breath smelled like clean, fresh mint.

"Now listen carefully, Hap," the man said, "because you seem to have some trouble sometimes, listening. You do *habla inglés,* yes?" He motioned to the others, and they stood away. "This little conversation is just our way of explaining to you that when your government asks you not to talk about certain things, we mean it. We trust there won't be a next time. If there is, well, let's just say we can't go on being lenient with you forever. See, next time it isn't going to be just a finger. I guess it'll have to be all of them. And it won't be just you. It'll be your mother

34

first. You'll get to watch, while we do her. Then we'll do you. Naturally, she'll get to watch that. Am I making myself clear?"

Hap, moaning, tried to speak but could not.

Jerry patted him on the cheek, softly, as he had before. "I'll take that as a yes. Now, you ought to get over to the infirmary and get somebody to take you into town and get that finger looked at properly. You'll explain that it was an accident, you'll say you managed to cauterize it yourself. I think they'll admire your presence of mind and your courage for that, don't you?"

Hap, running a jacket sleeve across his face several times to try to clear his eyes, made an effort again to speak, but when he looked up, no one was there.

He did get the infirmary personnel to take him into town, but there wasn't much they could do for him at the hospital other than just clean and dress the wound and give him some pain pills. He said nothing, of course, about the way the "accident" had really happened; he knew better. It was nearly dawn when he got back to his room at the station, and by then someone had pried his locker open and ransacked it. The Cervantes volume sprawled open on the floor amid a tumble of other books, but the searchers hadn't found the metal foil.

Hap never saw the man again who had called himself Jerry Weller. At the orderly room the duty sergeant would later say that the man had only arrived at the station a day or two before Hap, and now had suddenly gotten special orders relocating him someplace, nobody knew exactly where.

It was the last time Hap ever, his whole life, felt that he could trust anybody wholeheartedly.

It was the last time he ever felt that he had his life reasonably under control, that he was more or less in charge of his affairs, that he could face the future with a fair amount of confidence.

It was the last time that he was ever really innocent enough to feel that his government in the final analysis had its citizens' best interests, the American people's best interests, at heart.

It was the last time he ever felt altogether good about much of anything, actually.

# # # #

And, he mused--running a fingertip now over the ancient smooth stub of what even at this late date should still have been a finger--that was the time, those many awful years ago, when he had first started drinking heavily.

35

5

Lucy Trujillo and the Mesa Bookshop

She always enjoyed her walk up to the bookshop on Guadalupe Street, from where she parked her car. It gave her a bit of exercise, gave her a chance to fill her lungs with fresh morning air before starting work, gave her time to think about things in general before spending the rest of the day talking to customers about books and authors. Not that she minded. The store was her long-time dream, after all, and it was a delight to run, most of the time. The location was excellent for her; this neighborhood was her favorite part of Santa Fe. A little distance away, you had the Plaza and the Governor's Palace (Indians displaying their wares on blankets along the sidewalk), and these were an eternal part of the local landscape. Further across town, Canyon Road was a meandering fascination of art galleries, and the churches and museums were venerable monuments to New Mexico history, and she loved it all-- but she especially loved this little section of shops and cafés, with her adobe-visaged secondhand book store nestling among them like a quiet, thoughtful child in the midst of more boisterous folk. She was that rarest of souls, the person who really honest-to-God didn't mind going to work in the morning. She had her share of problems, no question about that, but she knew that overall she was very lucky. It was a beautiful morning, and she felt damned good.

"God, much more along that line of thinking and I'm going to have to burst into song," she said to herself, laughing. A young Hispanic couple passed her on the sidewalk and seemed to find her good cheer contagious. "*Pase buen día*," the man said to her, smiling, and she tossed her hair and said, "*Igualmente*." And here she was, at her door now, where multicolor volumes peeked from the show window beside the door. In the shadow of the metal sculpture of Kokopelli bent over his flute, a woodcut edition of *David Copperfield* vied for window space with a first edition of *Cannery Row,* while nearby Ernest Hemingway rubbed elbows with Shirley Jackson, and Hawthorne and Melville and Jane Austen and Amy Lowell jostled each other, flaunting their covers. A damned lively crowd, these literary folk.

Yes indeed, Mesa Bookshop: her baby now for going-on two years.

She unlocked the door, went inside, turned on the lights, made her way through the maze of bookcases to the kitchenette in the back and put on a pot of coffee. She barely had herself settled behind her desk up front, coffee steaming, computer screen up and glowing, doughnuts from the bakery next door spread out on wax paper beside her coffee, when the first customers came in, two elderly ladies looking for some Agatha Christie mysteries. Lucy had what they needed on the shelf, and rang up a sale. As the morning progressed, she sold a young woman a dog-eared paperback copy of Steinbeck's *The Winter of our Discontent,* and three chattering college students appeared on a quest for some Tony Hillerman novels, but mostly it was missionless browsers who came in, and they would sometimes happen upon some treasure, sometimes not; the gentle art of browsing was very much encouraged here in any case. The flow of customers was lighter now than it had been a few weeks before, because by now, the third week in October, the tourist trade had pretty much dwindled for the season. The shop did well enough all year round for her to make at least a meager living from it, but it always seemed quiet in the shops in Santa Fe when summertime was over.

This relatively slow pace gave her, between customers, some time to think, even a little time to write. That was one of the things she loved about the job, usually.

But sometimes she didn't feel in the mood to write, and sometimes her thoughts had a way of turning somber.

This, she reflected, slipping back to the kitchenette to pour another cup of coffee, this was going to be one of those times.

Back at her desk, the shop empty of customers at the moment, she peered at the locked glass display case to her left, in the recess behind the desk. Here were a few special volumes--a rare first edition of Faulkner's *Light in August,* an early edition of Poe, a signed copy of Joyce Carol Oates's *Wonderland,* a rare Arkham House edition of H. P. Lovecraft, several other items.

Including, wedged incongruously between the Faulkner and the Poe, an old leatherbound volume of Cervantes: *Don Quixote de la Mancha.*

Dad.

That was always what it was, wasn't it? When disquieting thoughts and memories threatened to seep into the sunlit cheer of her day. Thoughts of Dad. And of those--matters.

She looked at the Cervantes, inconspicuous there behind the glass. She kept a stock card in it, just as if it were any other book, and, should anyone for any reason ask to see it, she was ready to reply that it had been a special-search order and the customer was going to be picking it up.

Sometimes she thought about taking it out in the alley and burning it. But she knew she would not. There wouldn't be any point to it anyway, because only the book would burn. Besides, she felt an obligation to keep the thing, an obligation to Dad. And beyond that, she held a faint, vague hope that someday, somehow, everything would come out in the open--that the object hidden in those pages would turn out to be not just worrisome but important, that someone would have to pay for what the whole affair had done to her father, to her family.

In any case, just the sight of the volume flooded her mind with thoughts she would rather not have entertained just now.

Dad. Was she *so* bad, not to go out to Wichita Falls to see him more often? She hadn't just stuck him in a home, the way some people did their parents; he had been placed there as part of the release plan, from the state hospital. She did write to him, didn't she, and did call him once a month? And she'd been out to see him the past two Christmases. It wasn't her fault, the way things were.

It hadn't been easy, for her or for Mom, living all those years with an unreformed alcoholic. She tried not to dwell on the bad times, but sometimes they edged into her mind like sly little goblins, little scenes she did not want to see--the times he had come home roaring drunk, the verbal abuse, the arguments, the times he had slapped Mom, slapped his daughter. Afterward he would blubber, would overflow with penitence, would beg to be forgiven, and they would do their best, she and Mom, to forgive him, but it didn't make what they had any more of a real home, a real family. Dad had made something of a mess of his own life and theirs too.

Well--that wasn't quite fair. First, she was only now beginning to realize, being thirty-seven and divorced and childless and barely making a living, that since she hadn't done a flawless job arranging her own life, she might not have a whole lot of right to comment on anyone else's, including her father's; when you got right down to it, it wasn't easy, actually, this strange business of living. Second, it wasn't altogether true that Dad had made a mess of his life. To a considerable extent, others had made it for him. Mom saw it that way, and had said so, to her, though Dad plainly discouraged her talking about such things at all. Mom and Dad. What a pair they had been. A little while after whatever it was that had happened to Dad in Montana (something he refused to describe in any detail, though it had had something to do with losing his finger) he had been transferred by the Army Air Corps--no, by then it had officially become the United States Air Force--transferred to the air base in Wichita Falls, Texas, where he was discharged in 1949, met Juanita Melendez in 1956 and married her the following year. Lucy knew the story well. Her father, after getting out of the Air Force, had been working at a variety of odd jobs, all he would ever work at really, and had met her mother standing in line at a movie house. They were both waiting to see, and ended up seeing together, *Earth Vs. the Flying Saucers,* a film which, despite its ridiculous melodrama, affected Dad oddly, her mother would later say. During this period his drinking was not so pronounced as it would come to be, and Mom had been enchanted with him, and for good reason; he had been, and in some ways still was, a very charming man. He was strangely troubled, though, even back then, and it showed; but Mom had been understanding enough to stick by him rather than let his occasional drinking or moodiness drive her away. They were married the following spring, in 1957, and Lucy was born in 1958.

Dad had had the copy of *Don Quixote de la Mancha* with him for years, ever since joining the service, and he had it stuffed into the bottom of a dusty box of books at the back of a closet in his apartment when he married Mom. They rented a house in Wichita Falls, the house on Harrison Street where Lucy would be born, where she would grow up, and upon their moving into the house the books from the old closet got unpacked; Mom insisted on buying bookshelves and displaying all the books they had between them--only a few, for Dad's part, but she had brought with her quite a number of volumes of her own. Telling Lucy this, years later, Mom would smile; the story was an innocent reminiscence so far, the story of any couple's early life together. Mom had bought the shelves, unpacked all the books, and lovingly arranged them. For some time the Cervantes volume rested among the others on the middle shelf in their living room, and Dad didn't seem to mind, but after a while Mom from time to time would see him staring at the bookshelf, evidently in an uneasy mood, for reasons she couldn't then imagine, and if she asked him what was the matter, he would only shrug. When he was in these moods she was a little afraid to pester him with questions. Then one night, unaccountably, he got up from reading his evening paper, plucked the book from the shelf, and without a word stored it away in a box containing some other old things he had been planning to take up to the attic. Mom had thought that the book was handsomely bound and looked nice, and was a classic after all and should stay on the shelf, but again she thought it best to let the matter drop.

That had been that; the book went into the box of odds and ends, and the box went to the attic.

It would only be gradually, over a period of two years and more, that she would come to know anything of the truth about the book.

# # # #

The bell on the door jangled now, and a customer came in, drawing her thoughts back to the present. He was tall, lanky, late forty-ish, a rather attractive man, and he browsed the shelves for a while and ended up buying a shelfworn little hardcover copy of Shakespeare's *Titus Andronicus*. She counted out his change, and he nodded to her and smiled and went out. And she went back to the solitude of her thoughts.

# # # #

Dad's mood improved slightly when the Cervantes volume was out of sight, but only slightly, and only for a short while. Things gradually got worse. Dad didn't sleep well; Lucy remembered even from early childhood the sounds, from their bedroom next to hers, the sounds of his thrashing about, his sometimes crying out in his sleep. He drank-- not too unreasonably at first, but by the time Lucy was in her middle teens, the drinking had become a problem. Dad tended to drift from job to job, doing a little carpentry here, a little roofing there, a little of this and that somewhere else, but never seemed to settle on anything; more than once, his drinking had gotten him into trouble on the job, and more and more often he was drunk at home, and not just on weekends. Mom was a saint, through all this; she talked gently with him, she stood by him even when he was becoming abusive, she took his later apologies, she held him, she showed him, unfailingly, that she loved him. But whatever it was that was tormenting him would not let him rest, and his state of mind continued to deteriorate.

And, a little bit at a time, he began to tell Mom what it was that bothered him from his past. He told her a good bit more, apparently, than she was willing ever to say anything about, herself, and indeed it was plain that he insisted that she never speak of it at all, to anyone, not even Lucy. She promised, and for a while kept her promise.

But one night when Lucy was seventeen and had brought a date home after a movie, Dad had come in after a drinking bout and had caused an embarrassing scene in front of the boyfriend. Later that night, after the boyfriend was gone and after Dad had long since passed out in bed and was snoring loudly, Lucy had tearfully confronted her mother.

"I'm so ashamed! Why does he *do* it? What's the *matter* with him? And why do you put up with it?"

Mom had put her arm around her. "Lucy dear, let's go out for a walk. You'll feel better, and we can talk. *Vámonos.*"

They put on sweaters and went for a walk in the park, and Mom began talking about the problem with Dad.

"He's been through a lot of pain, Lucy. It started when he was in the service. He was stationed in New Mexico in 1947 with the Bomb Group at Roswell Field, and--" She stopped, and seemed to be collecting her thoughts, or to be deciding whether she would be believed in what she was about to say.

"Go, on, Mom," Lucy said. It was late, and getting cold, and the only light in the park was a pallid lamp goosenecked out over the sidewalk behind them. But Lucy wanted to hear the story.

"Well, your father told me that some kind of--spaceship, I guess-- crashed in the desert outside of town."

Lucy giggled. "Oh, Mom! A flying saucer?"

"Don't laugh. Let me tell you. Your father was one of the soldiers sent out to gather up the wreckage. It was all over the ground, acres of it. They told them that it was all a big government secret, the Army, you know, and hushed it all up, and told everybody it was only a weather balloon but it was top secret anyway, and they said if the men ever talked about what they'd seen, the government would do terrible things to them and to their families, and if anybody tried to take any of the pieces away, they'd be in big trouble. But your father slipped a piece of the stuff into his boot, and they never knew. He said it looked to him like a little piece of tinfoil."

"But--"

"Wait, that's not all. Later that night your father was at the hospital, back at the base, because he'd cut his hand."

"His finger--"

"No, that was later, up in Montana. The night I'm talking about, when he had just got back to the base with his buddies, he was at the hospital, and he saw them bringing in--" She shook her head, as if to say: why bother, you're not going to believe me, and I couldn't blame you.

"Go on, Mom."

"He saw them bringing in a--well, a little man."

"A midget?"

"No, dear. A little creature something *like* a man."

Now Lucy couldn't keep from cackling outright. "Mom. Little green men, like in the movies? Surely you don't--" She stopped when she noticed that her mother's face was dead serious.

41

"It wasn't human, Lucy."

"You're serious."

"Yes, dear," her mother said. "Yes, I am. Your father saw it, but he wasn't supposed to. He wasn't supposed to be there at all. There were colonels and generals and government people all over the place, and when they saw your father there looking at the--thing--they made terrible threats, they told him they'd do horrible things to his folks--"

"To Gramma and Grampa?" At first Lucy was more shocked at this than at anything else she'd heard so far.

"They made your father swear never to tell. Then they shipped him out, and all his buddies, but different places, so they couldn't talk to each other. That's when your Dad got in trouble in Montana, for talking about it to somebody he met up there. He's never said much about that part, and I'm afraid to ask him any more, because he gets a look in his eye like: don't *ever* ask me about that. Anyway, that's when he started really drinking. He feels like someone is always watching him, and he feels like he can't trust anybody. Sometimes I think he doesn't even trust me. He's a very unhappy man, deep down. This thing has put a shadow on his life."

"And that piece of--"

"I'll tell you more about it, another time. We'd better get back, it's really getting cold. I'll say this, though; I wish to God he didn't have the thing. I think he wishes so too, but can't bring himself to get rid of it."

"Well, what's the big deal, Mom, about a piece of--"

Her mother was plainly annoyed by the girl's naïveté. "About a piece of foil he picked up in the desert? Well, I just think that *is* a big deal, Lucy. It's a big deal because it's from another world. I'd say that's a big deal. Wouldn't you? And it's a big deal because the government is keeping it all secret and they can't afford to have anything like that sitting around, because it's evidence that they've been lying to everybody."

They were both silent during the walk back. Lucy wanted to ask a lot of questions--had Mom herself seen the piece of foil? where was it now?--but she remained quiet. Just before they got to the house, her mother turned to her and said, "Listen to me, Lucy. Never talk about this in the house."

"But why?"

"Because I'm scared, that's why. That's why Dad never says much around the house, I think. Because he's afraid somebody might be listening."

# # # #

42

Customers had come in, a couple of leisurely browsers. They stayed for a while, chatting quietly about books, and one of them bought a copy of Mary Shelley's *Frankenstein.*

As they went out the door, Lucy, her mood pretty much altered for the day, reflected: if only mad scientists were the sole creators of monsters.

She ate her sandwich for lunch, had some more coffee, and drifted back under the sway of memories that would not be still.

# # # #

The seventeen-year-old Lucy had had to learn a new way of thinking about some things, from the moment she realized that her mother had had a special reason to ask her to go for a walk to talk about Dad's problems, rather than just staying home and talking about them. It was a bit of a shock, to hear your mother say she was afraid to talk about such things in the house because there might be electronic eavesdroppers. By that time the world had seen the Watergate scandal and had come to think of eavesdropping technology as commonplace, and while Lucy at that point did not really think that their house was "bugged" with microphones and hidden transmitters, she found it disturbing that her parents *did* think so, or at least suspected so, or were unwilling to take a chance on it. The thought was an outrage, that a family might even have to worry about such things, true or not.

She was itching to ask her mother--or, better, her father, since he'd *seen* these things--more about the crashed object, the threats, the coverup, the debris.

The piece of foil.

But she followed Mom's advice and never said anything about any of it around the house, and never anything to her father under any circumstances; she suspected he didn't know she knew anything about it, because Mom might well not have had the nerve to tell him he'd told her.

And was still telling her--they had their further walks in the park, from time to time, and Lucy learned more. Dad had hidden the piece of debris in a book, a copy of *Don Quixote de la Mancha,* and that book even now was in a box of odds and ends up in the dusty shadows of the attic. Dad had carefully, craftily pasted two pages together making a sort of envelope with the metal foil inside. Lucy asked: had her mom ever seen the foil itself? No, she hadn't. The pasted-together pages had never been opened since that time in Montana, twenty-eight years ago now. Dad wouldn't talk much about it, Mom said, and of course wouldn't say anything at all in the house, or even in the car, but on the few occasions when he'd talked a little about the foil--out in the open, where there could scarcely be hidden microphones--he had suggested that as

43

much as it scared him still to have the thing, he felt bound to keep it, because maybe someday the whole secret would come out somehow, maybe he could then come forward with it and not have to be afraid. Maybe they would declassify the whole affair, make it public knowledge. Somehow he thought this unlikely, but he had to hope, and even in the event that the affair was never declassified and publicized, it might be important for someone--someone on the outside, someone with no stake in the coverup--to have a piece of the debris. Why, exactly, he couldn't say, and he had no idea what he would ever do, if anything, with his secret prize from the debris field. But somehow he had to keep it, and he certainly had to keep it hidden.

These occasional walks-and-talks with Mom were in 1975 and 1976, and after that they almost never talked about it; there just wasn't anything left to say. And in 1978--on September 23rd, a date burned into Lucy's mind like a cattle brand--the terrible auto accident had come to claim her mother's life. Lucy, then an English major starting her junior year at Midwestern State University in Wichita Falls, had just come home after taking an exam that afternoon, when the uniformed officer came to the door, and her world collapsed.

Or so it seemed at the time. She pulled herself partly out of her state of grief over a period of days, if only because someone had to have the presence of mind to see after Dad. The grandparents (chalky, tragic faces at the funeral) were old and ill, and lived too far away to be able to stay around and help. Dad had never been terribly stable, and this unthinkable loss was all he needed really to go over the edge. His drinking now was frightful, the eternal, hopeless drinking of a man lost to despair--this wraith, Despair, was now the third party living in the house, a wretched substitute for the warm, loving person who had left it. This third party, the omnipresent bottle, the vomit-sour breath, was the presence that edged Lucy's mother's very ghost away, the usurping presence that stood between Lucy and her father like a truculent bully bent on separating them. But she stayed home, somehow managing to live with Dad, somehow managing to finish college the spring of 1980, and she even stayed at home another year to watch after him. He still worked, but only sometimes, and drifted from one inconsequential job to another. She herself was working in town, as the editor of a small company's corporate magazine, and paying a good many of the household bills; her life was hectic but manageable overall.

But a time had to come when she wanted something more out of life, wanted a life of her own. She met Paul Sandoval in the spring of 1981 at a business conference, and they were married that summer. Paul was an accountant and made good money, but Lucy kept working, since they needed all the money both of them could earn. She feared for her father's survival, moving out of his house and leaving him pretty much to fend for himself, but she and Paul lived nearby, in an old house on Tenth Street, and they looked in on him as often as they could. He was not getting better; his drinking continued, and his moods, at times, were not anything pleasant to contemplate. In spite of everything she and Paul could do, he didn't eat regularly or healthfully, and they were afraid he was becoming malnourished. Forcing him to see a doctor, they discovered, not entirely to their surprise, that he had liver problems. As time went on, his sense of responsibility and sense of connectedness to the world around him seemed to diminish, his mind seemed to wander more and more, his behavior became increasingly erratic. In 1983 Lucy and Paul, as sad a task as it was, had him certified mentally incompetent, had him committed to the state hospital, and sold his house to help pay off the welter of bills he had left behind and to save for the expenses that no doubt lay ahead.

It was when they went through his house prior to selling that she brought the box of odds and ends down from the attic, and took it home to the house on Tenth Street, telling Paul only that it was a bunch of family memorabilia that she didn't want to part with.

She left it all packed as it was, and never told Paul about the Cervantes volume. It wasn't that she didn't trust him, but--

# # # #

The telephone rang--someone asking if she had a copy of Burton's *The Anatomy of Melancholy*. No, she didn't, but she would try to find one. A group of ladies came in and browsed, and ended up buying some mysteries--Amanda Cross, Michael Innes, Margery Allingham. Lucy rang up a goodly sale, but her thoughts were still melancholy themselves, *Anatomy of Melancholy* or no. It wasn't that she hadn't trusted Paul--

# # # #

Yes, it *was* that she didn't trust him, and for good reason, as it turned out.

At first it was just a vague feeling, but by 1985 she had started to suspect, in earnest, that he was having an affair. Their intimate life together had seemed to fade early on, for reasons she could not entirely comprehend, and she began to notice a pattern to his working late, a pattern to his absences due to unspecified or implausible errands on weekends, a pattern to his seeming to be exhausted when there should have been little reason. In the winter of 1986 she confronted him with her suspicions, and there was a big ugly scene; later that year she caught him at it outright. The whole thing almost ended in divorce court at that point, but they went to counselors, and Paul went to therapy, and as rocky as it was, they managed to get through it together at least, though

45

one could hardly say unscathed. Things seemed tolerable, almost normal, for a couple of years, and it happened again; a different "other woman" this time, a new bout of denials and excuses. From that point, the marriage was essentially over, though the divorce did not come till 1991, a week before what would have been their tenth wedding anniversary, as irony would have it. Within a year, Paul had married one of his girlfriends and they had moved away--California somewhere, Lucy thought.

Since there were no children, and since she was still perfectly capable of supporting herself if she lived (in Thoreau's words) "close to the bone," she asked no financial support from him. He was out of her life, and good riddance; she was Lucy Trujillo once more.

Had always been Lucy Trujillo, she realized now.

Thank heaven she hadn't told him about the book, about the piece of foil. She hadn't ever said much of anything to Paul, in fact, about the sources of her father's problems. She hadn't ever been sure, even at the start, that she wanted to tell him secrets as scary as those, and it only went to show how right her intuitions had been.

Since there wasn't much she could do at this point for her father, she no longer felt bound to stay in Wichita Falls; indeed, she felt the distinct need for a change. Selling most of her belongings and packing the rest into a U-Haul trailer, she got in her Dodge Colt and moved to Santa Fe, New Mexico, and had never regretted it. She had always rather wanted to run a bookshop, and by 1993 she was doing it.

# # # #

And now the Cervantes volume sat wedged between Poe and Faulkner behind the glass in a bookcase in a little shop in Santa Fe, nursing a bizarre secret in its musty paper womb. Like Poe's purloined letter, it was in plain view, this brooding secret that had helped to drive her father mad.

Just what any sleepy little bookstore needs, Lucy thought, sighing--a deadly secret, a quiet little relic that some people might well kill you for.

A piece of tinfoil.

An intelligently manufactured thing not of this earth.

6

Roger Wynn and Shakespeare

He hated this place.

Not the motel. The region. The culture, if you wanted to call it that.

The motel was all right. It was probably the best of the bunch on Cerillos Road, possibly the best of the bunch in Santa Fe for that matter. But that wasn't saying much, as far as Roger Wynn was concerned, not when you were a hearty New York lad born and bred, and tired of looking at adobe and cactus and Mexicans and Indians.

He hated the goddamn Indians. He hated the goddamn Mexicans. Oh yes, you were supposed to call them Hispanics, weren't you? He had only contempt for them by whatever name. Some of the women were okay, though. He wouldn't mind crawling into the sack with some of them. He *had* crawled into the sack from time to time, on the road, with women of various ethnic persuasions (he wasn't *that* prejudiced), the sorts of evenings you paid good hard-earned taxpayer-donated money for. Tonight he was too tired to go looking for such amusements, however refreshing they could be. Yeah, some of these desert wenches were okay. But basically he hated the people here, hated their "laid-back" lazy goddamn life-style, hated the cutesy little adobe buildings and the coyote fences, hated the sagebrush and the tumbleweeds, hated just about everything about the goddamn desert. It was no place for a real man. New York, Detroit, Chicago--now *those* were places for a real man. Nothing should live down here but the fucking lizards.

Still, something other than lizards did live here. Various clients, one might say. Carlos "Hap" Trujillo's diddly-ass daughter Lucy, for one. She wasn't half bad looking, actually, and he thought he just might be taking advantage of that fact at some point, you never could tell. He could get away with whatever he decided to do, and that much was pure fact. Right now he just wanted some rest.

No, the motel itself wasn't too bad, even if it was designed to look like a miniature Mexican village in earth-colored adobe and brightly painted trim with Indian designs like every other damned place around here. The room was comfortable, the bar down off the lobby was well equipped with libations at least as good as his own traveling stock, and the place was relatively quiet. He was only going to be here this one more night anyway, till the next time, because after checking on a few other things on his mental list he'd be driving back down to Albuquerque and then flying to Wichita Falls, Texas again tomorrow.

For now, he'd had a pretty decent dinner at a place down the road--real food, steak and potatoes, not that gut-wrenching Mexican shit-- and he was going to read for a while and hit the pillow, since he'd be wanting to get on the road fairly early in the morning.

He peered at himself in the full-length mirror in the passageway to the bathroom and hated how he looked: the slightly faded jeans, the open-neck Western shirt with the fake pearl snaps, the turquoise bolo tie, the cowboy boots. He loathed all this crap, but the one thing he never wanted to do was *look* like a government type. None of those plain off-the-rack suits like in the movie stereotypes, those quietly efficient dark suits, the sort of thing he'd actually rather be wearing. In New Mexico and Texas, day to day on the street, this corny Western getup was the closest thing there was to being invisible.

But, by God, he didn't have to wear this stuff while nobody was looking. He stripped down to his underwear and stretched out on the bed, cradling a glass of gin in one hand and reaching for his book with the other. Invigorating, the oddly timeless comforts of that wily old gentleman William Shakespeare. He flipped open the copy of *Titus Andronicus* he'd bought in the Trujillo broad's bookshop and began to read. He'd read it before, of course, but hadn't had a copy of it for a long time, and looked forward to getting back into it.

A strange diversion, some people would probably say, a peculiar enthusiasm for a government man sunk deeper in secret activities than most of the population could even have imagined. (Certainly the very existence of Group Epsilon was unsuspected even among most top-secret clearance holders in government service, let alone the general public. There were Presidents who never knew of it, and a couple who ended up wishing they hadn't.) But it wasn't so strange, this oblique fondness for Shakespeare. He'd derived much of his inspiration, over the years, from

48

the Bard. Not the kind of inspiration his teachers had wanted him to derive, he feared; no, a darker, less mentionable kind of inspiration. Just as he liked all of Shakespeare's most evil and loathsome characters--Iago in *Othello,* Lear's greedy and pitilessly grudging bitch daughters Goneril and Regan--he liked the characters in the play *Titus Andronicus* for their very villainy and baseness. Imagine, Emperor Saturninus promising to spare Titus's sons from the executioner's ax if Titus would cut off his own hand and send it to him in tribute, and receiving the hand from Titus, and sending it back to him with the sons' severed heads, the ultimate gesture of derision and contempt and arrogance. Imagine, in turn, Titus killing Empress Tamora's sons for revenge and baking their heads into meat pies for Tamora to eat. God, Roger Wynn loved these people.

Somehow they were more real to him than just about anyone he'd ever really known, or known of. A few real-life people came close. Take Carlos Trujillo's case, for example. He'd never known the operative, of course, out in Montana, who had posed as Trujillo's roommate and waited till Trujillo loosened up and talked about the crash site and then had taught him a quaint little lesson in obedience by cutting one of his fingers off. Hell, that had been five *decades* ago, before Roger Wynn's mother had given birth to a pink-faced baby destined to become a first-class bastard himself. But Roger felt as if he'd known the guy in Montana as a soulmate. He liked his style--uncompromising, unmerciful. You had to be that way with these people, these private citizens. They were peasants, basically; you had to keep them in line, and you had to never forget, even for a moment, your superiority to them. If only one could get by not even having such people around. That was unrealistic, of course; unfortunately, there had to be a general populace, if only to pay the taxes.

Then again, he reflected, there was a certain enjoyable flavor to this line of work precisely because there *were* the Trujillos and all the rest of them. Occasionally, when tired and a little disillusioned on the road somewhere, he caught himself thinking that maybe the Group should just quietly have all of them killed, that maybe it wasn't worth the effort keeping an eye on them. But in the next moment he would always admit to himself that that wasn't true--that it was, on the contrary, very much worth it. Just a year ago there had been that affair about the photograph. Someone back at Roswell in 1947, an enlisted man named Ortez, had whipped out a cheap little camera and snapped a black-and-white photo of a truckload of metal debris before it was secured in the hangar to await shipment to Fort Worth and ultimately to Wright Field (later Wright-Patterson Air Force Base) in Ohio. The photo, along with any number of unauthorized comments of a classified nature, no doubt, was passed through various family members, unknown to Roger's people until a grandson was overheard mentioning it on a computer bulletin board. Roger had not only retrieved the photo but eliminated everyone, so far as Group Epsilon could discover, who knew anything about what was in the photo. Thank heaven the bulletin board remarks had been vague enough not to really give anything away on the computer network.

This was the way it had to be. The Group simply could not allow any evidence of this kind to remain in circulation. So even if it meant seemingly fruitless travels, things like popping into Lucy Trujillo's bookshop, or into the barber shops and cabs and workplaces of dozens of other peripheral figures in this sprawling drama, it all had to be done. Sooner or later, you found something out. Sooner or later. That's why the Group didn't just kill all these people; to do so might be to snuff out information that they could ultimately provide.

It was a lot of legwork, overall. And the thing was, at this level, you did the legwork yourself, even if you were one of the highest-level operatives alive.

There simply weren't that many people you could trust.

He sloshed the rest of his drink around in the glass and finished it at a gulp, and set his book aside and switched off the light, and lay back and tried to get to sleep. But for well over an hour, he found it was no use; he lay in the dark with his eyes wide open, wondering what was keeping him from sleeping. It wasn't for lack of being tired. At length he realized that he was lying there listening. Listening for what? Somewhere off in the dark out there, some dogs were barking, and he could just hear the faint swish of late-evening traffic on Cerillos Road, a sound soft enough not to be a bother from this far back in the motel complex. What was he listening for?

No, the question was, what was he listening *to?* He must have been tired, he reflected, not to realize that it wasn't really a sound at all-- that it came from inside his own head. It was a sort of music, a plaintive, lilting, nondescript sort of song, so subtle and free-flowing that it was almost like listening to the wind. Or some primitive instrument that sounded reedy like the wind. This was strange, because even though all his life he had heard people say that they had songs on their mind that they couldn't stop thinking of, he had never been one to have that experience. Till now. It was crazy--he was a nuts-and-bolts guy, practical, purposeful, no time for silly songs.

But this song wasn't silly--it was haunting. It made him feel like laughing; then the next moment, just as he began a quiet self-reproach for such a foolish notion, the song's effect would turn sad, and damned if he didn't feel almost like crying. The feeling would pass, and the song would seem happy again, then sad again.

He sighed, wondering if maybe it was true what some people said about this line of work--that in most cases you were well over the hill, done, finished, history, by the age of fifty, and often a good bit ahead of that age.

Well no, God damn it, forty-eight was still plenty young, young enough. He could run dizzying circles around most operatives fifteen years his junior. Why let a song, a damned song that kept running through his head, make him think that he was losing it? Why did it bother him at all?

Because, another corner of his mind replied, you don't like not understanding, not knowing exactly what's going on, what's happening with your reactions.

It was true; that was why the song bothered him. Why else?

He finally began to drift off to sleep, but not before it occurred to him that something, some undefinable something about the song felt--*old*. Very, very old. He would have chided himself for that notion, would have told himself that he was letting his guard down, that he was too inclined to let spending so much time in the desert begin to tell on him; but he was asleep before he could form the thought, and his dreams were modulated by the feather-soft tones of a flute, like the burring of the wind in an arroyo.

7

Sage

The desert was cold tonight. Sage poked another dry branch from a creosote bush into the flickering fire as the chilly wind moaned its way through and sent little swirls of sparks dancing against the stars. He pulled himself up closer to the fire, filled his pipe with the special medicine he had prepared, and, lighting it with a twig from the fire, puffed an undulating curtain of gray smoke out on the air.

His wrinkled hand went up and touched the medicine bag hanging on its leather thong around his neck, felt and caressed the ancient pouch that had been with him always, the timeless pouch that contained a lifetime's gatherings of desert magic, his own individual medicines representing many, many years of sifting and choosing. His medicines were powerful. Powerful.

Tonight his dreams would begin to tell him what he needed to know.

It was only October, but another winter would be coming on, and it would be the seventy-ninth for the man whom people in the towns and pueblos called Sage, the man who couldn't even remember who it was who had first given him that name but answered to it all the same, even though he called himself by far other names, or by none at all. Yes, nearly eighty winters moaned and creaked in these bones. They were still serviceable, still took him where he wanted to go, but sometimes they felt weary, these bones, and they felt weary tonight, crouched in an angular pile beside the fire like so much kindling. Old bones in an old desert. This seemingly somber thought always warmed him. Let the Anglos and the Spanish and even his own brothers in the pueblos worry about their homes; to Sage, the desert was, had always been, would always be, his home--it would be home even when these bones moved no more. Maybe especially then.

As if in response to this last thought, the wind, carrying dry memories of chamisa and sagebrush, swelled into a moan. But the spirits were not come to carry him off just yet. There were things, important things to be done, long before then. Sage knew that, felt it.

As he puffed the mixture in his pipe, he gradually saw the cold light of the stars subtly brighten, the colors clarifying themselves, the very sand reflecting them where the wind drew its fingers through the drifting grains and resettled the sand in an ever-changing painting of starlight. It was time now; he would sleep, and dream.

He would dream the telling dreams, and would know what things he ought to do; and in doing them--who could tell?--he might well have to dream the Dream that Makes the World.

His mind settled into quiet caverns, into shadow. But the caverns were not entirely quiet, the shadows not altogether unbroken. What things stirred here?

In his mind he saw, coming out of a swirl of mixed darkness and light, the great bright object again, the great silver thing that had fallen from the sky many years before. Sage, then a young man, had seen it fall, and he saw it before him now, a resplendent memory made new. He seemed once again to be that young Indian from Jemez Pueblo, the outcast, the self-exiled visionary who was one day to be a *brujo,* a feared man among those who knew what such a *brujo* was, a man not to be trifled with, a man in touch with the world, not the white man's world but the real world of the desert. He seemed again now to be that young renegade who crouched in the shadows and watched the great bright object fall from the night sky, emitting a roaring sound as it passed overhead, splitting open to spill its strange entrails in the sand near where Sage watched, and falling to earth somewhere beyond a distant ridge. In his dream, the sight, the sounds were real again, as if no time had passed.

He saw himself stopping for a moment among the pieces of debris, then saw himself walking over the littered sand, walking and then running toward the place where he had seen the thing come down. When he came around the ridge and down into the hollow where the thing lay, he found little people, little crushed bodies sprawled upon the sand near the silver craft--lifeless little bodies with great round heads and eyes like almonds, eyes dark and deep but staring at nothing now, staring in the stony quiet of death.

But no, one of the little people lying on the ground was still alive. Its scrawny little sparrow-chest hitched slightly, and it blinked its big eyes

53

and turned its head to look at him. And in that instant, for Sage, it was like looking into all time and space, into all the mysteries of the world, to look into those dark almond eyes.

Things were said, understandings were exchanged, that no words alone could have conveyed. *I am in pain,* the bottomless eyes seemed to say; *you must help me.*

The young Indian's hand, first pressing the then newer medicine bag to his chest, reached across and touched the little child-face, the face of the little child that was not a child. He knew what he had to do. Gesturing to the sky-child that he must rest and wait for his return, Sage went off into the night to gather what he needed from the plants in the desert, things that not ten *brujos* in the land would have known of. When he returned, he made preparations from the plants, said the words of power over them, and ministered to the fragile creature lying before him on the ground. By the time the sun was coming up, the creature was visibly recovering, and a real and lasting bond of mutual understanding was developing between them; but there were distant sounds of motors, and Sage knew that the white man was nearby, that others had seen the lights in the night sky, had heard the explosion--he knew that they were coming to investigate. And in some subtle way he understood even then that he must not be here when they came, must not let them know that he had been here, or that he had seen the sky-child. He knew the minds of the Anglos too well for that. By the time they came in their Army jeeps and trucks, Sage was gone.

The scene faded, and his mind swirled away now into other regions, regions less clear because this time they were not memories but other kinds of images. He saw a woman, not young exactly but not old, with a pretty Hispanic face, a face, however, subtly shadowed over with some dark worry. The woman was surrounded with books, hundreds or maybe thousands of them, their multitudinous spines ranged around her like fantastic rows of teeth; but he sensed that there was no menace in this image, because the woman loved the books. Except that there were dark thoughts connected with one of them, one that he could almost but not quite see in his shimmering vision, some ponderous tome that held a vital and dangerous secret. Was it true, then, that in the Anglo world the things printed in books were often regarded as more "real" than the realities around one in everyday life?

No; as vague as the vision was, he sensed that the menace emanating from this strange book came not from the printed words on the pages, but from--something else, something somehow associated with the book.

Something, oddly enough, important in his own life.

And looming over this dream-scene was another strangeness, a shadow of more palpable menace. It was a man, an Anglo who watched the woman, who would in time come to her and do her harm. Somehow Sage felt that this man was an embodiment of all that was sinister, all that was evil in the Anglo world.

As the wind from the desert expanses rose slightly to moan through the chaparral like the whispered notes of a magic flute, Sage drew his blanket around him for warmth and slept again beside the pale embers, with one more thought before slumber eased up around him. It seemed to him that the shadow in the dream-image was that of a man without a soul.

8

The Tech Interviewer

In the little underground room with the soft blue light Dr. Anne Hawk watched yet again, one more time among countless times, as the inner door opened to admit a faint whiff of slightly different air, the canned and treated air prepared with tiny, subtle adjustments for the Crewman's comfort and health. He could breathe ordinary air well enough, but in time he would have had some difficulties without this barely discernible adjustment to the mix of gases: very slightly less oxygen, very slightly more nitrogen, tiny reproportionings of trace gases. The door swung fully open and the Crewman came in, nodding in his eternal way to Anne and, today, to the other interviewer.

For today Anne was not alone with her friend. Beside her at the little table sat Dr. Scott Harris, one of the tech interviewers who periodically came to talk with the Crewman. This was the part Anne hated, having these people here, not having the Crewman to herself. It was when they were alone together that the deepest understandings came, and the understandings with the most noble motives, the motives concerned with understanding for its own sake, not with the sort of "cultural gain" that these technocrats liked to talk about. With Anne, the reasons for her sessions with the Crewman had to do with changing the whole way one thought about language and communication and thought; with these tech people, the motives were altogether another matter. Anne could never say anything about how she felt, or even let her face betray her thoughts, but in many ways she hated these people. There would be no discussion of the semi-endo-resultative aspect of the L-1 quasi-verb this morning, certainly.

"Good morning, Anne," the Crewman said, blinking his large dark eyes once, slowly.

56

"Good morning," Anne said. In the presence of a tech interviewer, they would skip their customary pleasantries. The Crewman nodded, a little stiffly, to Dr. Harris, who, opening up folders of papers and spreading them around on the table, got right to the point.

"You mentioned to me last time," he said, "that you were soon going to be taking us into some more new territory, and opening us up to a whole new concept of circuit design."

The Crewman just looked at him, rather as if this prologue had been repetitive and unnecessary, though (Anne reflected as always) when one tried to deal with this creature's mind, one could never be sure about motivations and feelings.

"Well, uh," Dr. Harris continued, coughing as if a little embarrassed by the Crewman's silence, "I'd like to start exploring that new concept of design with you."

You mean, Anne thought, you'd like to move on to the next level of picking this noble creature's brain. But the Crewman this time was responding, in English and through oral means, speaking in his reedy voice through that thin, seemingly vestigial mouth.

"This will take some considerable time."

Dr. Harris shrugged, shuffling among his papers. "We have all the time in the world."

Yeah, Anne thought, *you* have, but would you ever consider this creature's desires? Does he want to be here at all, and has he not been essentially a prisoner all these years? That was a whole area of concern that Anne had never entirely been able to make sense of. What were the Crewman's real feelings about being here? Was he stranded among overbearing strangers? Or was he in the midst of something he saw as a grand adventure? Or was his notion of the situation something different altogether? She had at times tried to ask him about these things, but had never entirely understood his responses, and had always to keep reminding herself that when it came to the Crewman's psychology, she was eternally the beginner; it was always, in many respects, the first day of kindergarten. And it was always dangerous to think that one had achieved any meaningful analysis or reached any really valid interpretation of the Crewman's motives or wishes or preferences; indeed, even such terms as "motive" were suspect. But she could never quite abstain from wondering whether the Crewman would be capable somehow of leaving the complex if he ever wanted to, whatever "wanted to" meant for him. In what ways did it matter, or did it matter, to this creature, that he had been kept in secret places by humankind for half a century? What did time mean to him? Or was time a human metaphor merely?   But Dr. Harris was asking some questions of his own.

"You've said that this new phase is going to take a lot of time," he said, the tone of his voice nearly accusatory. "I can't help wondering why you say that. However complex these new concepts are, I think it's fair to say that we're very capable learners."

The Crewman gazed at him for a long time without speaking, as Anne looked on, somewhat amused. It was impossible, even for her, to read expressions in the Crewman's face with any accuracy, but Anne liked to think, just now, that he was enormously amused by the tech interviewer's egocentric remark. At length the Crewman responded.

"Yes, you are fairly good learners, over time. But we must take up these matters gradually to deal properly with them."

Dr. Harris snorted at this. "Really, I think you underestimate us. I think you've underestimated us all these years. You've dribbled technological information out to us much more slowly than was necessary. I have to take exception. In 1947, shortly after our sessions with you began, when you provided the inspiration for the invention of the transistor, could you not at that point have taken us farther along? What would have been wrong with showing us the fundamentals of printed circuit designs? What would have been wrong with teaching us the theory of fiber optics, years earlier than you did?"

"You would not have been as ready to receive such ideas," the Crewman said, speaking slowly, "as you were when more properly prepared by digesting preliminary stages of the technology first."

Harris was visibly annoyed. "Again, I have to take exception to this condescending attitude of yours."

"Let me ask *you* a question," the Crewman said. "You have the contents of the crashed spacecraft, well preserved somewhere, and have studied them along with the technological principles that you have been acquiring. To this day, do you fully understand the things you found inside the craft?"

At this, Harris got up and paced the floor behind Anne's line of sight, and seemingly had to, to contain his annoyance. Finally he sat heavily in his chair and glared at the Crewman. "No, we do not fully understand those things. But we're working on it, and I think we've come a long way."

The Crewman looked at him in silence for several seconds, and said, flatly, "You have come a little way."

Harris appeared to be rendered speechless by this response. He merely sat and scowled. Good, Anne thought. It was up to the Crewman to pick up the conversation. "We digress," he said. "We were going to begin talking about the next phase. With this, you stand upon the threshold of some real knowledge. But as I have said, and as you must expect, these things will take time."

Harris at length recovered his composure, asked a few preliminary questions, and took notes as the Crewman began a slow, patient-sounding explanation of some technical principles of which Anne had very little comprehension. She at least felt no discomfort over this lack of comprehension; Harris, she reflected, wouldn't understand the first thing about the language L-1 either, or about linguistics generally, and indeed she had the satisfaction of knowing that the process of communication here very much required her presence. For even though the exchange was taking place primarily in English (possibly with some mind-transference involved, Anne could never be sure), there were points at which clarifications were necessary, points even at which the process would have to wait for Anne and the Crewman to exchange some remarks in L-1 for attempted translation, then, into English. At these times, what Anne thought of as the "something-like principle" came into play, for some notions natural to L-1 were exceedingly tricky to express in English, and indeed would have been exceedingly tricky to import into any human language, though American Indian languages would often have been the readier receptacles.

"What he is saying," Anne at one point explained to Dr. Harris, "is that the principle on which the, ah, something-like proto-new circuit depends, is one that requires not only thinking beyond binary logic but something-like rethinking the thinking-beyond, rather as if the logical process were folded back upon itself."

Harris looked puzzled. "Could we see some examples?"

The discussion meandered on through mazes of discussion that seemed not only to leave Anne behind most of the time but also to push Harris to his limits. "You're right," he finally conceded, "this is all going to take some time. Let me just ask you: how different, ultimately, are these new circuit designs going to be from the most advanced designs we have now?"

The Crewman took some time to respond, blinking his large eyes and meeting Anne's gaze once before turning back to Harris and speaking metaphorically. "You have learned a good portion of the alphabet," he said. "At the farther levels, we are talking about reading *Finnegans Wake*."

With this response it gratified Dr. Anne Hawk to see, clearly, in the tech interviewer's face, that the Crewman knew more about English literature than the interviewer did. Narrow, disgusting people, Anne thought: driven only by monolithic motives.

59

"I think that's enough for this morning," Harris was saying as he gathered up his notes and prepared to leave. "I just have one more thing to say. I'm not pleased with the tone of some of the things that have been said here this morning. As I've indicated, I resent your condescending attitude, and I object to the fact that you've played out the facts to us all these years a great deal more slowly than I think would have been necessary, and you're still doing it." (How can the stupid son of a bitch say that, Anne thought, when clearly he hasn't understood half of what he's heard here this morning?) "I think it's only right to tell you," Harris continued, speaking to the Crewman as if Anne were not even present, "that if we perceive you as not coöperating with us, we may become less interested, than we have been in the past, in seeing to your comforts. It's trouble and expense to us, you know, to keep up your environmental specifications as carefully as we have regulated them. The very mix of air that you breathe in your quarters is a privilege that we dispense to you, not an absolute right. I trust that you will never give us reason to suppose that in your coöperation with our inquiries, you are trying less hard than you might."

Anne found these remarks profoundly shocking, even for these people. When Harris was gone, she turned to the Crewman. "I'm sorry, I'm sorry about this, as a human being and a friend. I'm ashamed of my species sometimes." That would end up on videotape, but she didn't care.

The Crewman looked at her, long and fixedly, and reached across the table and lay a dry, leathery little hand upon her hand for a second. She wished, for the thousandth time, that she could fathom the expression in those sable eyes. But, she reflected, maybe the consolation is in knowing this: that it is wiser to realize that one cannot fathom those expressions. She smiled to the Crewman, who nodded and withdrew to the door and into the hallway beyond.

This can't go on, she thought, a dull ember of anger glowing within her somewhere. Not if they're going to start treating him like this. Now that he's apparently got them technologically on the verge of something really spectacular, they're beginning to feel desperate to get on with it, and it's going to come out in the form of their being unkind to him. And this after all he has done for them, for us all! she thought, suddenly furious. The main reason for the secrecy, all these years, she reflected--besides the awkwardness of admitting that the armed forces of the United States do not control the airways if creatures from the outside decide to come calling--the main reason is a selfishness over the technology, a desire to be first, and to try to monopolize, as long as possible, each new advance, to try to be the sole beneficiaries. The irony of this, of course, was that sooner or later other countries, other societies did get in on the benefits; maybe the knowledge that that would be the case was a good part of the reason why the Crewman dispensed this information at all. She had often speculated on his motives, knowing as usual that it was all up for grabs, psychologically; seemingly, he wanted to bring humankind along to a certain level of sophistication, perhaps hoping that it would improve their collective character. But what was "wanting" and what was "hoping," when one was talking about the Crewman?

In any event, she was beginning to know what *she* wanted. She wanted these technology-hungry secret-hoarders to leave her friend the hell alone.

But it was dangerous for her, in her position, even to think such things. Her loyalty had to be beyond question.

How much longer, though, she wondered--how much longer *could* she be loyal to them?

9

A Face from the Past

Anne drove back to Alamogordo that afternoon in only a very little better frame of mind than she had been in earlier, when watching Dr. Harris with the Crewman. Her own afternoon session with the Crewman, though it had reverted happily to matters of linguistics and the philosophy of language, hadn't done as much as she had hoped, in the long run, to cheer her up after the morning session. Damn the arrogance of these people! What gave them the *right?* What made them think they owned the Crewman's mind outright, what made them think that they were justified in doing anything they felt like doing to attain their ends? It was disgraceful, the way that asshole Harris had talked to the Crewman. Disgraceful.

But driving through the lower outskirts of town with their garish clusters of fast food places, tourist bric-a-brac shops, used car lots, and motels, she reflected, forcing honesty upon herself, that only part of her growing concern was for the Crewman. A large part was also for herself.

She worked at a level of security clearance held by very few people. She was a person privy to government secrets of such extreme sensitivity that any suggestion of impaired loyalty on her part could lead to consequences she wouldn't even want to think about.

What, she sometimes wondered, had really happened to her predecessor George Quintana? Perhaps, under similar circumstances, he had grown squeamish at some point, had begun to balk at the whole process, had led the powers-that-be to conclude that he could no longer be trusted. What about the people who had preceded him? She felt like a sort of orphan, a lone figure whose forebears have been lost in some unfathomable mist of time, and in fact it gave her gooseflesh, at times, to realize that there was no trace left, anywhere, so far as she could determine, of anyone who had ever worked as a linguist with the Crewman. No trace left of anyone but herself.

That wasn't a happy inheritance altogether, when you thought about it.

To put it to herself bluntly: was she going to be next? If they ever decided that they could make do without her. . . .

Coming into town, she turned up Tenth Street and headed toward her home near the foothills out on the east side, but decided to stop at Cantina Zia, her favorite little bar in town, and have a drink before going home. She needed it. She really did. Parking her car in the lot, she reflected grimly that at no time, not even at this moment, could she assume that they weren't watching her. For all she knew, there would be a note in some report somewhere on somebody's desk by this time tomorrow, if not sooner, mentioning what kind of drink she'd had this afternoon at the bar. God, she thought--am I getting paranoid! But maybe not; she'd been in this business too long to be naïve.

Inside, the little room was shadowy and pleasant; she enjoyed the sensation of being away from light and cameras and scrutiny, even if the feeling was only evanescent if not downright deluded. Here, details were mercifully obscure, sharp corners rounded in dimness, anxieties put at ease. She sat at the nearly deserted bar--there were only four or five people in the place--and exchanged greetings with Mauricio, the bartender, and ordered a margarita.

"You look like you had a hard day, Anne," Mauricio said, setting the drink down in front of her. "*Trabajas demasiado. Debieras relajar.*"

She laughed. "Yes, I know I ought to relax more. *Pero es cosa más fácil decir que hacer,* Mauricio," she said. "Easier said than done. Gotta make a living, you know."

Mauricio smiled, shaking his head, and went back to polishing glasses.

She was halfway through her margarita when she became aware that a man seated a few feet down the bar from her was watching her.

The sense of being watched was so constantly a part of her life that at first she paid little attention, but after a moment, following some impulse, she looked over, and her eyes and the man's eyes met.

The man's mouth fell open. "Anne? Anne Hawk! I'll be damned, I *thought* it looked like you!"

She could scarcely believe it. "Eric? This is--my God, what are you doing here?" Eric Hayes. It was really Eric Hayes. How long, how many years--? She was off her bar stool, he was off his, and they were hugging and laughing.

63

Still holding her, he drew back as if to see her better. "I haven't seen you since Yale. Damn, that's been a lot of years, but I swear you don't look a day older. Do you live in Alamogordo?"

She gave him another squeeze and they sat back down, this time on adjacent bar stools. He was still as handsome as ever, his brown hair just beginning to show inroads of gray, his face broad and honest and full of character; he was wearing jeans and a western shirt, and he looked good in them. "Yes, I've been down here for twelve years now. I work at Holloman Air Force Base, government job. How about you?" Several years older than she was, Eric had been finishing his doctorate in anthropology at Yale about the same time she'd been finishing hers in linguistics, and the last she'd heard, he had been teaching in some university in Idaho or somewhere. "Still teaching anthropology?"

"Yes," he said, "Mesa Linda College, up in Albuquerque. Been there eight years now. I'm on sabbatical this term, came down to do some research on the Indian petroglyphs up the road here, the Three Rivers site up past Tularosa. But how about you? Still into languages?"

She took a sip of her drink and nodded. "Yeah, up to my ears." If you only knew, she thought. "Have you, ah, I mean, are you--"

"Married?" He finished the question for her, grinning. "Divorced, a couple of years ago. You know, just one of those things. No kids, but it was rough anyway. I've pretty well gotten over it, though. How about you? You, ah--"

She shook her head. "Never got married. I was always moving around from one job assignment to another and everything, all over the world, never stayed in one place for very long at a time until I came to Alamogordo, and never have gotten involved with anybody." Anybody human, she thought. "Guess I never found anyone who could put up with me."

He laughed, a goodhearted, pleasant, musical sound, and took a swallow of his drink. "Listen, I just got back from the petroglyph site half an hour ago and haven't had a chance to shake off the trail dust yet, so I've got to go back to my motel room and get cleaned up. I was wondering if you'd like to have dinner with me."

She finished her drink. "I'd love to. We can talk about old times." Inwardly she almost winced at having added this, wondering how it would sound to him. As exciting as it was to see him again, she rather thought that she shouldn't sound too eager. Their romance had been over, after all, for many years; the man had been married, in between, to someone else, for God's sakes. But he seemed not to find anything strange in her quick response.

"I'm not that familiar with Alamogordo," he said. "Any good restaurants?"

"There's a little place on the north side that probably serves the best barbecue on the planet," she said. "Place called Cholla Lounge."

"Well," he said, evidently pleased, "it's a date. Let's see, it's nearly five now. I could pick you up--"

"Why don't I just meet you there?" she said. "The Cholla is just north of the park, on the east side of the road." She had her reasons for hesitating to have him come to her house, and they had nothing to do with any mistrust of *him*. She knew she was almost always being watched, and somehow felt that this arrangement might afford them a shade more privacy, though for all she knew the powers-that-be were already taking all of this in. Well, let them, she thought; why should I have to hide, for Christ's sake, don't I have a right to some life of my own?

"Okay," Eric was saying, taking her hand and giving it a squeeze. "See you there at seven."

# # # #

They had a corner booth, dimly and cozily illumined by a candle in a little lantern on the table, and ordered a drink before dinner. She ordinarily never had two drinks on any given day, and passingly wondered if she was going to be in danger of getting sloshed. "Tell me," she said, "about yourself."

He shrugged. "Not much to tell. Pretty comfy teaching job at Mesa Linda, a mix of graduate and undergrad courses, get to direct a master's thesis now and then. Have been using my sabbatical to do some research on mythic motifs in Indian petroglyphs, which is what brings me down here to the Three Rivers site. Mogollon petroglyphs. I could take you out there and show them to you sometime, but just talking about them makes for pretty dull listening, actually. I'd rather hear about you."

"Well," she said. As always, she had to be careful to stick to the cover stories, or at least to the truthful but unclassified and thus uninformative job descriptions. "I do translation work, basically. Secret stuff, you know. Talk about dull."

"There's nothing about you," he said, and the look in his eye suggested sincerity, "nothing whatever that could ever be considered dull."

She laughed. "So you say. You barely know me any more, Eric. I'm going to turn forty in a few weeks. I'm not that lively young chick you knew at Yale."

"Aren't you?"

"Well, I don't *think* I am. That was a long time ago. Let's see, good heavens--eighteen years ago. I was twenty-two when I got my degree."

65

"And," he added, "as a prodigy, the envy of everyone on campus. Including me."

This was the closest they came, at this point, to talking about those times years ago, those faraway days in New Haven when they had had a promising-looking romance, a romance that somehow just never worked out. Blame it on what you would--diverging career aspirations, whatever--it just never worked out, and they had parted awkwardly, painfully. They had exchanged a few letters after that, but had quickly lost track of each other when Anne started travelling with her job. She wanted, now, to talk about those days, because the memories of them had often bothered her since. But just now they were ordering dinner, and the conversation turned to other things.

Over dessert, and after glancing around the room a bit to try to see whether they were being overheard, she leaned a little closer to him across the table, lowered her voice, and said, "I don't have to work tomorrow. Could we take a ride somewhere tonight? To talk some more? Out in the desert someplace?"

He looked surprised, but pleasantly so. "Certainly. You bet. Go in my car?"

"That'd be fine," she replied. And safer, she thought: probably nobody has bugged *your* car, and in any case I'm not talking about anything that matters, anything that I don't want overheard, not until we're out of the car and in the open somewhere, under the sky. "I just think it'd be nice to get out in the desert," she said. "I know you've been spending all your time out there--"

"But not with you," he said. "And not usually at night. It'll probably be cold out there, but I've got blankets in the car. You know something? People who have never been out on the desert at night have never really seen the stars the way they're supposed to look. I love it out there."

She smiled at him. "You're my kind of folks."

# # # #

A little after nine, they both drove back to Anne's house to leave her car in the driveway, and she got into his car, a light brown Subaru. "Fourwheel drive," he said. "It's great for unpaved roads, or no roads at all, the places I have to go sometimes." He stopped at a stop sign. "Where would you like to go?"

"Could you take me up to the petroglyph site?"

He shrugged. "Well, I could, but you can't really see much of anything up there at night. I'll take you there in daylight, first chance. Promise."

"Well," she said, "for now, then, let's just head north on Route 54, toward Tularosa, and maybe take some side roads."

"You got it."

They drove out of town, past the motels and auto dealerships and shopping centers of the north end, and were soon on the open road, where there was practically no traffic. As the moon wasn't up, it was too dark to see anything past the periphery of Eric's headlights, where the pale wash of illumination showed only the beginnings of what Anne knew was a limitless sea of sand and sagebrush stretching away in both directions from the road. They drove without speaking; Anne felt very comfortable, just being here with Eric, and was sure that Eric felt that way too, his face wanly lit by the glow of the instrument panel as the ribbon of road slipped beneath them. In a little while they were passing through the sleepy little town of Tularosa and then heading farther north, toward Three Rivers.

"There's a side road," Anne said, pointing ahead of them to the right.

"Let's see where it goes," Eric said, slowing the car and turning onto the little road, which was roughly surfaced with gravel. They bumped along for perhaps two or three miles, seeing nothing on either side but more sand and sagebrush and, occasionally, clumps of cactus. After a while another little road, even more primitive, because not paved at all, meandered off to the left, and Eric eased the car in that direction.

"Might as well get really lost while we're at it," he said, grinning.

They followed this road for maybe a mile, seeing it grow narrower and bumpier, and then it seemed to play out altogether. Eric stopped the car, shut off the headlights, and they got out and walked out across the sand, through the darkness, guided in their steps only by starlight, there being not the faintest suggestion of electric lights anywhere. The sky was a dense wonderland of stars against velvety black, cloven through the middle by a Milky Way more brilliant than anything Anne had ever seen. They stopped walking and just stood for a few moments looking up at the stars. Somewhere off in the night the wind sighed, putting Anne in mind of flute-notes. She took Eric's hand. There was no need for words. But finally Eric broke the silence; he spoke softly, as if not wanting to disturb the tranquillity around them.

"I've always wondered why things back in New Haven didn't work out for us," he said.

"Me too," she said. "I don't know. Life is funny. If I haven't learned much else over the years, I've learned that there aren't any easy answers."

Eric sighed. "I guess it was my fault. I might have been a hotshot doctoral candidate in those days, but in some ways I was an idiot."

She squeezed his hand. "Don't be too tough on yourself. I don't think things are always necessarily anybody's fault. Not altogether. It was as much me as you. Maybe more. I was pretty selfish, you know. I had my career to think of."

"Nothing wrong with that," he said. "I'll bet you've had a brilliant career."

She shrugged, and was quiet for a long time. "Yeah, well."

He moved around to face her more squarely. Now that her eyes were more adjusted to the dark, she could see concern in his face. "Somehow I get the feeling," he said, "that you're not too happy. Something's bothering you."

She put her arms around him, drawing him to her. "Just hold me for a minute." He held her close. A little dance of wind swirled around their feet, sought the darkness, and was gone. At length she leaned back, still holding him, to look into his face.

"You're right, you know. You always could tell when something was bothering me."

"Is it something you can talk about?"

"No," she said. "In my line of work there isn't much of anything you can talk about. But you know something? I've made up my mind. Maybe I'm *losing* my mind. I'm probably crazy as a bedbug. I'm probably rabbit-ass, batshit crazy even to be thinking about doing this. I'm probably signing my own goddamn death warrant. No, what's bothering me isn't anything I can talk about. But it's something I'm *going* to talk about."

"Are you sure--I mean, I don't want to--"

She gave him a quick hug, drew apart, pulled her coat collar tighter against the chilly air, buttoned Eric's coat tighter to his chest, and pointed to an expanse of bare sand nearby, pausing to see that it was free of snakeholes. "Let's sit. I've got a long story to tell you."

# # # #

By the time she had told him about the Roswell crash of 1947 and had told him what she knew of the coverup operations, they were getting cold, and Eric was saying, "Maybe we'd better go sit in the car." But she shook her head.

"No. It's got to be out here." So Eric went to the car and came back with the blankets, and they bundled themselves up warm, and Anne went on with her story.

By the time she finished telling him everything, the first rays of dawn were beginning to sneak into the night sky.

He just sat, for a long while, shaking his head, looking at her, then looking away, then looking at her and looking away again. "Dear God," he muttered, getting to his feet, unwinding himself from his blanket, dusting himself off, standing stiffly after so many hours' sitting on the cold sand, and staring off across the desert plains. "Dear God."

Anne too got up and dusted herself off, her eyes burning now for lack of sleep. She moved up behind Eric and took his hand. "We'd better go back to town," she said.

He sighed and turned to face her, his own eyes looking bloodshot. "Yeah. Back to town." He sounded as if he were asleep and dreaming; he probably wonders if he is, she thought.

"Before I forget to warn you," she said, "don't say anything about any of this once we get back in the car. I don't *think* they'll already have bugged your car, but you never can tell." Her life, she sensed, was different now, from this morning on; she was going to have to be vigilant, careful, circumspect--always.

"Just one thing I don't understand," he said.

"Only one?" she asked, and tried to chuckle, but it came out as a dry throaty sound without humor.

"From what you've said about the security and everything, you're really putting your life on the line to tell me all this. Why? How do you know you can trust me?"

She swallowed hard and tightened her hold on his hand. "Because sometimes a person has to stop thinking and start feeling," she said. "And because I had to tell someone. I don't mean," she added after a moment, "I don't mean just anyone. I'm glad it was you. I'm not sure I've done you any favors telling you, though. You'd really be better off not knowing, believe me. I guess it's essentially a very selfish thing I've done, now that I think about it. I've put you in a lot of danger to make me feel better. That's not a kind thing to do."

He leaned and kissed her, the first time they had kissed for eighteen years. "I'll be the judge of that," he said. "Now let's get you back to town; you need some sleep. I'm going to try to catch three or four hours' sleep and then get cleaned up and drive back up to Three Rivers. You want to come with me to the site?"

"What do you think," she said.

10

The Visiting Hour

Daydreams mixed and mingled with dreams, which mixed and mingled with waking thoughts. Hap Trujillo sat drowsing in the chair beside his bed, drowsing and waking, half listening to the old women down the way chattering about the weather, half preoccupying himself with his own dark and cavernous thoughts. It was an evening like any other, full of haunting memories, memories that weren't much company, because even in their swarming presence, he was still lonely. Lonely as only those in rest homes can be--bypassed by life, sidestepped by a busy world, lost in the slipstream. He did still have those memories, and sometimes he oddly cherished them, but often they seemed to smack only of despair. Sometimes they seemed colored with outright horror. Unwittingly, he put a comforting hand up to his own hand, covering and caressing the stub of what should have been a finger, and withdrawing a little more into himself.

Other people had visitors. He saw them come, saw them go. Mrs. Olney, your son is here. Mr. Morgan, your brother is here. Mrs. Beck, your daughter and her husband are here. Mrs. White, your granddaughter is here. "Mr. Trujillo." That was what he never heard.

"Mr. Trujillo?"

But he *was* hearing it. Wasn't he? He looked up, pulling his mind out of a maze of reflections.

It was that plump Miss Taylor, who worked here; she had a tall gentleman by her side. "Mr. Trujillo. You have a visitor. It's Mr. Ross."

The tall stranger was dressed in western pants and a western shirt, and wearing a turquoise bolo and boots. Ah, but he wasn't altogether a stranger, now that Hap remembered; he had been here before. Hap extended a bony hand, the hand that had all its fingers. "Hello, Mr. Ross. It's good to see you again."

The man smiled and sat on the edge of the bed facing Hap. "It's good to see you too, Hap."

It was awkward, downright embarrassing in fact, getting so old and rundown that you could no longer remember vital things--like who this fellow was, other than just his name. For the life of him, Hap couldn't recall how he had come to know him, or when, or exactly what the man had to do with the family. Some old friend, perhaps, from back when Juanita was still living. That must be it, if the fellow still cared enough to come visiting. Even so, it was embarrassing, not knowing exactly where he knew the man from. He felt obliged to cover up his ignorance, felt compelled to make conversation to give the impression of remembering all that he should be remembering, though he could not.

"It's been a while," he said.

The man shrugged. "Not so very long, Hap," he said. "Just a few weeks. I was here to see you in late August, I think it was. Yes, just before Labor Day. How have you been feeling?"

"Oh," Hap said, "*no puedo quejarme.*" Oddly, from the expression that Hap glimpsed in his face for a second, the fellow looked as if he didn't understand; it was an expression he had seen before, in countless faces, all his life in fact. But hadn't all of his and Juanita's friends, even most of the Anglos, known a little Spanish? Apparently this one did not. Hap was going to ask *¿Y usted?* but in his embarrassment over not recalling exactly who the man was or how he was supposed to know him, he realized that he didn't even know whether to address him more formally as *usted* or, more informally, as *tu.* "How about you?" he finally asked, taking refuge in the ambiguity of the English pronoun.

"I'm fine," the man said. "I saw your daughter Lucy the other day."

Hap brightened at this. "Lucy? It was--I don't know how long it was since I saw her."

"Surely she comes to visit from time to time."

"No," Hap said, "it's been--I can't remember. A long time. I think last time was Christmas, maybe. When you get old you think your children will think of you, but sometimes you find that they don't."

"How sharper than a serpent's tooth it is to have a thankless child," the visitor said, shaking his head.

"Sir?"

"Nothing, nothing."

"But how is my Lucy?" Hap asked.

"Oh, she's doing very well," the man replied.

Just then, Miss Taylor stepped up with a saucer and teacup. "I'm sorry to interrupt, but it's time for Mr. Trujillo to have his evening tea. Sweetener and a drop of milk, just as you like it, Mr. Trujillo."

Hap took the cup of tea and set it on the little table beside his chair; it would be too hot to drink, he liked to let it cool off a little first. "Yes, thank you, Miss Taylor." He turned back to face Mr. Ross, and sighed. "Like I said, Lucy never comes to see me."

"Well," the visitor said, "you know, she's very busy working. It takes a lot of time, running a business."

"Business?"

"Her bookshop."

"Oh. Yes. Bookshop." Had he forgotten that Lucy was working in a bookshop? It must have slipped his mind just momentarily. "The bookshop in--"

"Santa Fe. The Mesa Bookshop."

"Yes, yes," Hap said, though in truth the name didn't sound familiar to him. He must try to remember it now, something told him; must remember it, must etch it into his mind. He couldn't lose all the threads, couldn't let himself be detached from Lucy altogether. But didn't he have Lucy's phone numbers, at home and at work, somewhere? He thought he did, hoped he did.

"Is anything the matter?" the visitor was asking. "You seem preoccupied."

What was the matter? Hap's mind echoed the question ironically. My whole life is the matter, he thought.

"Your whole life?" the man asked, looking surprised. Had Hap spoken out loud?

"I--" Hap was confused now. What turn had the conversation taken? "Lucy--"

"Are you worried about Lucy, Hap?" the visitor asked, or seemed to ask; was the question only in Hap's mind? He gazed out the window at the darkness, or thought or dreamed that he did.

Worried? Worried about Lucy. Well, yes, when you've made the kind of mess of things that I have, Hap thought, there comes a time when you worry about what you've done to those you love. It wasn't enough that I gave poor Juanita so unpleasant a life, my dear Juanita who would be so early taken to her grave. No, that wasn't enough; I had to make trouble for Lucy too, Lucy and her husband both, but especially poor Lucy, after Juanita's death. *Dios mío*, Juanita had died, Juanita who knew about--things. And what ever happened to the piece of foil from the debris field? The piece of foil hidden in the book? He must have wondered about this before, but he couldn't remember. Everything was so confused sometimes. Most of the time. Did Lucy have the book, now, with the piece of foil? If she had it, did she *know* she had it? Had Juanita ever told her what the foil was, why it was important, how it was

72

concealed in the book? He scrabbled through his mind, his vague and unkempt memories, trying to remember. Where, where had the foil been, the last he knew, and where was it now? "Cervantes." Why was someone pronouncing this name? Had *he* said it?

"Cervantes?" a voice asked.

Suddenly a shroud of cold horror seemed to wrap itself around Hap's mind, chilling him, warning him. Was there a stranger here beside him? Ah, he remembered, he had been talking to Mr. Ross. But who *was* this Mr. Ross? Who was he really? Had Hap spoken to him? All this time, how much had he merely thought, how much had he said in his head, how much had he said aloud? "Mr. Ross, I--"

But the visitor was making ready to leave. "You were dozing off, and it's my fault, I shouldn't be imposing on you when you need your rest. Here, Miss Taylor asked me to remind you to finish your tea." He reached over and stirred the tea a little and handed the cup and saucer to Hap. "I'll be leaving now, but I'll be sure to give Lucy your regards when I see her, which will be very soon."

He stepped toward the door but turned to look back at Hap, shaking his head sadly. "O, what a noble mind is here o'erthrown," he said, and was gone.

Dear God in heaven, Hap thought, what have I said to him? What have I done?

A mound of ice seemed to gather in his bowels. Desperately, he tried to reconstruct what had happened, what he had said only in the imagination, what he had said aloud when his attention wandered. If he had said anything like what he feared he may have said, Lucy was in terrible danger.

Getting up and putting on his glasses and rummaging through his belongings in the little bureau at the foot of his bed, he sifted through formless jumbles of paper trying to find Lucy's phone number. Two numbers, he had, surely--her number at home and at work. Surely to God he had them here somewhere, somewhere.

Yes--here. In the front of his dog-eared little address book, a scrap of paper, and a legend in his own faint and shaky handwriting: Lucy's name, her home address in Santa Fe, her phone number, followed by *Mesa Bookshop* and another phone number.

He'd call her at home. They frowned on your making long-distance calls here, but he thought he could persuade them that he had to talk to his daughter. It was late, but he would call her, right now.

Or perhaps, to settle his nerves a little, he'd have his tea first.

11

Lucy Trujillo and her Dad

It was always a little startling when the phone rang, because it so seldom did. Lucy had her share of friends in Santa Fe, but they rarely called. In her circle of acquaintances people just weren't of the "thought I'd give you a call" or "thought I'd just drop in since I was in the neighborhood" type. They generally didn't call or visit without a reason and without telling you they were going to, and anyway, you saw them around town enough to keep in touch. So if this jangling telephone was one of those damned telemarketers ("How are you this evening, we'd like to offer you a free vacation in Hawaii, if you'll just take a moment--") or one of those survey-takers disturbing her at nine o'clock at night just when she was settling down to a nice martini and a cozy volume of Hawthorne stories. . . .

She walked from the living room to the kitchen and picked up the phone. "Lucy Trujillo residence."

At first she didn't recognize the voice on the other end, it meandered and rambled so strangely. " . . . all the time he was here standing here in front of me I thought I was just dreaming or maybe I was awake and just thinking my own thoughts and not really talking not really saying those things out loud to him but dear Jesus if I said any of those things to him really out loud and he heard me and he's one of them and he knows now because I think that's part of what I was saying when I thought I was only thinking it about the book and everything and not knowing if your poor mother God grant her peace in heaven if your poor mother ever even told you about what was in that book and what happened to me and why it was there why I had to hide it from them but now if he knows. . . ." This meandering discourse wandered back and forth between English and Spanish.

74

"Dad?" Lucy shouted into the phone, but trying to stop him was like trying to stop a runaway horse. "Dad!"

" . . . and I think I said it I think I told him and he knows all about you and where you are and everything and about the bookshop dear God he mentioned the bookshop I think he even said he was going to see you. . . ."

"Dad! Please!" Finally, she heard her father fall silent. "Now just calm down, Dad. This is Lucy, I'm here, it's okay, everything's okay--"

"No!" her father said, and the tone of urgency and panic in his voice started a slow, cold feeling like an icy finger working up her spine. Something, something was dreadfully wrong. "No," her father repeated, "no, Lucy, everything is *not* all right!"

"Dad," Lucy said, gently, trying to let him hear warmth in her voice, because she sensed that for whatever reason, he very much needed it right now. "Please just relax and tell me what's wrong."

There was a long silence on the other end. Finally: "A man was here to see me, Lucy. He called himself Mr. Ross. He's one of *them*. He's been here before. Trying to see if he can get anything out of me, I think. I'm not too clear in the head sometimes, Lucy, I wander a little, and I think he's been trying to see if--but you don't even know, do you?"

"Know what?" Lucy said, though she had actually a pretty good idea what he was referring to.

"God in heaven, I don't even know if your dear mother ever even told you all the facts. About the book. About what's in it."

The icy finger didn't just touch her spine now; it gripped it in a sickening little cruel embrace. Sweet Jesus, this could be it, this could be the end of everything, if they did know--! But it was preposterous. On a moment's reflection, she felt fairly sure that he was upset over nothing. She took a deep breath and got some of her composure back. After all these years, it was a little hard to believe that someone would just pop in like that and try to drag secrets out of him, even considering the magnitude of the secret that existed, because how would they have any idea? How could they even suspect, decades later, that there was an illicit piece of debris, that he knew where it was? But she had to say something, and thought it had better be the truth. "Dad--Dad, yes, I know what you're talking about. Mom told me. Years ago. Now please, just--"

Her father, miles away in a rest home in Wichita Falls, Texas, was crying.

"Dad, please, it's going to be all right." She wasn't entirely sure that it was, but what could she say? "You've just had a bad dream. It's okay. Try to calm yourself."

75

After a moment he said, "*Si, conforme, mi hija.* Let me just take a sip of my tea."

"Good," Lucy said. "Just relax, now, and we'll talk some more. Listen, I know they don't like you using the phone, so you hang up and I'm going to call you right back, that way it'll be on my bill. Okay?"

"Yes, okay," her father said. "I'll just have my tea and wait for you to call." She could hear him sipping it. "Good warm tea. Good for the nerves. It tastes like almonds. *Llámame de vuelta, cariña,*" he said, and hung up.

She sprinted to the rolltop desk, got her address book out, and bounded back to the phone and dialed the number. The phone rang several times before someone picked it up, and it wasn't her father. It was a woman's voice, and it was babbling incoherently over what sounded like a great deal of confusion. Lucy had to shout over the noise.

"This is--I *said,* this is Lucy Trujillo, Carlos Trujillo's daughter, I'm calling from Santa Fe. Is my father all right? I was just talking to him a moment ago. Is he all right?"

The woman sounded out of breath, and her voice trembled. "Your father--something has happened--he just--he just--we don't know-- we've called the doctor."

Oh, dear God in heaven, don't let this be happening. Lucy's hands were shaking so badly that she almost dropped the phone. "Are you--hello! Are you still--"

"I'm going to have to hang up now to keep the line clear," the woman on the other end said. "Your number is right here on a piece of paper your father had by the phone. We'll call you as soon as we know anything. I'm sorry, dear. We'll call you." And the connection broke off.

Lucy stood for so long with the phone in her hand that at length the dial tone was replaced by an angry beeping sound, and she remembered to hang up. After a while she realized that she was pacing the floor in the kitchen, and had been pacing it for some time, and she collapsed in a chair at the kitchen table, and immediately stood up again, and sat again, her hands fidgeting, her mind twitching with frustration and indecision. Dear God, what was she supposed to be doing? What could she do? Suddenly she felt cold, so she went to the bedroom and put on her bathrobe over her nightgown and came back to the kitchen and sat down again. She looked up at the round bland face of the electric clock on the wall, its second hand sweeping in slow, meaningless arcs. After watching it for some time it registered on her that it was past nine-thirty now. When had she talked with her dad? She tried to remember-- around nine? Had half an hour gone by? Why didn't someone call back? Should she call them? But wasn't she supposed to stay off the line? She sat with her face in her hands, and the next time she looked up it was quarter to ten. She got up, tossed two teaspoons of instant coffee into a cup of tap water, stirred it, and stuck it in the microwave. The bell on the microwave rang simultaneously with the doorbell.

The doorbell? Not what she expected. What in the world?

Leaving the coffee steaming in the microwave she walked through the house to the front door, flipped on the outside light, and opened the door to see a middle-aged Hispanic man holding up a police badge for her to see. "Miss Trujillo?"

"Yes." Her stomach felt like a mound of lead.

"I'm Lieutenant Alvarez, Santa Fe Police. I hope I didn't frighten you. May I come in?"

Lucy must have let him in, though as she stood in her living room looking at him in the lamplight she had no recollection of doing so. The man looked nervous, apologetic, and seemed to be picking over his words before speaking. Finally:

"I have been asked to deliver a message to you from a Police Lieutenant Barrett of Wichita Falls, Texas. He didn't want to just tell you on the phone. I'm sorry to have to--"

"My father," she said, swallowing but not getting rid of the lump in her throat. "It's my father. He's dead."

Lieutenant Alvarez nodded. "Yes, ma'am. I'm sorry. Would you like to sit down?"

"Oh. Yes. I guess. All right." She sat down on the sofa and placed one trembling hand on the endtable nearest her. The lieutenant sat beside her, shaking his head.

"You know, this is the worst thing about my job. I never get used to giving people bad news."

Lucy nodded. She felt numb, disembodied, and thought she should be crying, but somehow could not. What she felt was too raw, too painful, too frightening for tears. The lieutenant went on.

"Here's the whole message as I received it from Wichita Falls. Lieutenant Barrett is in charge. He says the people at the nursing home told him that your father had just had a visitor, who left. Your father asked if he could make a long-distance phone call, and they said yes, and he called you and talked for a couple of minutes and hung up. He was drinking a cup of tea, and they said he sort of choked on it and dropped it, and just collapsed. They called a doctor and she came right away, but by that time he was gone."

"I--" She didn't even know what she had started to say, and lapsed into silence.

The lieutenant stood up. "Like I said, I'm very sorry, Miss Trujillo. If there's anything we can do--is there somebody we can call for you, to come over and stay with you?"

She shook her head. "I'll call someone." It wasn't a lie exactly. There was indeed someone she was going to call.

"Well, I'll be going then. Let us know if you need anything. We're here to help."

"Thank you." She showed him to the door, and then she was alone. Really, really alone.

A glow of anger began to fan itself to life somewhere within her like an ember, and she strode back to the kitchen and picked up the phone and went through an operator to connect to the Wichita Falls, Texas police. "I'd like to speak to a Lieutenant Barrett."

"Just a moment." She waited.

"Lieutenant Barrett. What can I do for you?"

"This is Lucy Trujillo. I'm calling from Santa Fe. I--I'm the daughter of--" She couldn't say his name.

"Oh, yes, Miss Trujillo," the voice on the other end said. "Did you--"

"I got your message," she said, trying to make her voice sound calm.

"I'm very sorry," Lieutenant Barrett said. "Your father--"

"Was murdered," she said.

"Ma'am?"

"Murdered," she repeated. "He'd just had a visitor, people saw him, people can describe him. I don't know how the son of a bitch did it, but he did. And what are you doing to catch him?"

There was silence on the line; then the lieutenant cleared his throat. "The matter is being investigated."

"What do you mean, it's being investigated?"

The man on the other end sounded as if he were caught in a tight spot. "It's being investigated," he said again, "but not by us. It's out of our hands."

The mound of lead in her stomach grew heavier and colder still. "Out of your hands?"

"Yes. It's--ah--it's apparently a federal matter."

"A federal matter? You mean, like the FBI or somebody? Why is it a federal matter?" She knew the answer much better than he, no doubt, but had to ask, to see what he would say.

"I've been--we've been told we're not at liberty to discuss the case. All I can say is, it's being handled."

"I'm sure it is," she said, and hung up.

78

This couldn't be happening. Couldn't be, couldn't be, couldn't be. But it was.

A medley of competing emotions swelled up in her with such force that she felt, for a moment, that her heart might stop--the anger, the grief, the bewilderment, the fear. Which one would have the upper hand?

It turned out to be the fear.

She paced about the house trying to clear her thoughts, but her mind scrambled like some panic-stricken creature tumbling end over end; she tried to make sense of this terrible night, tried in particular to remember what her father had said about the man who came visiting.

Hadn't he said that he was afraid he'd said something, in a moment when his mind wandered--afraid that he'd divulged something to the stranger about the book with the foil from the debris field hidden in it? Wasn't that part of what that long, formless rambling was all about? It had all happened so fast that she couldn't be sure, and even if that's what her dad had said, maybe he'd been wrong, maybe he really hadn't said anything to the man, maybe he only thought he had.

Yeah, sure, Lucy thought--that's why the bastard poisoned him. Killed him. Snuffed out the pitiable shell of remaining life in a tragic old man who had already suffered enough, far more than enough, because of this business.

Whoever he was, Lucy reflected, the visitor probably hadn't thought that her dad would have the presence of mind or the time to call her. Warn her.

But he had. And when she thought, now, about that warning, she was scared. Damned scared.

Because it was all true, then, all real, just the way her mom had told it to her. That little piece of metal foil was something these people weren't going to allow to remain in private hands. Whoever they were, they were sure to come after the book, the foil. It meant enough to them to murder people, for God's sake, just to be sure that the existence of the debris would remain a secret!

She had to get to the bookshop. Right now.

On her way driving across town to Guadalupe Street, she finally found a chance for the luxury of tears, the first she shed for her father. They ran freely down her face, and they were her honest feeling, her offering, her love, after all these years, for her father, these warm tears. But they quickly gave way to anger and determination.

Yes, these people were certain to come looking for the metal foil.

And she was God damned if they were going to have it.

12

Roger Wynn and his Colleagues

It was a little after nine-thirty, New Mexico time, when Roger Wynn's shuttle flight landed in Albuquerque. He hadn't bothered to set his watch an hour ahead during his few hours in Texas, so it still showed Mountain Time, not Central Time. Walking through the terminal with thoughts of being in Santa Fe in an hour or so, he smiled at the reflection that he took such professional pleasure in handling some things himself. He could readily have sent word to some of his underlings in the field, could easily enough have had them take care of the Lucy Trujillo matter, but this was something that he wanted, even at this hour of night, to handle personally.

In any case, there was no particular urgency; after one swallow of that tea, Hap Trujillo was history (Roger, once outside the door of the nursing home, had actually jumped down off the porch and sprinted away down the block, not wanting to be within sight any more when things started popping), and even though Lucy, Hap's diddly daughter, would no doubt have heard about his demise in short order, she would scarcely infer that she was going to have a visitor tonight to spice up her lagging social life. Roger had intended to have a routine wiretap put on her phone, but unfortunately had delayed doing so, not knowing that he was going to strike pay dirt earlier this evening on what seemed likely to be just another routine stop with the elder Trujillo. Roger felt a little lax about this, but told himself that it really didn't matter, because it was all going to work out perfectly anyway; a truly talented and experienced agent at this level should always be able to sense unconsciously when it was okay to vary procedures a bit. Roger most definitely had that rare and seasoned sense of what it took to get the job done.

He wasn't sure exactly what the old man's rambling, mind-wandering monologue meant, except that there had been mention of a piece of debris, something that had evidently been in the family all these years. And it had to be a strip of foil (he had seen bushels of the stuff), because Trujillo in his babbling had hinted at something about concealing it in the pages of a book, presumably a book that the daughter possessed; and, to make Roger's search a bit easier, he had mentioned Cervantes. (Roger couldn't have expected them to make it Shakespeare, he supposed, grudgingly. What did these taco-eaters know about the Bard?) From what the old man had said, Roger wasn't sure whether the daughter *knew* that she possessed a piece of alien debris, but all the better if she didn't-- in that case, she certainly wouldn't suspect, ahead of time, that she was going to be in trouble, and there was no question in Roger's mind that he could find the hidden metal foil without her help if need be.

All that remained to be done, then, to put closure to a perfectly satisfactory day, he reflected cheerfully, was to dispatch the Trujillo broad, maybe fuck her (not necessarily in that order, but he was open-minded), and go shopping in the Mesa Bookshop once more, this time at night--*try our new extended hours for your shopping convenience*--their flyers should say--this time looking for a volume of Cervantes that would sport a rather unusual bookmark. If he didn't find it there in the bookshop, well, there was always the house. It had to be somewhere, and when he recovered it, he would have tied up yet one more loose end, an important one. It was no small matter, recovering a piece of debris illicitly held in private hands; over the past five decades such recovery had occurred only a very few times. One more untidy detail made tidy; Roswell was going to *remain* covered up. Forever.

With this thought, he noticed that the air terminal people were paging a Mr. Jerome Shelby. As that was one of Roger's code names, he picked up the first courtesy phone he came to, listened to the voice on the other end, made a couple of mental notes, and hung up. After going down the escalator and retrieving his suitcase, he picked up the keys to his car, went outside, walked up the ramp, and proceeded to his rendezvous in the indicated spot, a far corner of the rental car parking area. At this hour, very few people were around, but Roger's distinguished colleagues Blake and Varelli were waiting for him, all right, standing under a sodium lamp. Splendid chaps, these; dependably ruthless, thoroughly unprincipled, fanatically dedicated, and competent without being terribly bright. Qualities Roger very much liked.

"We may have a little problem, chief," Varelli said. Roger particularly liked Varelli. He still rather looked like the cheap mafia goon he in fact had been before the Group recruited him, but of course after

81

all his training he was a great deal more sophisticated now. You wouldn't know it to look at him, though; essentially he still just looked like a goon.

"What kind of problem?" Roger asked.

"It's the language broad," Blake said. Roger liked Blake for different reasons; the man was something of a beanpole, deceptively rather scholarly-looking, almost wimpy-looking actually, but if need be, he wouldn't hesitate to push an ice pick up your nose or strangle a child with a strand of barbed wire. Charming fellow all around.

"Anne Hawk?" Roger asked, surprised. Surveillance of her had always been exceedingly close, and they'd never had any reason in particular to worry about her.

"Yeah," Blake said. "She's got a new boyfriend, looks like."

"Oh?"

"Old boyfriend, actually. We did some checking on him. Guy named Eric Hayes. Doctor Eric Hayes. Teaches anthropology here in Albuquerque. Mesa Linda College. Anne Hawk knew him back when they were at Yale together. They were kind of a number then, looks like, but it didn't work out. He's on leave from his college, and he's down in Alamogordo working on some kind of research up at Three Rivers. Something about Indian rock drawings. Anne Hawk ran into him in a bar in Alamogordo."

"What bar?"

"Cantina Zia. Later he took her to dinner at a place called the Cholla Lounge--"

"Star-cross'd lovers," Roger said.

Blake gaped at him. "Sir?"

"Nothing," Roger said. "Go on."

"Well, after that they went for a drive," Blake said. "While they were in the lounge we bugged his car, but there's nothing important on the tapes."

"What's funny is what's *not* on them," Varelli said.

"What do you mean?"

"Well, there's a lot of nothing. Silence, I mean. Like when they got to where they were going, they got out of the car and stayed away a long time. Like most of the night."

"Maybe they were off somewhere screwing," Roger said.

"Maybe," Varelli said, grinning. "That Hawk piece ain't half bad-looking."

"So," Roger said, "what we're talking about here is a *possible* problem. Right?"

"Right," the two said in unison, almost like schoolboys.

82

"Girl has lonely job, no boyfriends, no social life," Roger said. "Girl meets old boyfriend. Girl wants to talk to old boyfriend after all these years. Question is, now, what does she talk about? Maybe just old times, maybe just the weather, maybe how much she likes what he's got in his pants. But maybe she talks about things she shouldn't talk about." As always, he was being careful not to mention anything specific enough to be classified, out here in an open area like this; besides, there were limits to what these two men knew about Dr. Anne Hawk's official duties.

"Yeah," Varelli said, "anyway, we thought you ought to know right away, what was going on."

"Quite right," Roger said. "It may not turn out to be a problem, but we won't take any chances. She's been with the program for a lot of years now, and after a while people can crack, you know. People can start asking themselves if it's what they really want out of life, people can start thinking differently about their priorities, all that sort of crap. In other words, people can get dangerous. You fellows know that." He drew back and cleared his throat and looked hard at both of them. "I want first-rate surveillance."

"You got it, chief," Blake said.

"Meanwhile," Roger said, "I've got problems of my own."

He turned away, leaving Blake and Varelli there, and went to his car. He tossed his suitcase in the back, started the engine, drove out Gibson Boulevard, and headed north on Route 25, toward Santa Fe. It wouldn't be quite an hour's drive, but it would give him some time to think.

As the scintillating northern expanses of Albuquerque dropped behind him, he found himself wondering if some big changes weren't going to be in order. This in spite of the fact that things had gone fairly smoothly, overall, for a long time. Years ago, Anne Hawk's predecessor George Quintana had ended up being a problem, of course. That was the trouble with these egghead types newly acquired from outside, as opposed to properly indoctrinated people--they could always end up getting scruples, or finding that they had a conscience, or wanted to have some kind of a life outside of their commitment to secret government service. In other words, they could turn mushy, unreliable, potentially traitorous. Quintana had been on the brink of trying to expose the whole program, it seemed, when they had decided to move in and snuff him just to be sure he didn't. Other than that, though, there had been relatively little trouble, over the years, for a program of this sensitivity and this complexity. Except for an occasional illicit photo or the occasional turning up of an illicit piece of debris--and the necessity on these occasions of removing everyone who knew anything--except for these things, the program had gone quietly, smoothly, reasonably trouble-free, and of course had been immensely profitable from a number of points of view. But Roger had a feeling that some of this was changing.

And maybe it was going to be time to talk about changing perceptions of how the program should best proceed.

From what he could gather about the technological exploitation side of things, the Crewman, having already taken them through astonishing stages of development, was currently in the process of moving his exploiters on to something of a new plateau, an entirely new level of understanding that would make what he had shown them heretofore about microcircuit theory and computers look like so much Neanderthal drool. Roger couldn't imagine that anyone in the program would want to do anything to diminish that prospect, the prospect of moving along to an incredible new level of technology, and of being, for a while at least, the sole inheritors of it. But as soon as that new phase was in the process of becoming well digested, maybe it would be time to think differently about the whole thing.

How much technology was even possible? The changes that had taken place since the beginning of the computer era were already dizzying, and surely this new phase would represent the apex, the real limit to what the Crewman could impart. As soon as the tech interviewers had pretty well covered it, surely it would just be a matter, then, of letting the eggheads and engineers digest it, using good old human ingenuity.

And maybe not needing the Crewman any more.

Slipping through the black desert night, Roger reflected that the longer this all went on, and the longer they kept the Crewman under wraps, the more problems there were going to be. It would have been unthinkable, back in the early days when he was just beginning to show them the developments that would lead to microcomputer technology, it would have been unimaginable then to consider terminating him. And it would be unimaginable now, until the new phase got well under way. But once that happened, were they really going to be wise to keep running the risks that the Crewman's continued existence posed? This was, after all, the most stupendous coverup in history, and if all this ever became public knowledge, it would lead to unthinkable turmoil.

"That way madness lies," Roger muttered. "Ah, Lear, if you only knew the half of it. You thought *you* had problems."

It wasn't going to be Roger's decision to make, of course, but his views were respected in high places, even those half-mythical high places in government that were so secret that Presidents and senators and generals could be kept away from them. There were going to have to be

84

some high-level conferences pretty soon, Roger had a feeling. He hadn't said much to Varelli and Blake, but he had a suspicion that this new wrinkle with Anne Hawk was going to be something like the old George Quintana problem all over again. It could all have come crashing down with Quintana, and it all could come crashing down now. Varelli and Blake had better get it right, he thought; a little skillful surveillance could readily tell whether there was a problem or not. In any case, a problem could always develop, and some thought was going to have to be given to Anne Hawk's continued existence, even before anyone discussed the Crewman's future. Right now that bitch was the only real link they had to the Crewman's mind, but maybe they wouldn't always need a link.

Anyway, the lights of Santa Fe were looming ahead, and he had a job to do. Some things, at least, were easy.

13

Petroglyphs

Across the way, the sun was setting as it can set only in the desert, with a soundless explosion of delicious red-orange exuberance that made it seem that all the world over the horizon must be aflame, and telling its fiery tale to the heavens. But to Anne it seemed too soon for the daylight to be fading. It had been a rather short day, because while Eric had roused himself early enough to get some of his notes together, he hadn't called to wake Anne till late in the morning, somewhat after ten in fact, and by the time he had swung by to pick her up and they had stopped in Tularosa for breakfast and had driven the rest of the way up here, to the Three Rivers site, it had been noontime. Eric had had plenty of work to do, all day, photographing and taking copious notes on the countless Indian petroglyphs to be found on the rocks in these stark and jagged hills, so for the most part Anne had been willing just to leave him to it, asking few questions. But she had stayed close to him, all day, watching him work, and he had often paused to talk with her about the etchings on the rocks, explaining their history in terms of the Mogollon peoples and describing the controversies, vividly alive in professional circles, concerning what some of the figures represented. He talked fluently, freely, about his work, for which he clearly had a real and enduring passion.

She enjoyed listening to him, watching him. Somehow, in his now dusty jeans and open-neck shirt and his trail boots, and with his form silhouetted against the darkening turquoise canvas of the sky and his hair disheveled in the breeze like wisps of cloud, he looked--like someone she could learn to care about again. He wasn't the old Eric; he wasn't that brash young graduate student at Yale, the Eric who took her barhopping, the Eric who dragged her out at six o'clock on a blustery

86

winter morning to build a snowman in the middle of New Haven Green; he wasn't the Eric who popped open a bottle of champagne the afternoon she defended her doctoral dissertation, and took her to see the big bands at Woolsey Hall. He wasn't that bygone memory, but he wasn't the final bitter memories either--he was someone else now, not mellowed exactly, but rather ripened by life, and imbued with just enough of a shadow of that old Eric that she still knew him, yet could learn to know him anew. Maybe could learn to love him again, though with those darker matters lurking in the background she scarcely dared to think this way just yet. For now she contented herself with letting him work.

But now, with most of the sunlight gone, he wasn't taking any more pictures, and he had his notes for the day fairly well in order. He was relaxing into an even more talkative mood. They had, both of them, studiously avoided certain topics all day--anything to do with Anne's predicament--and Anne welcomed the way in which the wealth of discourse that these rock-drawings provided made it easy for them to talk about petroglyphs and petroglyphs only. Eric's work presented a world bristling with problems, but those problems felt refreshingly safe and academic and theoretical compared to the difficulties implied by Anne's whole situation--now Eric's and Anne's situation. Sooner or later, of course, they were going to have to talk about the deadly serious problem that lurked nearby, ready to spring upon them and overwhelm them if they weren't careful, and maybe even if they were. Sooner or later they were going to have to figure out what, if anything, they should do. But not right now.

However ghastly that more serious problem was, Anne was enjoying herself too much right now to think about it. Eric was giving her a sort of tour, walking around among the rocks on these bleak hills as he pointed out to her a certain group of widely scattered petroglyphs that seemed to have a great deal in common.

"Look at that," he said, pointing out a particularly intriguing petroglyph on a large rock face just off the footpath. "What exactly do you suppose that was supposed to represent?"

She stepped closer to look at it. Even in the waning light its outlines were clear: a rough circle several inches in diameter, with something inside that looked rather like the old "peace" symbol from the Vietnam War days, and with a ring of dots around the outer edge of the circle that gave the impression of something like light flashing or glowing. During the day, and just now as Eric took her around, she had seen several other similar petroglyphs, circular representations of something perhaps associated, she suspected, literally or metaphorically, with light.

"Well," she said, "what do the people in your field say?"

"Oh no you don't," he said, giving her a playful poke in the arm. "That's too easy a dodge, and you're not about to get away with it. Not with me. I want to know what *you* think. Your impression may be the most valuable of all, you know. Because you're coming to the problem with a fresh eye. The rest of us may be looking at things square in the face without seeing them, because we've been gazing at all these damn rocks too long. What does the thing look like to you?"

"I'd say," she ventured, "that it could be a sun symbol. These dots around the edge, here, are kind of like little radiating rays. It could easily enough be just a picture of the sun."

He sat on a rock and wiped his brow, shaking his head and smiling. "Mm. Yeah, that's the problem. It could *too* easily be that. It's an easy assumption to make, and in this business easy assumptions are often wrong. Not always, but often enough."

"So," she said, "I'm trying to oversimplify. Well, let me get a little more ambitious, then, and let's talk symbolism. It's the sun, but metaphorically; it's something like the mandala or circle-symbol, the return, the ring of nature, the eternal coming-around, the cycle of the world, that sort of thing."

He smiled again. "I like that better. That's the very sort of thing I came out here to look into, because I think the desert drawings all over this region do have mythic patterns that link them. But no, I think you were closer when you were trusting your simple reactions. I think it's more likely to be a straight picture of something, than a symbol."

"But a picture of what?"

"C'mon, Anne," he said. "What do you think? What does it really look like to you?"

She knew where this was heading; she had just wanted to verify that it was a shared perception, and not her own strained imagination. "Those dots around the perimeter. Not sun rays, you're saying."

He was steadfast. "I want to know what *you're* saying."

"All right," she said. "Not run rays. But they still suggest light, or radiance."

"Not light, exactly," he offered.

"Okay. Lights, plural," she said. "Individual lights. Something like the running lights on a boat."

He nodded. "Yeah, that's they way they look to me."

"Let's turn this around. What do *you* think it's a picture of?" she said. "I want to hear you say it."

"Well, funny thing, see," he said, "I want to hear you say it too. I want to know that we're both thinking what we're thinking. It looks like a picture of--"

And at his cue they finished the sentence simultaneously.

"A spaceship." "A flying saucer."

They laughed. "Whatever you want to call it," Eric said. "Yeah, maybe it's just what I've, ah, had on my mind"--Anne noted that he was being careful of what he said--"but damned if that doesn't look like a flying disk, with running lights all around it. I mean, I know how campy that would sound to a lot of people, after all that business years ago about the gods of the Incas really being flying saucer people and everything. But--"

"But all things considered," she said, "it's not a bad guess." She was picking her words with some care, too, because she still wasn't altogether comfortable with the notion of talking out in the open like this, even out here where they were a long distance away from anyone else. She cast her glance around, to see that they were indeed alone. They were getting close to things that were genuinely dangerous to talk about, and she was relieved to see, in Eric's face, that he understood this by reading her own expressions. But there could be no one near enough to overhear them.

As if in a perverse sort of response to this thought, a human figure moved somewhere down below them on the shadowy desert floor, perhaps two hundred yards out from the base of the hill, in the direction of the setting sun, whose spectacular afterglow had now dwindled to a departing memory in the western sky. It was Anne who saw the movement down there in the chaparral first, and she motioned with her head for Eric to look and see too.

Someone was approaching the hill.

On reflection, Anne concluded that this shouldn't be anything menacing. She knew the sorts of people whom one would regard as potentially a menace in this situation, and one thing was certain: no one would spy on her and Eric by boldly walking up to where they stood. But this was what the figure on the desert floor was doing, moving at a very slow but steady pace through the sagebrush, evidently watching the two of them as he (she?) came on, and finally climbing the rocky path up the hill at a pace slower still. When the figure came close enough for Anne to make it out clearly in the failing light, she saw that it was an old man, an Indian, dressed in a strange assortment of cloth rags and leather, with a sort of pack in hand and with a leather pouch hanging around his neck. The old man stepped up close to them, nodding to them slightly, but seeming to pay more notice to the nearby petroglyphs. Eric, evidently feeling it necessary to say something at least, cleared his throat.

"Hello. I'm Eric, Eric Hayes. This is my friend Anne Hawk."

The Indian nodded again. "They call me Sage," he said, in those beautiful broad-vowelled tones that Anne loved, the tones that reminded her who and what she originally was; life in the Anglo world had to some extent bred the true earth-tones out of her own voice, she feared. There was something in the man's voice, too, that seemed to say: that's what they call me, those who think it's important to call me anything. It wasn't hostile or bitter, just the deep and inscrutable intonations of an old man who has seen much and thought much and said little.

"We were just talking about these," Anne said, pointing to the nearest petroglyphs and indicating, in particular, the one with the ring of dots. "We were just saying how many different ideas there are, about what these things mean."

"Yes," Eric said. "We were trying to decide if it's really a picture of something. And if it is, of what?"

The old man gazed long at the petroglyph; there was something in his eyes that said that he did so not out of puzzlement, but out of a sort of reverence, as he had seen the drawing many times before, and others like it. He drew in a slow, deep breath, and quietly exhaled. The gentle breeze that seemed to come up around them with his exhalation, stirring the sandy soil upon the path at their feet, made a sound that was almost musical, and gave Anne a little shiver, not out of fear but from a kind of fascination, because it was an effect she had sensed before, at times. It was like the soft, subtle, reedy tone of some strange and enticing flute. The old man's lizardlike face creased out in a running bewilderment of wrinkles as his ancient mouth opened to speak.

"This is a picture," he said, nodding toward the petroglyph, "of the silver bird."

"The silver bird," Eric repeated, more nearly like a confirmation than a question.

"The great silver bird," Sage said, "that come in the old times."

"Tell us about it," Eric said, motioning for the old man to sit down. They all sat in a little circle on the ground. Eric took Anne's hand. The wind swelled a little, bringing a chill from somewhere across the great desert expanses, and Anne pulled the collar of her jacket tighter to her throat and fixed her attention upon the old Indian.

"They say in the old times the great silver bird come down out of the sky," he said, "and bring the sky-children."

Anne swallowed. Hard. Eric squeezed her hand, as if to say that he knew what she was feeling. "The sky-children?" he asked.

The old man declined even to nod, merely blinking his eyes one time, slowly, rather as if there were no need to repeat himself, but only a need to give the others time to think about what he was saying. "The sky-children bring the music."

"The music?" Anne said. She felt foolish, for herself and for Eric, because all the two of them seemed to be able to do, in the face of this old *brujo*, was to repeat everything he said, like children. She, an Indian herself, however long removed from tribal ways, should know better than to banter with one of her people in the manner of the Anglos; it was not the Indian way. In the Indian way, one person talked, others listened; later, another person talked. One at a time.

"The music of the trickster," Sage said. "The music of life. It's the music of the wind in the arroyos, when Brother Coyote stop to listen and the owl shake his feathers. You, me, we come, we live, we die. People say, them, they never really die. The music never die. All people remember, deep inside."

He fell silent, and Anne, having reflected upon it, did not urge him to say more, but knew that he would. Eric, too, seemed content just to wait. Another breeze twirled fine grains of sand in the path and brought mischievous little memories of sagebrush and piñon to play among the rocks. By now it was darker, and the old man was little more than a vague, tattered shape in the gloom. At length he spoke again.

"In the old times a hunter meet the sky-child, and the sky-child show him about making the music. Come, look." Sage pushed himself to his feet, in a surprisingly agile way for so old a man, and motioned for them to follow. He led them around a corner in the outcroppings of rocks on the near side of the hill, to a place recessed now in deep shadow. He pointed into the shadows, and Eric unlimbered a flashlight and shone it there, revealing, on the rock face within, one of the several variants, at this site, of the well-known motif of Kokopelli, the humpbacked fluteplayer. They all stood in silence for some time, as Eric's flashlight played upon the petroglyph. To Anne it all began to feel eerie, just now, being up here in the dark of night on this rock-strewn hill, knowing what she knew already, with an ancient *brujo*--she figured, from his accent, that he was a Pueblo Indian, probably from Jemez, and probably one of those strange, rare figures who wander the desert in perpetual exile, laden with lore too powerful and too frightening for their own people to accept. Beneath these reflections there stirred, of course, unquiet thoughts of those other, all too clearly related, matters that plagued her in her own life, and would plague her in whatever further life she tried to have. She was scared, but she resolved not to dwell on her fears.

"Kokopelli," Eric said, his face a half-illumined ghost in the periphery of the light.

"By whatever name," Sage said, turning to go back to the spot where they had been sitting on the path. Eric played his light over the path now, as it was darker even than when they had gotten up. As soon as they were all seated once more, with the flashlight settled in the space

91

between them so that they could more or less see each other's faces, Sage spoke.

"One day the sky-child come again," he said.

Anne reflected that considering the uncertainty as to his verb tenses, in English, that statement could mean a variety of different things. Did he mean prophetically "would one day come," or matter-of-factly "has already come"? She found herself very much wanting to hear him say these things in an Indian language. But he was continuing.

"Sky-child come again, like in old times, same medicine. Want only good. But then great trouble come, to some. I see this in visions. Some people, great suffering will come to them. I have a vision, not long ago, of young woman, and a strange man come to her, and man is bad trouble."

Anne couldn't help looking over at Eric and chuckling, as Eric returned the look and laughed as well. She hoped the old Indian would not feel that they were trifling with him; surely he must have sensed that she was Indian too, and knew better. "I'm sorry," she said, still smiling. "It's just that, if my admittedly strange friend here is going to be bad trouble--" Like a reproach to her levity, the wind rose with a howl, moaning and sad-sounding among the angular faces of the rocks perched around them in the dark.

"Woman in vision is not you," Sage said, unperturbed but clearly intent upon saying what he had to say. His voice had dropped nearly to a whisper, and it was hard to hear him now with the wind, which ruffled his floating white hair like spiderwebs. "Man in vision is not him," he said, indicating Eric. "But you two have troubles too. Different troubles."

As before, Anne wondered if he meant "will have" or "do have," and was about to see whether he spoke Tewa or Navajo by addressing him in one of those languages, but something in the expression in the old man's wizened face had changed. He had put a withered hand up to silence her, and seemed to be listening. The wind had dropped to a low stirring of the dust around the flashlight, and then not even that, but as Anne listened with the old man, she couldn't hear anything. Eric was watching, listening too. He looked at her and shrugged, but the old man shook his head, pointing off into the dark of the desert floor below the hill on the near side.

"What--" Eric began, but again Sage motioned for him not to speak.

They sat for a long while in silence, the flashlight making eerie phantoms of their faces. For some reason Anne's view of this scene now swept up and away like a movie camera; in her mind she retreated to some distance away and seemed to see the three of them, goblin faces in the near-dark, clustered around the wan illumination of the flashlight in a strange little island of light floating in a sea of illimitable darkness. When she brought her mind back to the immediate scene, with Eric sitting by her side and Sage not four feet in front of her, the impression lingered, the feeling that they were wrapped in a tight little ball of pale light with endless, whispering, menacing seas of blackness stretching away around them in all directions. The effect, to her, was unspeakably, disturbingly eerie. She had never before been frightened of the desert at night, but it frightened her now.

Sage had clasped the leather pouch around his neck and pressed it closer to his chest, and had raised his other hand to make odd circular motions with it. Some nervous corner of Anne's mind reflected that the movement he was making with his hand was something like polishing a car with a chamois. Only after a few moments did she notice that the old man was muttering under his breath, nearly inaudibly, and she strained to listen. Yes, sure enough, the language, from what she could hear, was Tewa, but it was full of strange and exotic and far-flung words and references of the sort that only a truly bizarre *brujo* would use, and even she had trouble making anything of it beyond vague references to the spirit world. Whatever he was saying, it was not to be taken lightly; if one was an Indian one knew that. The old man's words came faster and faster, but grew fainter as they did so, and finally Anne could hear only an incredible torrent of, to her, virtually meaningless language.

At some point she realized that while she had been straining to hear, gradual changes had been taking place in the scene around them. The wind seemed to have come back up, for one thing, but somehow it didn't feel or sound like normal wind; there was something almost-- purposeful--in it, as if when it touched one's face it touched it knowing that it did so, like a conscious and insinuating caress from the fingers of a stranger in the dark. The sound of this wind was disquietingly different too, as if from some scattered, unseen points in the distance a whole chorus of ululant flutes had taken up a faint and lilting song, a timeless song that seemed to speak to something too deep in one's mind to be acquaintance or memory. Listening, Anne was quite simply too fascinated to move. In a fierce and undefinable way, just at this moment, she deeply, intensely loved the old man, with a primal kind of love that mingled admiration and fear with emotions not even needing to be possessed of names. From the corner of her eye she could see the pallid ghost of Eric's face in the feeble light, and while he too seemed fascinated, he looked, for the most part, just plain scared.

This maelstrom of impressions--the odd insistence of the wind, the feeling that the very darkness had grown subtly and intriguingly melodic--continued for what felt like a long time, though it might not have been so long as it seemed. Anne felt that it might have been like a dream, hours long in the mind but maybe very fleeting in reality, whatever reality was. At length the sound of the wind dropped to a very low moan but didn't go away altogether, and Sage looked first at Eric, then at Anne, and spoke.

"Now we can talk more."

14

Blake and Varelli

Everything was going great. From where they sat with the rifle mike trained on the rocky hill across the way toward the northeast, they ought to pick up every word, Blake thought. No interference, no traffic sounds, nothing; quiet as a goddamn mausoleum out here. Just let the language broad and her egghead boyfriend chatter their heads off. The more the merrier.

He settled down more comfortably in the sand and looked at Varelli, who, lying belly-down a few feet away, was giving the rifle mike some final adjustments. They had brought the low tripod, so the whole thing was no more than a foot off the ground at any point, which was as it should be; everything had to be kept out of sight. The barrel of the mike was covered with a sand-colored canvas strip to keep the sunlight from glinting off it. Varelli had plugged in two sets of earphones with plenty of wire, and they were settled in for a long listen.

It had worked out well, getting set up like this. Considering what must be the panoramic view from that hill, Blake had been afraid that they might have to park several miles away and hike in, maybe still with some problems keeping out of sight. But as it turned out, the bug in the boyfriend's car had made it possible for Blake and Varelli to ascertain, following the woman and the boyfriend out of Alamogordo that morning, that they were headed up to Three Rivers as suspected. That was, after all, where the guy was supposed to be working. Luck would have it that the two had stopped in Tularosa to grab something to eat, so Blake and Varelli had simply gone on ahead the rest of the way to the Three Rivers site, and had driven off the road cross-country to the southwest of the

95

site, well short of the point where anyone near the park entrance would have seen them. They had pulled the car around behind a ridge where it wouldn't be visible from the hill--out here, the sun on that much metal could be seen for miles, if you weren't careful about these things. And then, with a good half hour to spare before the woman and the boyfriend arrived, they had set up camp in a little clear space in the sand, with enough sagebrush in front of them to conceal them nicely as long as they didn't stand up or move around too much. Anyway, it was at least a couple of hundred yards to the base of the hill, and they wouldn't be spotted.

Nor would they have to worry about running into tourists who came out here to see the petroglyphs; no sir, Uncle Fred and Aunt Fanny on vacation weren't about to wander out here in the chaparral where they could get their ass bit off by a rattlesnake, not that rattlesnakes were the most dangerous form of life to worry about, with a couple of not very social government operatives hunkered down here for the day. It was a good surveillance site, Blake thought, easing himself comfortably into the cool sand; a good site, and a nice assignment, just plopping down out here for the duration. Not a bad way to make a living, all told.

Then there was the hardware. Great stuff. This rifle mike was so sensitive that even at the distance they had to aim it across, it would pick up the sound of someone swallowing, the sound of breathing. It was a very sophisticated model, this gadget, much more sensitive than earlier versions. Of course the price you paid for the heightened sensitivity was that it was also extremely directional, so as the targets moved around on the hill Varelli would have to keep making minute adjustments to the angle of the mike to follow them. The mike was set up on a base something like a telescope mount, and could be adjusted with extreme fineness. Of course, if the targets moved far enough around on the other side of the hill they might go out of hearing for a while, so a second surveillance site out on the opposite side would have been better, but it was too late for that now. For one thing, Blake and Varelli only kept one rifle mike routinely on hand; this model carried a good five-figure price tag, and even the government wouldn't write you blank checks without limit these days, especially since assignments calling for rifle mikes virtually always necessitated using only one; this hill-in-the-desert scenario was pretty unusual. Anyway, the targets would probably stay within range for the most part.

To finish setting up, Blake had unlimbered the audio taping unit and plugged it in, before settling down to listen. Anything anybody said up on that hill would end up recorded. To save tape, the unit would automatically cut off if no one spoke for a certain amount of time, but was set to cut back in, cued by the frequencies of the human voice, within one five-hundredth of a second when anybody started to talk again.

Varelli was lighting a cigarette. Blake eyed him and said, "Think we ought to smoke here?"

Varelli shrugged and pushed the earphones a little away from one ear. "Why not? They won't see any smoke from this far out."

"Just keep in mind what the chief said he wanted," Blake said. "First-rate surveillance."

"He'll get it," Varelli said.

"He'd better," Blake said. "I kind of think that man'd tear you and me new assholes if he didn't get what he wanted. Don't know about you, but I don't particularly need a new asshole. The one I got works fine. Remind me to demonstrate it sometime."

"Piss off," Varelli said, grinning.

"Hell, I guess you're right," Blake said, "they couldn't see the smoke from up there." So he lit up too, and they sat and listened.

Varelli patted the radio mike. "This baby'd pick up a worm fart."

Blake sniffed, shaking his head. "Let's hope we get something more interesting than worm farts."

"Damn right," Varelli said. "At least some lizard farts."

"How about some Anne Hawk farts?" Blake said. "That'd turn you on, wouldn't it, Varelli?"

Varelli grinned an unctuous grin. "Blow chunks and die, Blake."

As the afternoon wore on, they at first heard little of interest from up on the hill. Hayes seemed to be doing his work up there mostly without saying much of anything, though once in a while he'd stop and talk to Anne Hawk about the rock drawings. Mogollon petroglyphs, he called them. What little he said had mostly to do with the history of the area, and studies that had been done on petroglyphs before, and comparisons between these petroglyphs and the ones found in other places upstate, like Chaco Canyon. But overall Hayes and the woman talked so sparsely that the recording unit, which was patched into the rifle mike through a cable and plug, used very little tape the whole afternoon. A couple of times the two targets did move around out of range, but were soon back; evidently, most of what Hayes needed to do was on this side of the hill, as Blake had thought.

Around two in the afternoon Hayes and the woman stopped and ate lunches they'd brought, but even then they didn't talk about much of anything. Blake got the feeling that they were being deliberately careful. Did they suspect they might be overheard? Blake thought not. You had to consider what Anne Hawk did for a living; the woman would naturally be used to watching what she said. It was a gut instinct, and you didn't last long in government service at that level of secrecy if you lacked that instinct. You ended up in a body bag. Without even a tag on your toe.

Blake and Varelli munched on some sandwiches, and had some coffee from a thermos. As the day wore on, it got cooler the way it tends to do in the desert, but they were prepared for that, having heavier jackets to slip on. They saw to it that one of them was always listening at the earphones, even when the coffee sent one or the other of them out to answer the call of nature. It was a bit of a trick to answer the eternal call, actually, out here like this, without standing up, but they were clever folks; the way Blake saw it, if you couldn't crawl among the sagebrush and avoid rattlesnake holes and take a whiz in the chaparral without sticking your head up in the air like a scarecrow, you just weren't cut out for serious work.

The day wore on toward evening. Finally, about the time the sun was setting, the talk from across the way got a little more interesting.

Eric Hayes had been questioning the woman about what she thought some petroglyph he was showing her was supposed to represent. Anne Hawk had first evaded the question, and had then said that she thought it might be a picture of the sun. She and Hayes proceeded to argue this point. So far nothing too dramatic, this exchange of disembodied voices piping in the earphones for Blake and Varelli to hear.

"*C'mon, Anne. What do you think? What does it really look like to you?*" Hayes was saying.

"*Those dots around the perimeter. Not sun rays, you're saying.*"

Something in this remark of the woman's made Varelli and Blake look at each other, and both sat a little more attentive.

"*Lights, plural. Individual lights.*"

Blake looked at Varelli, who was pressing an earphone tighter to his ear.

"*Something,*" Anne Hawk was saying, "*like the running lights on a boat.*"

Varelli looked up at Blake and started to say something, but Blake, glancing down to be sure the tape was running, motioned for him to be quiet and listen.

"*I want to know,*" Hayes was saying, "*that we're both thinking what we're thinking. It looks like a picture of--*"

And the woman and the man spoke at the same time: "*A flying saucer.*" "*A spaceship.*" And the earphones were filled with the light sound of laughter, almost like canned laughter on television.

"Shit," Varelli said. "Still don't mean anything. They could be--"
"Ssh," Blake said. "Shut up and listen."

"*Yeah,*" Hayes was saying, "*maybe it's just what I've, ah, got on my mind, but damned if that doesn't look like a flying disk, with running lights all around it.*"

As they looked at each other again from beneath their earphones, Blake knew that Varelli was thinking the same thing he was. What did Hayes mean, about having something like flying disks on his mind? Why would he have them on his mind? Unless of course flying disks had been the chief topic of dinner conversation recently, between him and the woman. The chief was sure as hell going to be interested in these tapes.

The talk had fallen off now, up there on the hill, though Blake thought he heard the woman draw in a sharp breath as if she were surprised about something. He started to nudge Varelli, but Varelli was nudging him first, and pointing out across the expanse of sagebrush to their north, to the left of the hill.

There was somebody walking, out there, a good distance out from the hill and approaching it. The sun was almost down now, and even from here Blake could see that the walking figure cast a long, lean shadow out in front of itself as it went.

"Who the hell is that?" Varelli whispered.

"Let's just watch and listen," Blake said. He couldn't see that far without binoculars, which they hadn't bothered to unlimber, since this was supposed to be an aural surveillance routine primarily. Blake rummaged in a bag near his feet in the sand and brought out the binoculars, which he trained across the chaparral.

"It's getting a little too dark to tell for sure, but it looks like an old Indian," he said. "And he looks like he's heading up the foot of the hill."

"Mm," Varelli said. "Well, what the hell. Let him join the party. The more talk, the better for us. Right?"

"Right," Blake said. "It's already gotten pretty damned interesting."

Hayes was introducing himself to the old Indian, who in turn was saying, "*They call me Sage.*" In the earphones, it all reminded Blake of times when he was a kid climbing up and hanging over the fence at the drive-in theater, listening to the soundtrack of the movie as it came out of the tinny speakers on the posts. There was something unreal about it, somehow, this conversation on the rocky hill, since the Indian had joined in.

Hayes and the woman were talking to him about the same petroglyph, evidently, that they had already been discussing; they were asking him what it looked like to him. At this point a bit of wind was coming up, and it tended to interfere with the signal a little, but Blake heard the old Indian say, "*This is a picture of the silver bird.*"

99

Not *a* silver bird, Blake reflected; *the* silver bird. He wasn't at all sure what any of this meant, since those rock drawings were supposed to be centuries old, and shouldn't have anything to do with current affairs; but he pressed the earphones flatter against his ears and listened intently in the gathering dark.

"*They say in the old times the great silver bird come down out of the sky,*" the old man was saying, "*and bring the sky-children.*"

Varelli and Blake looked at each other hard. Again Varelli started to speak but Blake motioned for him to listen.

The old man was saying something about the sky-children bringing the music. What the hell was he talking about? But no matter what he was talking about, the mention of sky-children was a problem all to itself, wasn't it? What did the old man mean by "in the old times"? Fifty years ago, when Roswell happened? In any case the chief was sure as shit going to be interested in all this.

"*In the old times,*" the old Indian was saying, "*a hunter meet the sky-child, and the sky-child show him about making the music. Come, look.*"

Blake could hear the people up there moving around, and thought the Indian was taking them somewhere else on the hill--not around to the far side, he hoped--to show them something. No, they were still within range; there seemed to be a slowly moving glint of light up there, as if someone were holding a flashlight. Hayes said something, then, that sounded like *Kokopelli,* whatever the hell that meant, and the old man said something that Blake didn't quite catch; no matter, it would all be on the tape. Then they all seemed to be moving back to where they had been before, and resettling themselves. Again, there was a dim suggestion of light, unmoving now, and Blake supposed that the three had sat down around the flashlight to talk. He pressed the earphones to his ears again and listened.

"*--great trouble come, to some,*" the old man was saying. "*I see this in visions. Some people, great suffering will come to them. I have a vision, not long ago, of young woman, and a strange man come to her, and man is bad trouble.*" Anne Hawk made some joking remarks about herself and Hayes, and the old man continued, "*Woman in vision is not you. Man in vision is not him. But you have troubles too.*"

You got that right, old buck, Blake said to himself; yeah, these two haven't actually said anything classified yet, but they're going to have some troubles, big time, and sooner than late, if they do. Maybe they already had said more than they should; the chief was going to have to hear the tapes to tell for certain. What did the old man mean, though, about another woman, another man? What was he talking about? At this point he had a feeling he'd better take everything the old buzzard said pretty seriously, since you never could--but wait, something was happening.

A sharp little wind had sprung up, twirling the sand around them where they lay. Varelli was shaking his head, and Blake knew what he was thinking: that the wind might play hell with the signal long enough for some of the talk up there on the hill to be lost. Sure enough, when Blake cupped his hands over the earphones and listened, what he heard was mostly the whistling of the wind.

The odd thing was, though, that it wasn't whistling, exactly, and it didn't sound quite the way wind would normally sound. He could see in Varelli's face that he had noticed it too. Varelli, in fact, looked over, shook his head, and pointed to his own earphones in evident puzzlement. Blake kept listening. No, it wasn't whistling, but something else hard to pin down, something almost--musical, in a weird kind of way. It sounded sibilant, hissing, yet there were faint tones buried in it, tones that made him think of something that he could almost but not quite remember. Then he did remember--it made him think of Indian flutes. His parents had taken him to one of the pueblos one year when he was a kid and he had seen the Indians do their rain dance, or corn dance, or something, and there had been flute music. Somehow that was what this windy sound in the earphones put him in mind of. It was foolishness, of course; maybe this damned rifle mike with its fancy price tag wasn't such hot shit after all, if it couldn't deal with sound any better than this.

But then again, it wasn't foolishness--this damned wind, or whatever it was, did sound oddly like the sighing and moaning of a bunch of Indian flutes. Something about the sound made his flesh crawl, and he shuddered, quickly wanting to suppress this reaction for fear that it would look weak or silly to his colleague if he noticed it. But Varelli, looking across at him, nodded, as much as to say: yeah, it strikes me that way too. They both concentrated on listening through the earphones, but all Blake could hear was the half moaning, half hissing sound covering up everything that was being said up there, if anything was. In the earphones there only remained that sound.

The moaning, hissing sound that should have been wind, but wasn't.

Undeniably, though, a real wind was still blowing, because it was still stirring the sand, sending little drifts of it to resettle around them, ruffling the dry sagebrush. After a while the wind mostly died down, and Blake sighed with relief; now maybe they'd be able to hear properly again.

But the odd thing was, when the wind died down, the sound in the earphones didn't, not altogether anyway; a low, somehow mournful tone, or set of tones, remained, like the distant formless ululation of strange wooden flutes. And Blake couldn't hear a damned word from up on the hill. Of course, the rifle mike might be on the fritz, though in all truth he doubted that. It might also be that no one was talking up there. But he wondered.

He wondered what the hell was really happening here. Whatever it was, he didn't like the feel of it. Didn't like it at all.

15

Sage and his Story

For all his professional training, and for all his years of experience, which most certainly should have given him a leg up on all this, Dr. Eric Hayes (M.A. Columbia University, Ph.D. Yale) was scared. Terrified. Fascinated, too, oh God yes; his professional instincts did kick in to that extent, somewhere deep in the spinning kaleidoscope of his mind--but the intrinsic fascination of the thing didn't seem to keep his hands from shaking as he retrieved the dying flashlight from the ground, unscrewed the cover, and worked at inserting fresh batteries. This procedure of course, especially with his uncertain grasp slowing things down, plunged them all into darkness, and Eric wasn't at all sure that protracted darkness was what he needed right now. The moon would be coming up in a little while, he thought, but he felt a certain undeniable urgency to get the flashlight back up and working, well before then.

Maybe it was true, then, maybe those primal vestiges of the savage that sometimes possessed you when you were a child--unreasoning fear of the dark, for one--were always mockingly ready, just below the surface, to reassert themselves. Maybe that veneer of sophistication, kept polished bright by civilization, was, as some people thought, just a thin coating of theatrical cowplop after all. Underneath that flimsy attempt to make oneself seem cultured and sane, maybe we were all still just fidgeting children, scared shitless when the light dimmed and the shadows began to jitter and dance and nameless things stirred in the dark. Maybe as Jung had said, the archetypes were always there, deep in the mind, whether one lived in London or Shanghai or Montevideo or Nairobi, whether one slept in a glass-and-steel high-rise or under a thatched roof, whether one fell asleep at night listening to television or to tribal drums.

One thing was certain--he had never felt more bewildered and insecure, more inadequately supported by the devices of civilization and urban life and sophisticated education, than he did at this moment.

What in God's name had happened here, was still happening here, tonight?

His fingers tried to hurry to get the flashlight working, but these thoughts did little to steady them, and the enduring blackness around him made him more nervous in turn, and the more he tried to hurry the more he fumbled. What do you *think* happened, Eric? a sector of his mind queried, like a catechism.

Well, he could try to answer that one. What he thought had happened was that an Indian *brujo*--medicine man, shaman, priest, wizard, witchdoctor, whatever you wanted to call it, but the Spanish word came closest to being adequate--a *brujo* had looked around, lifted his hands in the night air, and raised a windstorm. Among other things. Now, even to an anthropologist who had lived in the desertlands of the Southwest a good part of his life, that was a bit of a problem.

He was professionally open-minded about this sort of thing, no question about it. How many times had he chided his students in the freshman courses about open-mindedness? So-called "primitive" peoples, he had told them over and over, have their own kind of sophistication; it might not work on Madison Avenue, but it works for them. And how dare anyone call anyone else "primitive," anyway? As Eric had said a number of times in his various classes, the average New York stockbroker would probably consider Indians living in pueblos to be primitive; but, to turn the tables, what attitude toward the pathological, suicidal, bulging-eyed frenzy of the stock exchange could a silver-and-turquoise artisan living and working in Taos Pueblo be expected to have? Was either perception innately privileged over the other? Which world was the "primitive" world?

And how many times had Eric told his students that while urban sophisticates might scoff at the doings of medicine men and tribal witchdoctors, such scoffing was the height of ignorance. These people were never, never to be taken lightly. The funny thing about a medicine man shaking feathers at sick children to make them well, was that many times it *did* seem to make them well. Now, one could argue that it was all psychological, that the illness itself was perhaps psychosomatic, but that would just cover the issue over with labels, labels that fraudulently tried once again to assert the inherent superiority of one cultural viewpoint over another; in the end, a tribal witchdoctor's machinations might well have just as much validity, of their own kind, as a surgeon's. So-called primitive social systems were invariably replete with mysteries that no amount of ivy-league analysis could hope to comprehend. In particular, the desert seemed always to be a special repository of magical influences, and when an Indian *brujo* claimed to be able to heal the sick or to read the future in the clouds or to work changes in the weather, it was not terribly smart to laugh. Each culture, Eric had insisted countless times to those upturned student faces, each culture, however strange to outsiders, had its own internal logic, its own traditions, its own respectability. Its own magic.

Fine. But (Eric had to admit to himself now) all this was usually pretty theoretical. It was the platitudinal sort of thing that one stood up, as a smug and self-satisfied academician, and glibly intoned in the sheltered safety of the classroom--the sort of thing one usually didn't have to worry too much about actually confronting. Not on the way to a tea in the faculty lounge. Not at a Wednesday-afternoon meeting of the Curriculum Committee. Not at the supermarket. Not in real life.

But this *was* real life, here, now, tonight, and confronting the reality was going to be something else altogether.

This was a new reality.

Somewhere off in the night, it was hard to say how distant or how near, strange sounds whined and moaned, like some residue of the diminished wind. It was the howling of coyotes, Eric thought at first, but then again the more one listened, the more it sounded somehow more-- melodic--than that. Like the low, lugubrious moan of flute-notes, as if somewhere out there on the desert floor in a circle around the hill a chorus of wooden flutes were intoning a mind-lulling medley of notes that floated in on the darkness and made the very air on one's skin feel alive. Whatever it was, its effect was unsettling beyond words.

At last Eric succeeded in getting the flashlight back together, though when he flicked it on he wondered which was really worse, the darkness or the pale wash of light that showed him, again, the wrinkled lizard visage of the old *brujo,* the fellow human being who a few minutes before had apparently raised a windstorm with a gesture of the hands. The face was expressionless, as if the darkness and the light were a matter of indifference to the mind behind the face. Glancing at Anne, Eric saw in her face a mingling of emotions at which he could scarcely even guess. He started to speak, but found when he did so that his throat was so dry that no sound came out, and he had to swallow and try again.

"What's happening?" he asked. "You made--that--happen?"

The old Indian's mouth opened to set a maze of wrinkles fleeing, changing, coalescing. "Sage does nothing alone. The spirits help."

"But you're a--"

105

The Indian's face came as close as it ever seemed to come to smiling. "Those Spanish call me a *brujo*. My people have other words. She know," he said, nodding toward Anne. "But *brujo* needs all the spirits. Work together."

Eric's impulse was to ask him something further, but he really couldn't think what to ask. Besides, he had the feeling that the old man was going to open up and talk some more of his own volition, and the feeling turned out to be right.

"I was not always *brujo*," Sage said. "When I was a child I was like others. Had to learn and grow, same like others. When young man, start to have visions. Like dreams, but not just dreams. Visions tell me about my power. Power I was going to have. Talk with elders in the pueblo, they help me understand my power. The power grow up faster than the young man. Some people who have power, all alike. Indians, we see power like that at work in life, every day. But Sage's power not the same. Strange, different. My own people afraid of me. One day I know what I must do, and I leave the pueblo, go away. Sometimes go into town, work a little, but live in the desert. Sleep under the stars, live close to the spirits. Years go by. Spirits take my power and shape it, like my father shape pots out of clay. Visions grow, every night. Power grow. Every day, more strong. Then something happen."

The old man paused, and Eric resisted his natural impulse to ask what happened; the thing to do was just let the man speak.

"One night, out in the desert, over near Roswell. Outside of Corona. Just sitting. Something come flying over, with lights like stars. Silver bird. Great sound like thunder, silver bird spill her insides on the sands near where I sit. Great bird fall to earth not far away. Everywhere on the sand, little silver pieces of the bird. I walk to where the bird fall to earth, and find the sky-child."

Eric shot a glance at Anne, whose mouth had fallen open.

"Sky-child alive on the ground, but hurt. Others near him, not alive. I leave him there, go out and find plants for special medicine, strong medicine. Takes time, put those things together so they work. Call upon all the things I have learned, use all my powers, to make this medicine. Sit up with sky-child all the night, making him well. In the morning, hear others come. Them Anglo Army people. I have to go before they see me."

"Jesus," Anne said under her breath.

"But that was time when I get most of my power. All the time I try to make sky-child well, sky-child and me talk, not using words. His head, my head. Just talk. Just know what he want to say, he know what I want to say. I give him something, making him well. He give me something too. From that time, sky-child and I have a--" The old man seemed to be searching for the right word.

"Link?" Eric suggested. "Relation? Connection?"

"Yes," the old man said. "It's like we still talk. I don't hear all he think, but I know he's alive. I can feel it. I know he's there."

"Know he's where?" Anne said. The moon was rising, and Eric, switching off the flashlight, wondered if it was just the bone-white wan radiance that made Anne's face so white. He thought not.

"Where them Army people keep him," the old man said simply. And he added three words that brought a little gasp from Anne. "Where you know."

They sat in silence for a long while. Eric reflected that the old man no doubt understood very well that he had given them quite enough to digest for the moment, and was waiting before he said anything else. Eric's own mind was racing, trying to make sense of everything. His acquaintance with Anne's situation was still so newly acquired that he wasn't at all sure he could handle these new revelations. He felt that his whole understanding of things had changed, radically and forever, twice in as many evenings. As an anthropologist he was supposed to be flexible enough to spring back no matter what unsettling new matters he encountered, but he realized now that in practical reality he was not much more capable of absorbing what he was now trying to absorb than most other people would have been. He was just another academic guy whose life, fleshed out by class schedules and by file cabinets full of lecture notes, was pretty much the same one year to the next. But now that old comfortable life was over. Things were never going to be the same. He was so immersed in this reflection that he jumped, a nervous reflex, when the old man spoke again.

"This was not the first time the sky-children come," he said. Again he lapsed into a few moments' silence, as if to let the import of this remark sink in.

"Not the first time?" Eric said. "When did they come before?"

"Many, many years ago," Sage said. "Before all them Anglo cities. Before the Spanish come to New Mexico. When my people still live in Chaco."

Damn, Eric thought. Before the Spanish--Coronado had come through New Mexico in 1540. But then, he reflected, if this earlier contact was during the time when the Anasazi, the ancestors of the present Pueblo peoples, still lived in the settlements of Chaco Canyon, well then hell--we were talking about a time maybe five centuries before Coronado. In other words, nearly a thousand years ago.

"But how do you know they came before?" Anne asked. No doubt she too knew that the aliens had been here before, if indeed they had,

107

Eric thought; the Crewman must at some point have intimated as much. Anne was no doubt just trying to piece things together.

The old man sat for a long time without speaking, his face pensive, his eyes nearly lost in their nests of wrinkles, where they seemed to withdraw like the heads of turtles, just beyond reach. Eric sensed that his answer to Anne's question was not going to be a simple one.

"The stories of our people," he finally said, "live a long time." Eric wondered if *our people* was meant to include Anne, as much as to say, to her: you well ought to understand this, even if you do live your life among the Anglos. Eric of course knew the importance of storytelling to Native American peoples; it often represented virtually unbroken strains of lore stretching back for countless centuries, and it was natural that for some Indian peoples the most common motif in sculpture was the figure of the Storyteller, usually a woman with her mouth shaped in an *O* and with numerous diminutive listeners perched in her lap and up and down her arms. To Indians, storytelling was an integral part of life, a way of continually reasserting the fundamentals of your understanding of the world, a way of being connected to your past, to the world around you, to your Mother the Earth, to your real identity. Telling a story wasn't just telling a story; it was a making-still-alive of what the story said. But Sage, himself like a Storyteller sculpture come to life now, was continuing his response to Anne.

"Not everyone know all these stories. Some stories, only certain elders know. One story says when the sky-children come, that time before, they bring the music. Hunter see them come down out of the sky, and then him and his people come down from the mesa, and the sky-children make the music for them. Story says, music was so beautiful it make the hunter cry, eyes full of tears. Hunter go back up the mesa and carve picture of sky-child fluteplayer in the rock. People call him Kokopelli. Many stories about him. Say he brings rain. Say he make the corn to grow. Say he make the babies to grow in women's bellies. You go around this land, see pictures of him in the rocks, everywhere."

It was true, certainly, Eric thought; to this day in all likelihood not all of the Kokopelli carvings and drawings had been found or catalogued. There were hundreds of them known.

"Him that people call Kokopelli," the old man was saying, "live everywhere in the desert, not just in rocks. Live all around, like spirit. Some of you Anglos," he added, looking at Eric, "say he is the Trickster. Brother Coyote is the Trickster too. Brother Coyote, Kokopelli with his flute, lots of others, same spirits. Some people even say Sage is the Trickster." Here the faintest glint of amusement seemed to flicker in the old man's watery eyes. "Sage sits here, talks to you. Maybe Trickster sits here, talks to you. But Trickster does not live just in one place, one time. Spirit of the Trickster rides," the old man said with a slow sweep of his hand, "on the wind."

This remark roused Eric to ask a question that had been bothering him. "Before, when you--when you and the spirits of the spirit world--made the wind come up, and the sound that stayed when the wind died down. Why did you do that?"

"Because," Sage said, "somebody out there"--he lifted an arm and pointed to the west--"try to listen to what we say."

"God damn," Anne said, clearly startled by this revelation, especially coming now after all that had been said. Eric saw that her eyes were wide, unblinking, frightened-looking, with somehow a subtle trace of anger in them too. Some corner of his mind reflected, even now, that it was surprising how well he still knew her, still understood her facial expressions, her moods, her feelings, even after all these years. He half suspected, in fact, that he understood her now more than ever before, in a way that might have made a difference back then when they were younger, in New Haven. For certain, Anne was disturbed by this last remark of Sage's, and for good reason. Eric noted that she had to swallow hard and catch a breath before speaking again. "You mean--" But she lapsed into silence, obviously having second thoughts about saying anything else at all. It occurred to Eric to wonder how the old man had known that someone out there on the desert floor was listening. It didn't occur to him to question whether it was true; he was sure it was, all things considered. And he wasn't going to ask how the old man knew. By now, he could accept the fact that he just knew. No explanations were possible. Maybe none were necessary.

"After the wind come up," Sage said, "and the music, nobody out there hear nothing." In seeming corroboration of this, the barely perceptible wind lifted a little, bringing on it a vague low mingling of ululant sounds, as if a weirdly playful confluence of wooden flutes had made antiphonal response, like the chorus in a Greek tragedy. Eric realized, though, that the sounds had been there, nearly below the level of audibility, right along.

"Are you sure? Are you sure nobody could hear?" he asked, but felt a little foolish asking it, especially when Sage didn't even bother to reply. Of course he was sure. Anyway, he'd damned well *better* be sure. They might all be in serious trouble, even so. They would most certainly all be in trouble if any of this last round of talk had been overheard. Eric's mind fairly reeled when he allowed himself to think of some of the implications of what he and Anne had heard here tonight. In a way, it felt good to know that Sage *knew*--that he might be just a penniless old

Indian living in the desert but he apparently knew things that only Anne and her shadowy government employers were supposed to know, in their unimaginable dark labyrinths of secrecy. The Indian knew! It made Eric feel as if he and Anne weren't so alone after all with their own terrible knowledge. Then again, maybe this meant that they were all in trouble, that yet another human being, a gentle old Indian who just happened to have the curious knack of raising a wind when he felt like it, another innocent human being was just possibly going to get drawn into the foul pit of trouble that this business must surely spawn. That trouble might already have started, for all any of them knew.

Suddenly the old man was standing up and making ready to leave. "I go now," he said. "You should go too. All need rest." Eric suddenly realized that there were a lot more questions he needed to ask. But without waiting for any further conversation, Sage turned and began making his way back down the path in the ivory moonlight, picking his steps slowly, surely. When he was a little distance away, he turned and looked back up the path at them, and made a curious gesture. Slightly raising his hand, with the thumb and first two fingers together, he dropped the hand level with a little bounce, a kind of pointing, a little like a child gesturing with a toy gun, but with none of the levity that that would have entailed. Somehow the effect was sobering, almost grandiose. It all happened in a second, and the old man had turned and was walking away again, but Eric felt that the gesture was a special moment to him, to Anne, to all three of them. In a way, it was like being marked. Marked by the Trickster, in a gesture that meant a medley of things: *you're the ones, we're you and I connected now, you must do the right things, good luck to you.*

Eric took Anne's hand, and they watched the old man dwindle down the rocky path, watched him walk out onto the desert floor beyond the foot of the hill, watched as a veil of cloud drifted over the moon and seemed to fold the small moving figure out there into a pocket of darkness. The wind still stirred from time to time, carrying rumors of dry sage and pungent cedar, and mingling with the sound, seemingly all around them, low but discernible, of half-hinted musical notes, notes that could have been just some half-imagined part of the wind's caprice among the rocks. When the clouds scudded on by and the moon cast its full chalk-white radiance once again upon the desert sands, they could see the old man no more.

16

The Arroyo

As the night wore on, Varelli, flat on the sand beside Blake in the shadows, felt more and more that his blood was coming to a nice roiling simmer beneath his skin. Quite simply, he was pissed, and that was putting it lightly. Sure, having a little technical glitch arise and losing a line or two of sparkling dialogue up there on the hill would have been one thing, but this was fucking ridiculous. He didn't know what had gone wrong here, but whatever it was, it had royally screwed up the surveillance, and he didn't think the chief was going to dance a dance of joy about that, exactly.

In fact, he tended to think the chief was going to be inclined to kick some serious ass, and there was no question whose. In the scenario to follow, there was going to be Blake-ass, and then there was going to be Varelli-ass, and it was all going to have nice livid shoeprints on it. Or, to judge from the way he'd last seen the chief attired, bootprints.

Well, hell, it wasn't their fault. Not that that was going to make any difference to the chief, or to his higher-ups, but it really wasn't their fault. They hadn't caused it. What *had* caused it, he didn't have much of an idea. Somehow he had the feeling that there was something unnatural, something truly bizarre going on here, and he didn't like it a damned bit. He'd seen the same thoughts in Blake's face, too, since the moon had come up, sending them both hunkering lower into the sand and the ragged shadows of sagebrush, to keep from being visible from the hill. Blake's face, mostly in shadow but pasty-white in the glow of the gibbous moon when he looked up, showed that he didn't like this development either, and Varelli didn't think Blake had any clue what was causing the problem, any more than he did.

Just when things had started to get interesting, too. Shit! Wouldn't you know it? Varelli, in his mind, ran back over what they had heard, before the problem arose. Hayes and the woman up there had said that one of the petroglyphs looked like a flying saucer. That was interesting--not classified, of itself, but interesting, in a sinister sort of way, considering Anne Hawk's position. Even in the realm of the unclassified, there were things you should talk about and things you shouldn't, and flying saucers just might be the biggest "shouldn't" of them all, on Anne Hawk's list, it seemed to Varelli. She was getting a little reckless, from the sound of it, even to mention such a thing as that when--well, when things were the way they were. Christ, this was no parlor game; there were deadly-serious considerations of secrecy here, more secrecy than had ever been attached to anything, Varelli thought, in all of history. So what was this bitch doing running her mouth off about flying saucers?

But *then* the old Indian had come up, and things had gotten more interesting still. The old man had actually stood right up there on that hill, looking at that petroglyph (damn, Varelli wanted to have a look at that himself) and talking about a great "silver bird" coming down out of the sky and bringing the "sky-children," and then a little later talking about the likelihood that Eric and the woman were going to have "troubles." What kind of troubles, and why would the old fart say that? And if that "sky-child" business wasn't a reference to the Crewman, Varelli told himself, then just what the hell was it? To think that they had been lying out here in the sand with the rifle mike, hearing some old Indian walk up out of the desert and practically say in so many words that he knew classified information, information that was so highly classified that practically nobody on the goddamn *planet* could know it, information that even he and Blake and other operatives had only sketchy knowledge of, just as much as they needed to know to do their jobs. And they had been on the verge of hearing the rest of what the Indian was going to say, when--when whatever happened happened. At first Varelli had thought it was the wind somehow screwing up the sound, but then when the wind had pretty much died down, that *other* sound had stayed: low, vague in the earphones, just enough to destroy the signal, so that from that point they hadn't heard a damned word. Varelli knew that Blake was still taping everything, but he also knew that the damned tape was going to be blank, or was only to have that strange sound on it, the sound like weird, howling, tuneless but somehow depressing music being played on flutes, the sound he had been hearing all goddamn evening now and was still hearing.

And he also knew that the chief was going to ask: why? Why, gentlemen, did the surveillance go to seed? And instead of waiting for an answer--well, you know, the mike just went on the fritz, chief, we, huh-huh, told you not to buy the Sears economy model--the chief was going to supply an answer himself: it all went to hell because you two turkeys screwed up, real, real bad. Because as your chief I had the spectacularly poor judgment to send you on an assignment that would require an operative to have, let us say at the very least, a brain stem. It all went wrong because you two cretins can't be trusted with assignments of this importance. It all went to hell in a basket, because you seem to enjoy getting your butts kicked, and having your career plans adjusted by a slight deflection from your intended trajectory, to the effect that you will soon be dragging out your days in government service scrubbing shit-smeared toilets in the most flyblown hellhole we can find for you, if you're lucky enough to still be alive, that is, my lads--and if you can call that luck.

Well, whatever had happened, at least the two of them could corroborate the story for each other, even as inconclusive and senseless as it was. But then the chief would no doubt have the rifle mike checked out, and if there wasn't anything wrong with it, well, then Varelli and Blake would probably be in deep shit, toilet-scrubbing reassignments or no. It made Varelli furious, to think of it, of how damned unfair it was. He'd never screwed up an assignment yet, anywhere, anytime, and he wasn't screwing *this* one up, either.

He had an idea.

He resolved to tell Blake about it as soon as the little party up on the hill was over, whatever the hell was going on up there.

And it wasn't long before that appeared to be happening. He and Blake were still getting no intelligible speech in the earphones, only that weird moaning sound that, one time you thought of it, sounded like coyotes howling, and the next time sounded like Indian flutes playing some surrealistic Zombie Song from Hell or something. But even though no speech was coming through to help them figure out what was happening, it appeared, in the wash of pale moonlight that illumined the rocky hill, that the old Indian was getting up and moving off down the path, while the others were staying put as far as Varelli could see in the uncertain light. He reached across and nudged Blake, but Blake waved him off, indicating that he'd already seen it. Blake was still pressing his earphones to his head, as if in some last-ditch hopeless effort to hear something. The Indian seemed to stop for a moment, maybe saying something to Anne Hawk and the boyfriend, and then moved off again, making his slow way down to the bottom of the hill.

"Blake, listen," Varelli said, gesturing for Blake to push his earphones off far enough to listen. "That old man is a problem. Big time."

"Step to the head of the class," Blake said. "You think I haven't been thinking the same thing? Yeah, damn right he's a problem. Our problem. So what are we going to do about him?"

"Well, hell," Varelli said, "there's no question. We have to take him in."

Blake nodded, keeping one earphone in place, apparently still hoping that the sound would clear. "You're right. I don't know how he knows what he knows, but I think there are folks that can find out, don't you? It may not be just him, who knows, it may be all kinds of people he's talked to. We have ourselves a fucking serious security-leak situation here. Here's what we do."

"I got my own ideas," Varelli said, "but what do you say?"

"It looks to me like the guy and the girl are getting ready to leave, and when they do, I'm going to take the car and follow them back to town," Blake said.

"And I'm going to stay and--"

"Let's say, ah, interview our friend the Indian," Blake finished for him, smiling.

"Just what I had in mind," Varelli said.

"Don't kill him, for Christ's sake," Blake said, his grin shading off into a kind of never-can-quite-take-you-anywhere look. "We've got to take him in alive. They're going to want him to talk his head off. That's the whole point."

"Hey," Varelli said, "do I look like the kind of guy would kill a feeble-ass old Indian geezer?"

Blake snorted. "Shit, Varelli, you'd kill your own mother and eat the body."

"Well, yeah," Varelli said, "but that don't mean I'd kill a feeble-ass old Indian geezer." Now that they had a plan to pursue, and a pretty promising one, he was feeling a lot better. Surely, he thought, if they get the old man to talk they'll piece together whatever the hell it was that happened out here tonight, and the assignment won't be an abortion after all, or not altogether, anyway.

The point was, he and Blake would be off the hook.

"There they go," Blake was saying, nodding in the direction of the hill. He was already packing up the rifle mike and shoving other odds and ends into one of the canvas bags. "They're heading down to their car. As soon as they go and they've had enough of a start, I'll pull out of here behind them. And the minute I take off, you haul ass after that Indian. When you get him, wait right here for me to come back for you. The old

114

man can't move very fast, it looks like, so I think even you can handle this."

"Hey, piss off." Damn, he hated it when Blake (and other people) treated him like the village idiot. Just because we was a good old-fashioned mafia type from the concrete jungles of Rhode Island didn't mean he was stupid. Some of the greatest people in the world were of his particular ethnic persuasion, for God's sakes, didn't everybody know that? Varelli thought this smart-ass Blake might be surprised to learn that his partner the Galloping Guinea knew a thing or two, if anybody ever gave him half a chance to show it. "I can handle it," he told Blake.

"Well, I'm just telling you," Blake said, "you screw this up, Varelli, and you might as well just hand the chief your balls to save time, because he's going to staple you to the wall by them, for everybody to come and see. You get the picture."

"Yeah, yeah, Christ on a crutch, it's just a piss-ass old Indian," Varelli said.

Blake's teeth were clenched as he poked Varelli in the arm with a forefinger. "*Don't* fuck this up."

Over in the parking area near the base of the hill, car doors were slamming, and an engine faltered and then started up. Without another word Blake was scuttling across the sand, keeping his head down, dragging equipment bags by the straps, making his way around behind the ridge where they had hidden their car. Across the way, a car crunched and bumped its way down the road to the south, the twin yellow cones of its headlights poking the dark like twitching antennae. Immediately, Blake had started the car behind the ridge and was easing it back across the chaparral, with the headlights off, toward the road. Not even waiting for Blake to be out of sight with the car, Varelli got up and started walking in the direction the Indian had gone, feeling a real urgency to do what had to be done.

Blake had been right: he'd damned well better not screw this up. But what chance? The old fartface couldn't be more than a hundred yards away by now, and catching up with him was going to be like chasing a snail. No prob, friends and neighbors. Piece-a-cake. Done before you know it.

He was going to enjoy this, in fact. Blake was right, he shouldn't seriously hurt the old man, not enough to keep him from being able to talk, but he was going to enjoy this little outing anyway. Sometimes he had a real talent for working with people, he reflected, chuckling to himself; by all logic, he should have been a social worker.

He wove his way among the clumps of sagebrush, letting the moonlight guide his way, watching all the while for snake holes and giving them wide berth when he saw them. He felt around the small of his back for the leather scabbard he kept there, and drummed his fingers momentarily against the hard, cold handle of the hunting knife that lodged in it. An old friend, a gentle persuader when you most needed one. He'd had this knife since he was a leering fifteen-year-old street punk back in Providence. Following the old man's trail now, he suddenly remembered a scene from that time, years ago, the occasion of another pursuit, when he and four of his scowling cronies had chased a scrawny bookish-looking kid down South Main Street one afternoon, brandishing knives and yelling. Varelli had had this very knife in his hand that day. They had chased the kid up an alleyway and back up onto Benefit Street, then up Meeting Street where it dead-ended, and finally cornered him there by the old concrete steps at the end, where he cowered in every expectation of being sliced to shreds. But instead, Varelli and his four companions had unzipped their pants, unlimbered themselves, and hosed the kid down good and proper, howling with laughter all the while, at length zipping themselves back up and striding off down the street, leaving the kid collapsed against the steps, whimpering and spluttering and choking, dripping wet from top to toe, half-drowned in a stinking pool of urine. To this day, it tickled Varelli to think of it.

Now, this was a different kind of pursuit, here tonight, but he still had a feeling it was going to be good wholesome fun. He scanned the landscape around and ahead of him. Aside from the hill, whose craggy shape rose in the moonlight like some strange humped sea creature coming up for air, there was nothing as far as the eye could see but desert followed by more desert, followed in point of fact by more desert, off to the horizon in every direction. It looked stark, bleak, dead in the moonlight, like some landscape on the surface of the moon itself. But far off ahead and to Varelli's left, a dim figure moved across the chaparral. The old man was in plain sight now, maybe a hundred yards ahead, and moving at a hobble. Easy prey. No need to hurry too much. Still, Varelli didn't want to take all night doing this. The sooner he had the old man in hand, the better. He'd just herd him back to the camp site by the ridge and tie him up, and they'd wait there for Blake to come back with the car, or to send somebody back if he got too busy listening in on the woman and the boyfriend. All in all, it was destined to end up a pleasant and profitable evening, and a good return on the taxpayer's hard-earned dollar, Varelli thought, feeling warm inside.

Stepping up his pace a bit, he began to close the distance between himself and the shuffling old man, whose form up ahead in the wan light reminded Varelli, in some bizarre comic way, of the movements of a crow wobbling along in the moonglow. Soon he was only fifty feet behind the Indian, who seemed either not to have noticed or not to have chosen to pay any attention. If he knew he was being followed and wasn't bothering to acknowledge it, Varelli thought, now *that* was a little spooky, and there had been enough spooky stuff about this whole night not to require anything else along those lines, thank you ever so much. Probably, he told himself, the old man's hard of hearing and just doesn't know anybody else is out here. That was okay; Varelli would soon enough make his presence known.

When he walked a little farther along, into an area where the ground was becoming uneven, he saw that the old man was coming to the mouth of--what did they call these things?--an arroyo, one of those dry riverbeds that sometimes twist and turn through the desert floor for miles. Varelli had been on assignment down here long enough to have seen them many times before. In some instances they were just shallow rivercourses, which you could step in and out of, all up and down their lengths, but sometimes they were deep trenches eroded into the desert like miniature canyons with twin walls of sand and twisted vegetation, walls so high that if you were walking in the arroyo you couldn't see up onto the desert floor on either side.

This appeared to be one of those deep, high-walled arroyos, and it looked as if the old man had it in mind to step into it.

Varelli really didn't want him to do that. As long as he had him out here in the moonlight where he could see him, things were simple, and he liked them that way. "Hey!" he called after the old man. "Hey! Hold it right there."

The Indian gave no sign of having heard him, and took a hobbling step into the mouth of the arroyo.

"I *said*, hold up! I want to talk to you."

The Indian strode into the arroyo, and was soon only visible, from where Varelli stood, from about the waste up, and then only from the shoulders up. He seemed to be moving along faster now, and would be out of sight in a few more seconds, from this vantage point anyway.

"Damn." Varelli sprinted the rest of the way up to the entrance to the arroyo and fetched up a little short of going in. He glanced inside, seeing that the riverbed was perhaps fifteen feet wide, and that it started shallow, with sandy walls only three feet high on each side at first. But it quickly deepened, so that if you walked fifty or sixty feet in, you would have walls on each side of you too high to see over. The moon was directly ahead as he faced into the arroyo, but the chalky moonlight only penetrated just so far down those higher walls of sand and cedar roots, so that the depths of the dry rivercourse were cloaked in deep, cold shadow, and by the time Varelli started into the arroyo himself, he couldn't see the old man ahead of him at all.

117

This was not what he'd had in mind.

He trotted into the arroyo with the feeling that when he caught up to the old fart he was just possibly going to give him an extra kick in the balls or something for putting him to this kind of trouble. The old man couldn't be very bright. Did he honestly think he would get away? These arroyos were sometimes long, sometimes miles long, in fact, but they didn't go on forever, and whichever path in the maze you chose to follow after the rivercourse started branching and fragmenting, you generally would find the path dead-ending not too far up ahead of you somewhere. Let the old man have his fun, it wasn't going to last.

Inside, the riverbed was a meandering walled expanse of silky sand punctuated here and there by tufts of sagebrush or chamisa, or by dusky snake holes that looked like moaning mouths in the sand. *O-O-O*, they said, as if anticipating that response in the visitor. Varelli tacked his way along, swearing under his breath. Clearly, he had to watch where he put his feet in here. His annoyance with the Indian was growing. This was supposed to be easy.

His frame of mind wasn't made any mellower by the sudden realization that that sound was still there, up on the desert floor but clearly audible even down here, in the arroyo--that dim, vague sound that was like coyotes howling, or maybe like the whine of some deranged chorus of distant flutes.

He found himself kind of hoping at this point that his next assignment might be in the Bronx, or in Philadelphia or Detroit. Good old urban squalor. He could deal with that, any day. He wasn't sure any more that he could deal with the desert. There was too much about it that was just plain damned weird. Hard work, he had no objection to. Dirty work, he had no problem with. Weirdness, he didn't need. No sir, not Mama Varelli's baby boy. Weirdness wasn't what he signed on for.

Rather like a perverse colophon to this thought, something stirred somewhere up ahead in the shadows. He had a glimpse of the old man-- there he was, just moving out of sight again around a bend in the arroyo wall.

"Hey," Varelli called after him, but without much enthusiasm this time; it was more like a commentary made to himself than a call to the old Indian. He trudged ahead, struggling to close the gap, and finding that it was harder to walk in this sand than it looked; the stuff was soft, and his feet sank in it, sometimes more than ankle deep, so that his shoes filled with grit. Well, it couldn't be much longer now; the old bastard had to be up ahead just around the bend.

But when Varelli himself rounded the turn, he found only more arroyo stretching ahead into the dark, with only frenzied shards of moonlight on the sandy walls to suggest what directions the riverbed took. The old man wasn't anywhere in sight.

"Damn!" Varelli bounded ahead, dodging around clumps of dry vegetation and feeling his feet sucked down by the sand. At this point the arroyo was tending to branch out, with little sidetracks that probably went in toward the walls a few yards and stopped, but he thought he could still see where the main course ran, and that was no doubt the track the old man would take; these desert types knew better than to blunder into a dead end, probably, even when they were as old as God's grandmother. Varelli trotted ahead, keeping to the main rivercourse and straining his eyes in the near-dark to catch sight of his prey. Finally he did see him, rounding another corner up ahead, his white hair trailing after him like a ghostly halo of vapor.

"God damn it, I said hold up!"

The Indian was gone again.

Varelli trudged on through the sand, navigating around little clumps of sage that poked their way up through the riverbed like withered hands with dry, gnarled knots of fingers that seemed to reach for his feet. How far did this damned arroyo *go*, anyway? Ahead he saw only more of the same, a seemingly endless pathway that stretched off into the night. It was like looking down a throat of darkness, and it felt almost that way, as if he were propelling himself not so much forward as downward, pitching himself into some unthinkable black well where nameless things stirred and where no one sane would want to go. Clearly, some corner of his mind retorted, you're letting the situation get to you, if you feel this way, Varelli, old boy. Firming up his resolve as best he could, he plunged onward into the blackness before him, and presently was rewarded with the old man's coming into view again.

There, maybe a hundred feet away--how did he get so far ahead, moving as slow as he moved? But there he was, a vaguely tattered-looking blotch of darkness against darker dark, moving away with shuffling steps. And (the gods be praised, Varelli thought) the Indian was not keeping to the main rivercourse this time, but edging off toward the right, into one of those jagged cul-de-sacs that would dead-end at the wall of the arroyo. At last. Varelli could feel himself doing the mental equivalent of licking his chops. The old man was worn down at last, and had made a serious mistake. He was going to trap himself in a blind, and would be easy picking. There would be nothing left to do but grab him out of there and haul ass with him back to the camp site before Blake got back with the car.

Excited now to bring the thing to a close, and more than a little steamed at the Indian for causing him so much exertion and bother,

Varelli sprinted across the remaining distance and came up to the branch of the arroyo into which the old man had blundered. He could see, already, a part of the arroyo wall at the back of this blind, which was only maybe fifteen feet deep and mostly in shadow, below the reach of the moonlight on the upper wall. This was it, there was no way out, the old man had indeed trapped himself neater than neat. Feeling very self-justified, Varelli plunged a couple of yards into the blind and halted.

And found the blind empty, except for himself and a formless assortment of sagebrush crouched against the bottom of the sandy wall.

He blinked and studied the darkness more carefully. The old man had to be here of course, no doubt hidden, momentarily, in the shadows. Varelli had seen him go in here. The wall at the end of the blind was too high for climbing over. There was no way out. The old man had to be here.

The problem with that was, he wasn't.

Varelli strode farther into the blind and turned this way and that, surveying the spot, nudging the sagebrush, running his hand over cedar roots that laced their way down through the crumbling sand of the arroyo wall. He went over the spot half a dozen times, to make sure he wasn't making a mistake, wasn't overlooking some hiding place the old man could have crawled into. But it was no use--the Indian simply wasn't here. Off in the distance, out on the desert floor above him somewhere, a whining chorus of sounds, sounds that had been there all along, he remembered, rose a little in volume now, playing on the air like wind, though there was no wind. The sounds were like the somehow melancholy keening of coyotes, but then again not quite like that, more like those damnable flute notes once more, that unplaceable idiot song that he couldn't seem to get away from, even in here, in a blind in an arroyo where he could fall down dead and nobody would know. He put his hands up to cover his ears, willing the sounds to go away. After a moment they seemed to recede, but did not cease altogether; a strangely lilting little residue remained, like some half-formed sheaf of thoughts in one's own brain.

And suddenly Varelli realized that in addition to his anger and frustration and puzzlement, he was immensely tired. He wasn't in as good shape as he had thought, and the pursuit across the sandy terrain had sapped his strength to an alarming degree. It took all the strength he could scratch together to turn and walk back out of the blind, into the main arroyo.

Where, to his astonishment, he felt lost.

And where, suddenly, he also felt very, very alone.

He looked to his left, which was the direction in which he had come. Wasn't it? But it somehow didn't look like the area he had passed

120

through to get here. Then again, what did that mean--desert looks like desert looks like desert, he mused. He looked to the right and found only more arroyo yawning away into the darkness, no more comforting a prospect than the other view. Finally he decided that his memory was correct on the point that he had followed the old man into a blind to the right, not to the left, so he had to turn left now and follow the arroyo back out onto the desert floor.

He set out walking, breathing heavily, needing to stop from time to time and catch his breath. Damn, he was tired, and, now that he thought about it, worried. Scared, even. Blake's words echoed in his brain: don't fuck this up, Varelli, or the chief is going to staple you to the wall by your balls. But he *had* fucked it up. He had let the Indian get away. Impossible--how, how? He had followed the man into the blind, for Christ's sake, into the damned blind, where there was no exit. It just couldn't be. The old man couldn't have *not* been in there, yet the blind had been empty. But was the chief going to take that for an excuse? God, no. Would anybody? Varelli had to admit it: he wouldn't buy a story like that himself. He wasn't sure he bought it now, and he had *seen* it.

But he had to admit something else too: it wasn't the chief's probable wrath that scared him now.

It was this damned place. The arroyo. The spooky old man. The whole situation.

Something about it was terribly, terribly wrong, and whatever it was, he was caught square in the middle of it.

He walked on and on through the sand, in the pale light, with a subtle wash of sound swirling around him, those mournful tones that were, necessarily, the wind or the crying of coyotes, but were in truth not the wind, not coyotes. With a gradually dawning awareness, he was puzzled to find that he seemed to be having to go farther to get back out than he had walked when coming in. That was horseshit, of course, in any sane world-view, but that didn't keep it from being true, did it? Not out here.

This place was haunted, he was ready to admit that to himself now. Anything was possible out here.

To make matters worse, a gathering of gray clouds had come up to cover the moon, and what little light had been filtering down into the arroyo was fast playing out, leaving him in nearly total darkness. Swearing in a raspy whisper, he staggered forward, feeling ahead of him with outstretched hands, sliding a foot ahead of him to test the ground. It was uncanny, how the failing of the light also seemed to take away his sense of time, for he thought he spent an hour or longer moving blindly forward, feeling the air, finding his slow way along--yet it couldn't have been anything like an hour. It couldn't have been, because now the patch of gray cloud was drifting past the moon and letting the pasty light down again to inch part of the way down the arroyo walls and dimly illumine the riverbed where he walked, but there had been only a scruffy little bit of cloud, and it couldn't have taken more than three or four minutes to drift past, in front of the moon, and on again. What he had thought was an hour or more, blundering forward in the darkness, could only have been a few minutes.

In any case, he noted with immense relief, the opening to the arroyo was visible ahead of him, and he quickened his pace and made for it.

And stopped.

And listened.

What had that been? That sound? The odd flutelike sound had subsided to a barely audible level now, just a thin, reedy suggestion on the air. That wasn't it. He had heard something else.

There it was again.

A dry, dry, ratchety little sound that part of his mind leaped to identify, while another part tried to deny it.

No question, really, what it was, though, and the thought itself made him jump with such force that when he started to take his next step, hoping to haul himself out of this wretched place as quickly as possible, his foot came down half on, half off a low clump of sage, and he lost his balance and sprawled forward face downward, burying his face in the sand, coming up spitting and choking. When enough of the sand fell away from his eyes for him to open them, he didn't much like what he saw.

It wasn't the first time he had ever seen a rattlesnake, but it was the first time he had seen one from the distance of eight or nine inches, its triangular head level with his face, which was precisely where the snake struck, hitting him with an open-mouthed jab of fangs in the left cheek and recoiling to strike again, which it did, hitting him in nearly the same spot before he'd even had time to react to the first strike. Or maybe it was one of the other snakes that struck the second time, and the third, it was hard to tell, because through his tears he thought he could see a number of snakes, it was impossible to tell how many, maybe ten or twelve, their rattlers alive in a buzzing nightmare of sound, their malevolent heads darting and retracting and darting again, their fangs sinking into his face and throat over and over. He seemed powerless to defend himself, for though he flung his arms up and tried to ward them off, the snakes found their way through, hitting him again and again, before finally withdrawing to a conclave of writhing and rattling a few feet away.

He managed to reflect, with what would be his last flicker of consciousness, that the venom must surely have derailed his mind, because in his final glimpse of the rattlesnakes as they recoiled and drew away, he could have sworn that one of them, the nearest and largest one, had around its wedge-shaped head a little halo of floating white hair.

17

Much Ado

Pulling the car off Route 25 a little after 11:00 P.M., Roger Wynn made his way through the nearly deserted streets of Santa Fe with such a sense of a mission-nearly-accomplished that he found himself whistling as he drove down Cerrillos Road and turned toward the southeast side of town: where Lucy Trujillo lived, out near the community college, and where she was about to receive a surprise visitor. He had decided to go to the house first rather than just trying the bookshop; if he was going shopping for a special edition of Cervantes, he would need a guide, someone who knew the shop's literary wares, and what better guide than the enterprising and shapely proprietor? Besides, she might have the book squirreled away at home, rather than at the shop.

What a hoot this would be, Roger thought; he actually winked at himself in the rear view mirror, and chuckled in anticipation. He might have been a carefree young college student on his way across town to pick up a date, looking forward to a little game of hand-up-the-leg later on. Who knew, it might end up that way, after a fashion.

He turned down the street where she lived and nosed the car along, peering at mailboxes and numbers on houses. He knew the address but hadn't actually seen her house before. Again, he felt a certain regret that he hadn't had her phone tapped, but dismissed the notion; after tonight it wasn't going to matter one way or the other. Where was the house? The way the numbers were running, it was still a block or two away, apparently.

All along the street, blinds were drawn against the night, and cozy lights shone through, bespeaking families at home, people together, while he prowled the street out here, a spectral lone-wolf figure haunting the dark like some dismal wraith. At times he wondered what it would

124

have been like, living a normal life, working at a normal job, coming home to a family in the evening and having dinner with a wife and a gaggle of kids and plunking down in a chair and reading the paper and watching the late news on television and going to bed with the same woman, night after night, and getting up and going to the same job at the same time morning after morning with his briefcase in his hand. Nah. Not for him, thanks. Now, where the hell was that house?

Ah. There it was, on his left, a trim little two-bedroomer, from the looks of it, with a short drive up to an attached garage, and with a front yard of sand and cactus and sage on both sides of the drive, the kind of yard these people loved, nothing but a wedge of desert left intact beside each house when the housing development went in, not a damn blade of grass or a real tree anywhere to be seen. You really had to be a desert type to live this way, he supposed. He'd take a good old noisy, overpopulated, smutty brick-and-concrete city back East any day. At least there you could feel as if you were in the real world.

Pulling into Lucy Trujillo's driveway, and killing the engine and turning off his headlights, he noticed two things. First, the lights shining throughout the house, spilling out from all the windows, strongly suggested that the woman was home. Second, the fact that the garage door was up, revealing a garage somewhat cluttered with household paraphernalia but otherwise empty, strongly suggested that the woman was *not* home. Well, Roger said to himself, even in New Mexico it can't be both ways, now, can it? He would see.

He got out of the car, closed the door quietly, and walked up onto the porch. The house was one of those fake-adobe jobs that seemed to be so common here, a stucco-type construction over a wooden frame; he remembered reading somewhere that all structures in the city, houses and public buildings alike, had to at least *look* like adobe, to preserve the Santa Fe look. More cutesy desert crap. Anyway, the lots here, scattered at odd angles around a curving street, were of fairly good size, and that was just as well; Lucy Trujillo had no neighbors any closer than a hundred yards, so if perchance there were to be any screaming. . . .

He was about to ring the doorbell when he noticed a third thing to add to (one) the woman's being home because the lights were all on and (two) the woman's not being home because there was no car in the garage. Thing number three: the front door was actually open a crack, letting a yellow sliver of living room light spill out over the right end of the porch.

Did that swing it favor of the woman's being home or not being home? The night air was a bit too cool to justify leaving the door open, if she was home, but presumably she wouldn't leave it that way and take off somewhere. Santa Fe, he was given to understand, had a fairly problematical amount of burglary. The conclusion would seem to be, he reflected, that she ought to be home, if you considered the matter on a two-counts-out-of-three basis. But then where was her car?

And another thought followed close behind this one, a less pleasant reflection.

What if she had indeed left, and left in a hurry? Enough of a hurry to neglect even to shut the front door, much less lock it?

Now, why would she do that?

Enough idle speculation for one autumn night; he pushed the door the rest of the way open and stepped inside.

Surveying the front room, he saw nothing out of the ordinary: just the kind of little nest a desert-minded single woman would keep, with issues of *New Mexico Magazine* and various Southwestern housekeeping magazines scattered across the coffee table, and with pastel prints of desert mountains and Indian pueblos here and there on the walls. The mousy little personality of Lucy Trujillo was everywhere here, but Lucy Trujillo herself evidently was not. Roger strode through the rest of the house, checking the kitchen, bathroom, and both bedrooms, to verify that the woman was indeed not home. He stopped in the kitchen long enough to note that there was an untouched cup of instant coffee sitting cold in the microwave, and that a rolltop desk nearby was open, with an address book sprawled open on it and various notes and papers scattered around it as if someone had hurriedly looked up a telephone number. Mulling this over, Roger headed back toward the living room.

And also noted now, in the little hallway that lead from the back part of the house to the front, that a closet door stood half open. Peering inside, he saw that a couple of coat hangers were spun around and stuck above the clothing bar, as if someone in a considerable hurry had grabbed a coat or something off its hanger, dislocating other hangers without stopping to straighten them back out. Roger proceeded to the living room with the reflection that this was all pretty consistent with a single hypothesis: that Lucy Trujillo had taken herself out of here sometime tonight in a good bit of a rush.

And of course he had to face it--if this were true, then there was another little problem. Two problems, actually. One was, he needed to get to her *now,* and get his hands on that book with the debris hidden in it. The other problem was, this all meant that he, Roger Wynn, also known in legend and song as several other people, had thoroughly, inexcusably screwed up. He had gotten careless, smug, overly confident, had simplified things too much in his mind. He had made assumptions that were turning out, it appeared, to be faulty. In this business, you couldn't afford to make this kind of mistake.

He continued piecing together the probable scenario as he began searching the house for the book. For some reason the woman had left in a hurry, and that suggested being forewarned. She could have been forewarned by her father, calling her from Wichita Falls; in that case he must have placed that call to her before actually taking that first deadly sip of his tea. To think that the little matter of the order in which a scatterbrained old drunk did things, could make the difference--the question of whether he sipped the tea first or picked up the telephone (on some presentiment that he had perhaps said too much to his visitor) and *then* sipped his tea. God damn! Of course, the news of her father's death, which must have reached her through the police, might have been enough to set her off, but he wondered. It depended on how much she knew, and he had only scraps of rambling monologue from a half-crazy old man with a mangled liver to tell him that.

He searched through the bookcases in the living room, looking for any book spine that carried the name Cervantes. Scattering the volumes to the floor as he went, he saw that there seemed to be just about everything here *but* Cervantes. Books in Spanish, books in English. Collections of poetry. Novels. Essays. Classics. Light literature. Collections of plays. Even the works of Shakespeare, he noted with a curious twinge of self-satisfaction that stood in danger of being swamped by that darker reflection: that he had screwed up too bad to have any right to feel good about himself this October evening.

Looking about him with growing alarm, he tried to think. The question of the extent of Lucy Trujillo's knowledge surfaced again. Would she necessarily even know that she *had* the book, the hidden strip of foil from the debris field northwest of Roswell? Would she even know about Roswell, about her father's connection to what had happened there? Even if he had called her with some kind of warning, could she not have simply fled, afraid only that she was in danger, yet not aware of the details? This could be--he might be in luck, she might just have run away and left the book behind. Then again, maybe she knew everything, in which case she was a very dangerous lady to leave running around loose, probably lugging the book with her. He had a nagging feeling that that was the most likely possibility. She knew, knew it all, and had the spunk to pick herself up and run away.

"Thou know'st no less but all; I have unclasp'd to thee the book even of my secret soul," he said to the missing woman. "*Twelfth Night*," he explained to the empty room.

But he felt no jocularity. After another ten or fifteen minutes' searching, he was fairly sure that the book was not in the house--it was not in any of the bookshelves, anyway, unless it had an altered cover, but there were hundreds of volumes here, too many. He knew where his next stop would have to be, and he would have the same problem there; if the bitch's house contained too many books to examine individually in the time he had, how was it going to be, looking for the damned thing at her bookshop? He'd need help. To that end, he had business to attend to right now.

He went back out to the car, retrieved the com unit from his bag, and returned to the house, where he found a phone jack in the living room and plugged the com unit into it. As soon as the little six-by-six-inch screen came up with its black-against-silver display, he took his ballpoint pen and typed in the codes needed to subvert the connection to the regular phone lines and program himself into the communication net. There, he made the necessary contacts and arrangements. A couple of operatives in the field would come over and do a more thorough search of the house, and a couple more would meet him at Mesa Bookshop to help him turn the place inside out; they would probably be people he didn't know, and he typed in some recognition codes for them to use. In the meantime, a complete description of Lucy Trujillo's Dodge Colt went out over the net, so that field operatives everywhere in the region would be looking out for it. Also, he set up an ongoing scan for her credit card numbers, should they pop up anywhere. Just about the time he was wrapping up these arrangements, the message indicator light came on, and he picked up the telephone receiver that was cradled into the unit's side.

"Chief. Blake here," the voice said. It was coming through a scrambler-descrambler process, and sounded tinny. "Got a problem."

"I don't need any more problems, Blake," Roger said. "What is it?"

"We were doing open-air surveillance on Anne Hawk and the boyfriend, up at Three Rivers where he's working. An old Indian who calls himself Sage came up and they all talked. There's a petroglyph up there, looks like a flying disk. Anne Hawk said so herself. I don't think she's actually said anything classified, but something, uh, went wrong and we lost the sound for a while. Anyway, I think you ought to listen to the tape. I can upload it to you."

"Do that," Roger said. "What else?"

"The Indian said some things about a silver bird coming down out of the sky and bringing a sky-child."

"No shit," Roger said. God damn, he really *didn't* need this.

"That's not all," Blake went on. "When the conversation broke up I followed Hawk and the boyfriend back to Alamogordo and left Varelli to bring in the old Indian. Hayes and the girl didn't talk about anything on the way back in their car, and I turned surveillance over to somebody else and went back for Varelli. But when I got back out to Three Rivers he wasn't there."

"He what?"

"He wasn't at the surveillance site. Don't see how he could have gone off very far, but I've looked around the area some, and haven't been able to find him. No sign of the Indian either. A cloud cover has come up and there's not much moonlight. I've got a flashlight, but--"

"I take it you're still out there," Roger said.

"Yeah, chief. I'm in the car. I had them patch me through to you."

"All right," Roger said, "now listen. We can't have this shit. I've got problems enough as it is. You've got my authorization to pull in some more people. I'll put the word out from here. Get whoever is available to come out there to help you search, and you find Varelli, and bring in that goddamn Indian. Right now."

"Yes sir, I'll--" But Roger was already cutting him off, and typing code onto the net for the authorization he had mentioned. Surely, surely to God, with enough help one halfwit should be able to find another in a little patch of desert. Those idiots, letting some old stumblebum of an Indian get away when he probably knew classified information!

But then Roger had to ask himself ruefully: what about you, old son? Talk about screwing up. He had made a number of errors in judgment here--not thinking Hap Trujillo's daughter was high enough on the list yet to merit a phone tap, not thinking that that damned old chili-eater over in Wichita Falls might get his head together enough to realize he'd spilled some beans, not thinking that he might call his daughter and warn her *before* he'd had his nicely laced cup of tea, not thinking that instead of planning to come back out to Santa Fe and do the thing himself (and maybe enjoy a tad of poontang into the bargain) Roger really should have had somebody in the area pick her up immediately. Not thinking, not thinking, not thinking. God damn, he had really blown it. You get too confident, he told himself now, too cocksure, and this is what happens. He had no right to feel superior to Blake and Varelli just now for letting the Indian slip away--a half-assed low-credibility old buck who quite possibly really wasn't too much of a menace--when he himself had let Lucy Trujillo slip away, Lucy Trujillo and her forbidden souvenir of alien debris, which most certainly *was* a menace.

Well--he'd see about this.

He disengaged the com unit, left the house without turning off any of the lights, and carried the com unit back to the car. By the time he was halfway across Santa Fe, heading for Guadalupe Street, he had had time to reflect that his ruminations on the way up here were pretty much on the mark after all.

Yeah, things were beginning to get out of hand all around. It was what he thought of as the complex system syndrome: the more complicated a situation got, and the longer it stayed that way, the more the lurking element of chaos would tend to rear its head and cause trouble. Things had gone along fine, overall, for a good number of years, and the technological crop that the system had harvested from the unknown presence of the Crewman had been phenomenal, had ushered in a whole new age. And now the Crewman was reportedly about to demonstrate that all of that was nurserytime stuff, and that it was time now for the first day of school and a whole quantum jump up to a new level of understanding. Fine and good, but if the Crewman's existence ever became public knowledge--if the public ever came to know that the government had perpetrated murder, torture, mutilation, assassination of a President, and an assortment of other such pleasantries to keep this the best-kept secret in history of humankind, then it was all over, all over for Roger, for his bosses, for all of them. The repercussions were difficult even to begin to imagine. No, it was going to be time, very soon, for the Group to think about bailing out. The honeymoon with the Crewman was just about over. Not much more was to be gained at this point. Let the Crewman take them to the next level, but then it was going to be time to blow the creepy little bastard away, burn the body, burn the other bodies in the labs, destroy all the wreckage, snuff all the low-level people who knew anything, and walk away whistling.

And draw pension money and sleep the sleep of the righteous.

No question, this bailout had to be his recommendation to the Group, the next chance he got, and he hoped to God they'd buy it, because if things went much farther along in the direction they were headed, it was all going to turn sour, just as sure as God made security clearances.

He pulled the car up in front of Mesa Bookshop, noting without surprise that two nondescript chaps were already waiting at the door to the shop, like customers who had misunderstood the hour. Well, gentlemen, not to worry, he thought: the shop is going to be open for your shopping convenience after all. He got out of the car and stepped up on the sidewalk.

"Someone said the bookshop was going to be closed for inventory," he said.

"Closed until Thanksgiving," one of the men replied.

"I guess I won't get my copy of *Much Ado About Nothing*, then," the other man added.

Since these were the correct responses, Roger nodded and began to jimmy the door, but found that it was already unlocked. This discovery did very little to calm his growing concerns, but he motioned for the two men to follow him inside, where he switched on a light and pulled the shades down.

"Okay, fellows," he said, "here's the deal. We're looking for a book by Cervantes."

"Who?" Mr. Thanksgiving asked.

"Cervantes, for Christ's sake," Roger said, "the Spanish author. *Don Quixote* is the title that comes to mind."

"If you say so, sir," Mr. Much Ado said.

"Just find it. Look alphabetically first, then if you don't see it, look everywhere, it could be out of place on the shelves. Could be anywhere." He wasn't about to tell them anything about what was concealed in the book they sought; they didn't need to know that.

They turned the rest of the lights on and began searching the shelves, pulling books onto the floor as they went, and stepping over growing mounds of them. Roger checked the drawers in the little desk up front but found no inventory catalog, nor any computer disks that might contain one. He turned the computer on, thinking that perhaps she had the inventory in a file on the hard drive, but upon examining the directory found nothing of the sort; anyway, how did he know she would even catalog the book?

Switching the computer off, he looked at the glass display case in front, by the desk, where there was a copy of William Faulkner's *Light in August* and a copy of Edgar Allan Poe's *Tales of the Grotesque and Arabesque*, with an intriguing space in between, across which the two volumes tried to lean toward each other like conspiratorial old friends on a park bench. It might not mean anything, of course, this space where a book might have been removed--in a bookshop you could go crazy chasing down every indication of that sort--but this obviously was the special display case, after all, and it didn't exactly cool his curiosity to notice that the glass door was unlocked and open, with the tiny key still actually dangling in the lock.

He had brought the com unit in, and while Mr. Thanksgiving and Mr. Much Ado searched the shelves farther back, he plugged it in and tried to keep an eye on the message indicator while he moved about, looking through the nearby shelves. He had a damned strong feeling, though, that he was too late. Shit! If the bitch had taken the book--

The thought was scarcely formed when there was a knock at the door to the shop, someone striking a knuckle against the glass inset.

Now what? For a crazy little moment he half thought that there really were customers out there on the sidewalk, hoping to find the shop open. But of course, it was obvious what the knock at the door really was. He went to answer it.

A policeman, who barely looked old enough to be out of high school, stood there in a neatly pressed blue uniform, his shadow long and angular in the glow of the streetlamp down the way, his nametag proclaiming J. NAVARRO in black letters against white, his Hispanic face the picture of duty-being-performed. Ah, youth. "Sir, I'll have to ask what you're doing on these premises," he said, a hand resting warily on the service revolver at his side.

"Certainly," Roger said, stepping aside. "Please come in."

The cop did so, but visibly bristled at having the response to his question delayed even this much. Looking around Roger, he peered into the back of the shop, where he must have been rather amazed to see two other people casually raking through the books on the shelves and pushing most of them onto the floor. His hand tightened on the grip of the revolver. "I'm going to ask you one more time--"

Roger put up a hand in a gesture of acquiescence and cooperation. "I admire your diligence, officer, and understand your concern," he said, producing an identification badge in a little leather folder. "I'm Julian Ford. United States Government, Special Security Services. My colleagues and I are here on official business, and it's something of an emergency. We would normally have alerted the local authorities of our presence first, but as I say, there hasn't been time." It was true--Roger, during his encoding session on the com unit back at Lucy Trujillo's house, could have set up a fake interface between federal and local agencies, informing the city and state authorities that federal officials were on the scene and must be allowed to operate without obstruction. In Wichita Falls, Texas, that had been his first act after leaving the nursing home, to move the responsibility for the investigation of Hap Trujillo's death into the territory of the feds, though of course no investigation would really be pursued. Here, as he had told Officer Navarro, there had simply been no time. No time to bother with it, was what he meant.

For a moment the cop looked a little stunned at the identification badge that Roger had shown him, but quickly recovered. "Oh. I see." He cast another uneasy glance toward the back of the store, where Mr. Much Ado and Mr. Thanksgiving were making a considerable mess for someone else to clean up. "If there's anything I can--"

"No, no, thank you, we'll take care of it." He concentrated on putting on his best conspiratorial face, as if taking the young officer into his confidence. "Don't say anything about this, but it's, ah, drugs. You understand. You'll really have to excuse me now."

"Yes sir," Officer Navarro said, touching the bill of his hat. "Like I said, if there's anything we can do." And he was out the door and gone.

Probably gone to check in with headquarters, Roger thought. So, even though Roger had told him there had been no time to inform the local authorities of the federal investigation he'd led the young cop to believe was happening, he thought it might be a good idea to set up an interface anyway. He didn't need any more complications tonight. Crouching over the com unit, he accessed the net and tapped in the necessary code. Now if Officer Navarro in his crisp clean blue uniform went back and asked headquarters if there was a federal drug search going on over on Guadalupe Street tonight, the dispatcher's answer would be yes, official notification just came in, so let the good gentlemen do their job.

Which the good gentlemen were doing anyway, but to no effect. Roger still had a feeling Lucy Trujillo had taken the Cervantes volume and made herself, and it, very scarce. He helped the other two finish the search, but, less than surprisingly, nothing turned up. The possibilities of course were many and disturbing--she could have taken the metal foil out of the Cervantes and hidden it anew somewhere else, somewhere that could take days or weeks to find. But Roger didn't think so. He didn't know much about her, but his intuition told him that if she was going to get up at this hour of the night and run away, she would take the book with her, wherever she had gone. He had to admit to himself that he had misassessed her; seeing her the first time here in this shop, he had thought she looked a bit mousy. Sexy too, yes, but still mousy, not the sort, you would have thought, to actually get up and bolt with a stolen piece of highly classified government property. Shows how wrong one can be, he mused. In a way, he had to kind of admire her spunk. Not that it was going to keep him from killing her, of course.

Messrs. Thanksgiving and Much Ado soon finished their interior redecoration job, a not particularly spectacular improvement over the shop's original decor. "Found these volumes of Cervantes," Mr. Much Ado said, handing three leatherbound books to Roger. He took them, sat down at the desk, and went over them very carefully, leafing slowly through each of them in turn, checking for sequentiality of page numbers, but found nothing. Had he found anything, he wouldn't have shown it to these characters.

"Look," he said, "I want you two to stay and go over this place again, and don't limit your search to Cervantes this time. Look everywhere."

"What are we looking for?" Mr. Thanksgiving asked.

"What I'm about to tell you is classified top secret. This'll sound a little strange to you, but I know what I'm doing. You're looking for a piece of tinfoil. Maybe hidden inside a book, maybe not." He wanted to keep them more in the dark than that, but he did need for them to search with some notion of what they were trying to find. It was just possible, after all, that the Trujillo woman had re-hidden the thing here somewhere before taking off. He didn't think so, but it was possible. These two didn't have to know, of course, that the foil they were looking for happened to be a Roswell, New Mexico debris-field souvenir from another solar system. "That's it. Just a little strip of metal foil. You're to discuss that with no one. I'm not sure that it's here, but if it is, find it."

"Yes, sir." Nearly in unison. Somehow these two reminded him of Tweedle-Dum and Tweedle-Dee, but he needed them to finish the search. It was after midnight now, and he was going to have to catch a few winks, as he had a feeling tomorrow was going to be a pretty busy day. The woman's car and other info had gone out on the net, and he'd get a jangle if anything happened during the night. "I'm going to be staying over on Cerrillos Road." He gave them the name of the motel where he had stayed the night before, and where he had already booked a room for tonight too. "You give me a phone call if you find anything, and I'll come back over, or meet you somewhere. Otherwise, don't call, your assignment is finished."

By the time he was settled into a room in the little adobe-village motel on Cerrillos Road, it was nearly one in the morning, and as he was planning to get moving again no later than six, he wasn't going to be reading any *Titus Andronicus* this time. He was dead tired, but before he turned in he ran the com unit up and put out an order on the net to scan the airlines' passenger lists and see if the woman had caught a flight anywhere; somehow he didn't think so, but you never could tell, and he would hear about it if her name showed up on the scan. That was enough for tonight. He had a shot of gin, got undressed, and stretched out on the bed. But just as he started to drowse, the message indicator on the com unit came to life.

"Yes?"

"Chief. This is Blake."

And it turned out Roger's day wasn't quite over after all.

18

Lucy Trujillo and Cervantes

It was a rather seedy motel on Central Avenue in Albuquerque, so low-key and nondescript in the way it showed its unpretentious little adobe front among the more elaborately neon-festooned storefronts and motels on the avenue that one could easily drive right past it without seeing it--unless one were looking for it specifically, or unless one were shopping for *any* motel that might be unobtrusive and obscure. Which was precisely why Lucy Trujillo, arriving in the city about a quarter after eleven at night, had chosen the place on sight--that, and the configuration of the cracked and poorly painted six-foot adobe walls that wrapped around in front of the motel on both sides of the little drive, blocking off the parking area. With this setup, she might hope that her car wouldn't be seen from the street, if someone came searching for it. A very real possibility, she had to assume.

Parking the car under a feeble neon sign ("O FICE") that spluttered as if suffering from some strange electrical disease of the circulation, she locked the car, opened the office door, and stepped inside. Standing in the tiny office, where the only light at the sign-in desk was a mangy-looking lamp that struggled to disperse a little illumination through its crumpled yellow shade, and where an elderly and very plump Hispanic woman was going through the ritual of renting Room 12 to her, Lucy let her mind run back over her panicky drive from Santa Fe, and realized that there wasn't much memory there to review. Except in a vague and jumbled sort of way, she really didn't remember driving down here tonight.

Now that she thought about it, she supposed she had unconsciously headed for Albuquerque, both because she obviously had to get out of Santa Fe and because Albuquerque, which she had only visited occasionally, was the largest city in the area, large enough for her to have a good shot at losing herself in it, or eluding pursuers, should there be any. She could have gone north to Española instead of here, but Española wasn't big enough to impart a sense of comfort when you were intent on losing yourself. Anyway, here she was.

"No baggage," the woman behind the counter said, and Lucy couldn't tell whether it was a question or an observation.

"No, uh, nothing really." She held up her purse by the strap, as if to say: this is it, I'm afraid. "I had an emergency and didn't have time to pack a suitcase," Lucy said. She wasn't sure what difference that made, and her mind was so tired and bewildered at this point that she didn't feel she had the mental energy to expend on the question.

"How will you be paying?" the woman asked.

Aha, that was it, she supposed. If you checked in without luggage it always looked a little suspicious; maybe they were afraid you'd run off without paying. She had very little experience with this kind of thing, she realized now. Up until tonight, she would never have thought she had exactly led a sheltered life--married, divorced, relocated, proprietor of her own business--but right now she didn't feel terribly cosmopolitan.

She could see, behind the woman, a door leading off into wanly lit but somehow cozy-looking spaces beyond, presumably the woman's own living quarters. For a moment, a grizzled old man in jeans and t-shirt appeared in the door, framed there like a painting, and nodded at her and withdrew. A faint aroma of coffee and fried tortillas and cigar smoke wafted out on the air. Suddenly Lucy felt dejected, filled with an ineffable sadness, and realized that "home and family" imagery was the last thing she could comfortably think about just now.

"*Señorita--*"

"Oh, I'm sorry. How am I going to pay, you said? I, ah--" She hadn't thought about it, but suddenly it came to her that it might make a great deal of difference. Leaving in the kind of hurry she had been in, she hadn't had a lot of cash on hand, so she needed to do some figuring and thinking. She fished her Visa card out of her purse and laid it on the counter. "I might want to put it on my card," she said, "so can you just run it through but not charge the room yet? I might decide in the morning to pay cash."

"Yes, sure, we can do that," the woman said. "*Por supuesto.* Are you staying just one night?"

"I--I think so. I'm not sure."

"*No importa,*" the woman said, brushing a renegade tangle of graying hair from her face. "You can have the room as long as you like. We're not expecting no big conventions here." She looked around her at the simple decor of the place and smiled a wry kind of smile, and the gesture made Lucy feel a little better, as if there were still a little humor, a little humanity left in the world after all.

"*Mil gracias,*" she said, and watched as the woman made an impression of her Visa card.

"I'm Teresa Morales," the woman said, handing the card back to her and looking at her with an expression that seemed to say: it looks to me like you're in some kind of trouble, girl, and I feel for you, but I think maybe it's none of my business to ask about it. "If there's anything we can do," she said, fixing her for a moment with that concerned look again.

"Thank you very much, I'll be fine," Lucy said, and realized a moment later that her very wording was an admission that not all was well. But, she reflected wearily, that must not be an unusual experience, for people who run a motel; every frustration, every anger, every disappointment, every sorrow in the world must at one time or another pass through here, emblazoned on a human face.

She took the key Mrs. Morales was handing her, smiled again, and stepped back outside. She found that even here in the shelter of the little court around which the tiny rooms wrapped themselves in a dusky semicircle, the night air had a chilling bite to it, so she didn't linger. Besides, the sooner she was behind a door and out of sight, the better she would feel. The place was nearly deserted; there were only two other cars in the parking area. She got in her own car, pulled it around to the space in front of Room 12, parked it, and retrieved her few belongings from the seat beside her. While it was true that she had packed no real luggage, she had at least been lucky enough to have brought along, unknowingly, a few things she needed, in a canvas overnight bag left over from a recent trip to a booksellers' convention in Taos; she'd never bothered to take it out of the car. That and a couple of pairs of jeans and a couple of tops from the hall closet. She'd have some fresh clothes to change into, if nothing else. Checking to see that the car was indeed out of sight to anyone driving past on Central Avenue, she grabbed up the bag and the jeans and tops. And the computer disk with her inventory file on it, which she slipped into her purse.

And of course the book.

Locking the car again, she opened the door to Room 12, stepped inside, switched on the light, and closed and locked the door behind her. The tiny room boasted only a single badly swaybacked twin bed, a rickety little table and chair, and a bathroom with a shower stall but no tub. She placed her overnight bag and clothes and purse on the table and sat heavily on the side of the bed, and realized that she was still clutching the book. The Cervantes: *Don Quixote de la Mancha.*

137

She put it down beside her on the faded bedspread and clasped her hands in her lap and took a couple of deep breaths to try to calm herself. What time was it? Sliding her coat sleeve up to look at her watch, she saw that it was about 11:40.

She tried to think. How long, how long since this all started?

The astonishing answer came to her: as nearly as she could figure, all this had started only two hours ago. A mere two hours ago, when her phone had rung, and when--

Her breath hitched with a sob that she couldn't suppress, nor would have wanted to suppress. Two hours ago, she had picked up the telephone in her own house and had heard her father's voice. And now-- the whole weight of it came crashing down on her, and she cried, harder than she had ever cried since her mom had died in the accident all those many years ago. But she had never, never in her life, felt a twist of emotions blacker or sicker than this. At least with her mom it had been an accident, a terrible, tragic one, yes, but an accident still. Shuddering with revulsion now, and wiping at her face with her hands, she looked square into the maw of darkness that the situation presented to her. This, this was no accident, no old man choking on a cup of tea. The sons of bitches had *killed* him, would kill her too, she felt quite sure, if they caught up with her. For all she knew, one of them might be standing outside this motel room door right now.

Gasping at the thought, she got up, pulled the ragged curtain an inch or two aside, and peered out. There was nothing out there but the cold neon light playing over the few cars parked in the little court, and an occasional murmur of passing traffic from out on the avenue. She dropped the curtain back in place, sat back down on the bed, and picked up the book.

For this, she thought, all for this. For this, I have lost my father. For this, I have left my home, I have left my shop, my work, I have become a fugitive. For this, I have come down to sitting in a dingy little motel room, alone in the world, without the faintest idea what I'm going to do. *Is it worth it?* her mind wanted to know.

She opened the book on her lap and flipped through its yellowed, musty-smelling pages, where the antique Spanish of Cervantes was punctuated here and there by droll but masterly illustrations. Ah--was this it? One page felt a tiny bit thicker, heavier than the others, the sort of thing only a long-time book fancier would notice, and then only if looking for it. She got up, holding the book open, retrieved her purse from the table, and sat down again on the bed. Marking the spot in the book with a shred of Kleenex, she turned back to the front of the book and studied the list of illustrations; flipping through the book, she found all of them but one that should have been around the middle of the volume somewhere. It should have been, she verified for herself now, about where the suspicious page was.

"Aha," she said, and was startled at the sound of her voice in the little room. It sounded like someone trying to deny some nearly overwhelming grief with a frail little show of bravado. But that wasn't altogether what she felt. What she felt was a certain belated admiration.

"Pretty crafty, Dad," she said. "You're all right."

Were all right, a nasty little voice in her mind corrected her. And she burst into tears again.

By the time she was through crying, for the moment anyway, she felt a little better for it, because she had needed to cry, and because it was true--her dad had been pretty damned clever, hiding the thing this way, keeping it hidden all these years.

Was it all really true then? Even now, she found it hard to believe, that what was hidden in the book in her lap was a little piece of something not from this world, a secret piece of something about which the government was so covetous that they would commit murder to *keep* it secret. But if this much was true, then the rest was too--the whole story that had been whispered down the years in her family, the story of what had happened in 1947 in Roswell, New Mexico, when her dad had been there, and when he had seen what he had seen.

The alien foil--she had it with her right here, right now.

Should she open up the pages and look at the thing?

Something told her no, don't do that. Dad has had it hidden this way for all these years, don't change that now. Maybe sometime. Not now. Not tonight. It rather surprised her that even now she wasn't overcome with curiosity to see the thing, but then she had been overcome by all kinds of other emotions these past few hours, and there was little room left for curiosity at the moment. For now there was just sadness, and anger. And remorse, and guilt. Right, Lucy? (The nasty little voice was back.) You never showed your dad the kind of love you really could have shown him, the last few years, did you? How often did you call? How often did you drive out to see him? And it's too late now, isn't it, Lucy? Too damned late.

"Yes," she told the stale air in the little room. "Yes, it's too late." But what overwhelmed her now was not the sadness or the anger or the guilt. What overwhelmed her now was mind-numbing fatigue. She was just plain tired, tired to death; yet there was something she had to do, and moving the book off her lap, she replaced it with her purse, which she rummaged through. Her checkbook, perversely enough, had run out of checks that morning and she had neglected to replenish them.

Counting her money, she found that she had a little under a hundred dollars with her. How long could she live on that? She had no cash cards and no cash-advance checks, because she had never been in the habit of using them. Well, one thing at least was certain; she was going to use her credit card to pay for the room in the morning, because she would need her money for food.

She got up and placed her purse and the book on the little table, and got undressed. Pulling back the bedcovers and turning off the light, she crawled into the bed in so weary a state that even the achy-eyed rawness of her misery seemed to be falling asleep. Within a few minutes she followed it, down into hollows where, at first, not even dreams chanced to stir.

19

The Tape

"Chief. This is Blake. I'm calling from Three Rivers."

Great, Roger thought: *now* what? He had just been lying back on the pillow and closing his eyes and savoring one of his favorite lines from *Macbeth*--"Sleep that knits up the ravell'd sleave of care"--when the call had come in and his vision of a few hours' uninterrupted rest had dissolved like a mist.

Blake's voice was sterile and cold in the telephone receiver connected to the com unit. He sounded like some flunky making a lackluster routine utterance with no heart in it. "Three Rivers" in this tone of voice could have been "three pounds of potatoes" on a grocery list. But something told Roger it wasn't anything like apathy he heard in this voice; it sounded more like a grim mingling of depression, puzzlement, and perhaps even fear. Whatever was up, it didn't sound to Roger like good news coming.

"What do you want, Blake?"

"Something's happened here," Blake said.

"Well for Christ's sake, what is it?" Roger said. "Can't I trust you people to do one simple--"

"Varelli's dead, chief." Now the voice, falling away in volume, was like a stone dropping down a well into foul black water. Roger wasn't even sure he had heard right.

"What did you say?"

"Varelli," Blake said. "I took two guys back up here, and we fanned out from the surveillance site and searched. It was me who found him. In a dry riverbed about a mile and a half from where we started. Lying face down in the sand. Dead as a fish."

141

Roger couldn't believe it. How, *how* could things get this shitted up in what ought to be a routine surveillance? "God damn you, man, what are you telling me? What happened to him?"

"He, ah, looks like he was bitten by a rattlesnake. Or maybe more than one rattlesnake. Maybe a lot of snakes. We found bites all over his face and throat. His head's puffed up all green and black, swollen so bad you almost wouldn't have recognized him. It made me want to puke."

"Rattlesnakes?" Roger bellowed into the receiver, then lowered his voice a little; he didn't want to be overheard through the motel room walls. "How could he be that stupid, to get himself--but what about the old Indian?"

"No sign of him yet, chief," Blake said. "Looks like the snakes got to Varelli before Varelli got to the Indian. We're still searching the area, but we're going to need more people. It's a big desert, and he's got a hell of a head start."

Roger sat shaking his head, a useless gesture. He thought about switching to a video connection, but remembered that Blake was getting patched through from his car unit and wouldn't have a video setup. Why bother anyway? If he couldn't bring these boneheads into line by the sound of his voice, he couldn't do it at all.

"Blake, you listen to me," he said, cradling the receiver between his head and his left shoulder, grabbing the bottle and the water glass on the table beside the bed, and pouring himself out a fresh shot of gin. "I can count the times on my fingers--on one hand, for God's sake--when I've ever in my life lost an operative in the field. There's no excuse for this shit. You should have called somebody in Alamogordo to switch over to, for the car surveillance on Hawk and her boyfriend, and *both* of you should have gone after the Indian. But then I can't trust you brain-dead assholes to make a decision like that, can I?" He realized he was speaking as if both of them were still alive. Then again, how could you tell the difference, with these cretins?

"Chief, we just did what seemed logical. He's only a piss-ass old Indian. Christ, he can hardly walk."

"Well, he seems to have done a splendid job of getting away from *you* pinheads," Roger said. "I get the impression he could have been in traction in a hospital bed and you two couldn't have caught him. I'm telling you something, Blake. You're in shit up to your eyes. You're going to answer to me for this. For the moment I'm leaving you in the field, only because somebody's got to look for the Indian, and you and your men are the ones who are out there to do it. Get whoever else you want to help search. I'll authorize it, I'm typing in the authorization code

142

already. But I'm telling you right now, if you don't have that frigging Indian in custody by dawn, I don't think you even want to imagine what our next little chat is going to be like. Am I getting across to you?"

"We're on it, chief. We'll find him. You'll see." Damned if Blake didn't sound almost like a browbeaten child; from his tone of voice he could have been saying: I'll hit the ball this time, coach, you'll see, you won't be ashamed of me any more. Damn, Roger thought, it was scary when you considered it--what could turn out to be some of the most important work in the world so often had a way of getting entrusted to people who in the final analysis were just that: people. Diddly little mediocre people, people with failings, people with limitations. But, an obnoxious little voice in Roger's head piped up: who the hell are you to say that, Roger Wynn, when you let the Trujillo woman get by you?

Well, not for long. The butterfly net was already out, ready to slip over *that* bitch's head.

"Chief?" Blake said. "Are you still on?"

"Yes," Roger said, and suddenly was glad he hadn't broken the connection to Blake, because he had something else he needed to ask him about. "Did you digitize that audiotape file and upload it to me like I told you?" He could check, but this was faster. Heaven and all the angels of the firmament help your poor soul, Blake, he thought, if you don't have the right answer to this one.

"Yes I did, chief. It should be there in your directory."

"All right. Get cracking. Keep me posted." He hung up.

He sat on the edge of the bed for a moment, took a sip of gin, and tried to organize his thoughts. He couldn't believe how the last twenty-four hours or so had gone. Couldn't believe it. How could they lose an operative, how could that fool Varelli get himself killed by rattlesnakes in a goddamn dry riverbed? Something about that didn't quite make sense. Sure, you could get bitten by a rattlesnake--bitten once, even twice, by *one* snake. Roger wasn't an expert on desert fauna, for sure, but he thought he was on solid ground in believing that snakes in the kind of place Blake had described didn't "nest" in huge numbers the way you always heard of them doing in caves and the like. Snakes out on the desert floor tended to live in individual snake holes; Roger had seen them. Maybe Varelli had run onto one rattlesnake, maybe that snake had bitten him many times. But somehow Roger didn't think so; even an imbecile like Varelli ought to have been able to get clear of *one* snake, after the first strike anyway. Christ, you had to be pretty slow on the uptake to get bitten by a rattlesnake at all; it wasn't as if they didn't warn you. But what use was it to ruminate about that now?

143

And he found himself wondering exactly how critical all this was really going to turn out to be--was it possible he was overassessing the importance of the threat to security that the old Indian might pose? To a great extent, that depended on what had been said earlier this evening up at Three Rivers.

He thought he'd better hear that audiotape file.

It was only a few seconds' work in the com unit's computer to retrieve it, and he sat sipping his gin and listening through the headset.

"C'mon, Anne. What do you think?" This would be the voice of Eric Hayes. *"What does it really look like to you?"* They were talking about that petroglyph. *"Those dots around the perimeter."* Anne Hawk's voice; Roger had met her on the infrequent occasions when he had actually seen the Crewman, back at Holloman. *"Individual lights."* Silly bitch shouldn't even be saying this much; she should be changing the subject before one thing led to another. *"Like the running lights on a boat."* Then Hayes was saying, *"It looks like a picture of–"* And they were chiming in together and laughing. *"A spaceship." "A flying saucer."* Yeah, actually laughing over it, having a grand old time. Of course nothing classified was actually being security-breached here, but. . . .

He listened to the part where the old Indian came up to greet them. *"They call me Sage."* It should have sounded half idiotic, like a line in some B-movie, but for some reason it didn't. Roger would of course put out a general information search on this character, but if he was just a desert vagabond it wasn't too likely there would already be a file on him anywhere. *"This,"* the old man was saying in Roger's earphones, *"is a picture of the silver bird. They say in the old times the great silver bird come down out of the sky and bring the sky-children."*

Roger cringed. Sure, there had always been popular talk about pear-headed aliens and the like; the aliens in some science-fiction movies could almost have been patterned after the Crewman, in fact. Usually Roger and his superiors took the attitude that all this popular "gray alien" subculture stuff was more useful to the government than otherwise: it kept the whole thing squarely in the realm of fantasy and movies and make-believe, so that the usual strategy of "deny and ridicule" worked the best, whenever anybody tried to make serious claims about alien visitations. But--we were talking about a conversation involving Anne Hawk here, and that made it a very, very different matter.

The conversation on the tape went on, something about the sky-child making music, and something about Kokopelli, whoever that was; the name sounded vaguely familiar to Roger, but he couldn't quite say why.

"I have a vision, not long ago," the old Indian was saying, *"of young woman, and a strange man come to her, and man is bad trouble."* Anne joked about Eric and herself, but the old man replied, *"Woman in vision is not you. Man in vision is not him."* Roger was forgetting to sip his gin.

"But you have troubles too."

Roger had barely begun to roll this around in his mind when it happened--after a few seconds of silence elapsed on the tape, the sound went all weird. Whatever the interference was, it did an infuriatingly efficient job of blotting out the voices on the tape, if anyone was saying anything more at this point, and substituting an uncanny kind of hissing or whistling, something that filled Roger's mind with a jumble of contradictory impressions. When he let his professional instincts kick in enough to calm himself and reflect upon his reactions, he found that he wasn't disturbed so much by the fact that the strange overlay of sound expunged the voices from the tape (a workover in one of the audio labs might succeed in recovering them), as by the quality of the sound itself. There was something positively eerie in the way one couldn't decide whether the sound most resembled some creepy, moaning wind hissing through desert sands, or a pack of coyotes howling somewhere off in the night, or a windy chorus of oddly articulated Indian flutes piping some distant song that the mind couldn't quite grasp. It was like all of these things, and yet not quite like any of them. It felt to him that there was something almost archetypal about it, as if it plucked weird strings deep down inside him somewhere, strings that he didn't know he possessed. That was nuts, of course. How could any sound do that?

Anyway, whatever it was, it had played hell with the tape, that much was for sure. Grimacing at the seemingly endless litany of ululant sound but listening to it clear through, he found that there was not another intelligible word on the tape.

So, exiting from the file and shutting the com unit down, he reflected that he would have to be satisfied with what little he had heard. And in some ways that little exchange disturbed him even more than the spectral qualities of what he thought of as "the flute sound." In some ways what the old man who called himself Sage had said were very disturbing indeed. Not so much the part about the flying disk pictured on the rock--hell, people were probably always speculating about that, and let them, who the hell cared?--and not even the part about the sky-child, though that one did give him a twinge.

What really dug into his mental shinbone a bit was that crack the old man had made about his vision *"of young woman, and a strange man come to her, and man is bad trouble."* And the old man had even gone on to add the colophon that the woman and man in the vision were not

Anne Hawk and Eric Hayes. No--he had seen some other woman, being visited by some other mysterious figure of a man.

If Roger didn't know better, he would half suspect that this was a reference to Lucy Trujillo, who was in fact due (overdue) a surprise visit from a mysterious man, a fellow named Roger Wynn. But that was crazy beyond belief--how could the Indian know anything about that? How? He couldn't, obviously.

But he sounded as if he did. So that problem interwove itself, in Roger's now aching head, with the others. With the problem that he now had an uppity Hispanic woman running around New Mexico somewhere (he hoped it was still New Mexico) with a piece of alien debris. With the problem that he now had a dead field operative to explain to the people upstairs. In his high position within the Group, Roger had enough autonomy to avoid making full reports for a while, but he couldn't keep them from knowing about Varelli's death, and it would look bad, would look wretchedly bad in fact, for a certain Mr. Wynn, when they found out about it. To all this, he could add the problem that he had a decrepit fart of an Indian, with probably the equivalent of a third-grade education, drifting around the desert loose somewhere, spewing out stories of flying saucers and sky-children, and talking about visions that sounded to Roger as if they ought to have TOP SECRET stamped on them. Surely, surely to God this last part was just a meaningless coincidence.

Nevertheless, sitting on the edge of a bed in the small hours of the morning in a cutesy little adobe motel in Santa Fe, with the faint, somehow chilling residue of an unplaceable song lingering in his head, Roger Wynn began counting up, in some idle corner of his mind, how long he had to go till retirement.

20

A Lesson in Grammar

Entering the little underground room where she had met the Crewman at least five or six days a week for the past twelve years, Anne felt as if she had been away for much longer than her one day off. Usually a day off didn't make much of a ripple in the flow or the continuity of her work with the Crewman. But this morning, for the first time she could remember in all her years of secret government service, she had felt genuinely nervous about coming to work and going through the security screenings on the way in.

She had half expected to be stopped at some point and told to report somewhere, and then told that her security clearance had been pulled. But why? Because someone may have overheard her saying to Eric that the petroglyph on the rock at Three Rivers looked like a flying saucer? Because the old Indian who called himself Sage had talked about flying disks and sky-children and problematical visions? Had anything classified actually been breached? She wasn't clear in her head about that, after last evening, which seemed more like a dream than anything that had ever happened to her--more like a dream, ironically, than working for all these years with the Crewman, whom she had more or less come to regard as a given, a constant in her life.

She hadn't seen Eric since he had driven her home last night; while they hadn't talked much in the car, knowing it wasn't safe to, they had formed a kind of silent understanding between them that they would not get together this morning, even for breakfast. Eric would go back up to the Three Rivers site, and Anne would go to work as usual. They were far from certain how things stood, after the events of the previous evening, and the unspoken understanding was that right now the more natural-looking their actions were, the better for Anne.

But no, she hadn't been stopped or challenged at the gate or at any of the checkpoints, hadn't been told to report to anybody's office, hadn't even had anyone look at her strangely. Not that that meant much, actually. But so far so good, she thought, pouring herself a cup of coffee and waiting for the Crewman to come through the door.

When he did come, with his usual nod to her, he was carrying things. Hardware. Little circuitboards of some kind, with odd-looking little attachments here and there.

"Good morning, Anne," he said, placing the items on the table between them and seating himself across from her. To this day it was difficult for her to read any particular expression in his face, with its tiny slit of a mouth and its huge eyes floating in a bland expanse of pale yellow-gray skin, but now she thought there might be just the faintest suggestion of what on a human face would have been a mischievous twinkle in the eye.

"Good morning," she said. "And what in the world is this stuff?"

The Crewman let his dark almond-shaped eyes play over the objects on the table, then flicked his gaze back up at Anne, as if to say: yes, look what I've been up to. His manner at this moment would have looked almost childlike to Anne at one time; it actually still did, but after all these years she knew better than to infer too much about expressions and emotionalities when one was dealing with the Crewman. His face revealed only subtle shifts of expression, and any speculations as to what feelings they indicated, even from the viewpoint of all of Anne's experience, all her history of interaction with him, were apt to lead to oversimplification.

"These are some demonstration circuits," he said. "You will recall that the day before yesterday, when the tech interviewer was here, we talked about going on to the next phase. After that talk, I began to think that from the outset this would require that I construct some illustrative materials, some teaching aids, if you will. That night I formulated an extensive list of parts that I would need, and asked for them to be brought to my living quarters so that I could begin work on them right away. The people to whom I directed this request were most helpful, and I spent yesterday working on the circuits."

Yeah, Anne thought, of course my superiors were helpful, because they want that further quantum-leap of theory so bad they can taste it. But what she said was: "This is something of a surprise."

"When you take a day off, Anne, all sorts of things happen," the Crewman said, and Anne felt rather than heard an undertone of humor in what he said, like a sort of tingle in her mind.

"Are you going to tell me about these things?" she asked, nodding at the peculiar objects ranged between them on the table, some of which

148

resembled ordinary printed circuit boards with little aluminum appendages like miniature satellite dishes clipped around the edges, interspersed with what seemed to be small but otherwise ordinary silver-backed mirrors. "Because if you *are* going to tell me about them, I can't guarantee I'll understand much of it. I'm a low-tech person, you know. My physics teacher in high school thought I was a moron."

"There is little to tell, as of yet," the Crewman said. "These are only the bare beginnings of some demonstration circuits. I merely wanted you to know that I am working on them, and hope to have them ready the next time the tech interviewers come. For now, I feel that there is something more to the point that we need to talk about."

"What would that be?" Anne asked, feeling an uneasy little twinge in her spine. What was it he thought he and she needed to talk about all of a sudden? Could he have any way of knowing about some of the things that had been happening on the outside the past day or two? And wouldn't he remember anyhow that all their conversations here were monitored, videotaped, filed, reviewed? Surely to God if he did know anything, he wouldn't let them be overheard talking about it. Somehow she couldn't shake the feeling, though, that he had more on his mind than the routine business of language.

But he replied: "There are several crucial points of verbal structure in L-1 that have continued to trouble you, to the point where I feel that we will have difficulty continuing until we have cleared them up for you. My special concern is that when I next speak with the tech interviewers and begin explaining the principles underlying the new circuit theory, we must look to your function as translator. You have done excellently up to this point, but from here on, there will be subtleties requiring that your command of L-1 be enhanced."

"I understand," Anne said, not sure that she did. "How do you suggest we proceed?"

"I think it best," he said, "that we have an extended conversation in L-1, along lines that I will more or less direct. I have given much thought to the linguistic structures that trouble you, and I feel that I can guide you through these difficulties by deliberately arranging for you to encounter them, one after the other, in a variety of conversational contexts. As you know, contextualization is everything. I think that by the time we complete the exercise, you will have mastered most of the points that have eluded you."

"That sounds good to me," Anne said. "Let's get started."

The Crewman nodded in his slow, graceful way, and began speaking in the softly flowing syntax of L-1.

"I am afraid, my old friend, that you are going to be a little disillusioned with me." As usual, he was partly speaking, partly boosting the effect of his reedy voice with mental projection. The people listening and recording and videotaping would of course hear his voice, weakly, whatever good it did them to hear it in L-1.

"Why?"

"Because you have never known me to resort to falsehood," he replied. At least she would have translated it "falsehood," had she been translating for someone else's benefit; the expression in L-1 actually meant something closer to "utterance variously directed, depending upon who hears it."

She peered at him across the table, searching his face but finding it devoid of clues. *"Why do you say that?"*

"Because my reasons for wanting a protracted exchange with you in my own language have little to do with the enhancement of your own command of the language, as you scarcely require that at this point, despite your own diffidence sometimes. Not," he added, *"that the exchange will not clear up a few remaining linguistic difficulties for you in the process."* With these words there again came across that tingly mental impression of unspoken humor of a wry and ineffably alien kind. And she felt the unspoken presence of a related question. The Crewman did not seem to entertain long communications in their entirety with thought transference, but often used it to supplement speech, imparting extra nuances to what he said.

"All right," Anne said, intrigued. *"First, you need not apologize for resorting to a little falsehood; heaven knows, my people thrive on indirection and insincerity and outright lies and worse. And I think I understand what you want to ask me first. You're asking me whether anyone else around here understands enough L-1 to follow this conversation. In this business one never really knows about things like that, but I can say that it's extremely unlikely. I've been here so long and have been such a free spirit with you, have been so devoted to linguistics and so unenthusiastic about their political causes, that I suspect they would have eliminated me by now if they had anyone else who could do the job."*

"This is my understanding as well," the Crewman replied. *"I will proceed under the assumption that, for the moment, we are safe."* This remark gave Anne an odd sort of thrill, not entirely pleasant, but not entirely unpleasant either; it was the first time she had ever heard him say anything of the sort.

"Go on," she said. *"I will try to make my part of the conversation sound, to the people listening, like my responses to a linguistic exercise. I'll*

try, I say. I'm not sure how good an actor I am. It may depend on what you tell me."

The Crewman paused for a few seconds. *"I have come to the conclusion that things cannot go on, for very much longer, the way they have been going. It is clear to me, from the behavior of the tech interviewers and from other sources of understanding available to me, that my good treatment here, in exchange for the technical information I impart, is not something that I may indefinitely take for granted. I am sure that you well understand, my friend, that the people for whom you work have no interest in the theory of linguistics or the theory of alien psychology; from their point of view you are here solely to facilitate their gaining the sort of information that has taken your civilization into the computer age and beyond, with a speed it would otherwise not have achieved."*

Anne was beginning to feel a little dizzy; this was vastly different from the kinds of things they had usually discussed, even when their conversations had turned philosophical. *"If you mean that in some scenarios my superiors might harm you, I am ashamed to admit that I fear you may be right,"* she said. *"I say it with a sense of being a little ashamed to be human."*

The Crewman blinked slowly and fixed her with his eyes for a long while before going on. *"It can be a noble thing to be human, Anne. I have tried to make it more so, these years I have been here. With what success, your own future history will have to tell."*

"I have always wondered about that," Anne said. *"About your reasons for helping us. Helping them. I am quickly coming not to think of myself as one of them. All they do is take, take, take from you. All you do is give, and you seem to expect nothing in return."* The very formulation of this was difficult in L-1, which did not have precisely the same concepts for giving and taking, tit-for-tat, as most human languages. *"But given their greed for what you can continue to impart to them, is it not probably true that they will treat you with some decency so long as they hope to keep on reaping the technological harvest?"* She said this with some ducking and nodding and smiling, as if she were struggling with linguistic points rather than what she was really struggling with.

"Yes," he replied, *"but I think they feel that the harvests, to use your delightful metaphor, are soon to be over, and the soil soon to be depleted. While they are unquestionably eager for this next phase of theory, they are inclined to believe, I suspect, that it represents the ultimate in what can be possible for them to learn. Nothing could be further from the truth, but such are the limitations of their imaginations. In any event, as soon as they have acquired the fundamentals of the new phase, they are likely to take the attitude that my services here are no longer required."*

151

She mulled this over, trying to remember to make it all look like a natural, routine, scholarly exchange of the sort they would expect of her. *"So what are we going to do?"* she asked. She felt that the question marked a decisive turning-point, that the Crewman must understand that for her as well as for him, there was no turning back now; she was committed to opposing the way her superiors were starting to treat him. *"What can we possibly do?"*

The Crewman blinked at her and, Anne felt, would have taken her hand, but for the video surveillance. *"You need do nothing just now,"* he said. *"Try not to worry about me."*

"How can I not worry?" She felt her eyes threatening to grow moist, and hoped to God it didn't show in the camera. To staunch what could get to be the fatal beginning of tears, she shifted the focus of her response. *"And what did you mean, before, when you said you had not only the behavior of the tech interviewers to judge from, but other sources of understanding available to you?"*

"It is difficult to explain," the Crewman said. *"For one thing, we have a mutual friend. One with whom I am, let us say, not entirely out of contact."*

It shouldn't have been altogether a surprise, given what she had already heard, the previous evening, but hearing the Crewman himself refer to it, she found the connection reasserting itself to her like a slap in the face--a compassionate slap, of the sort that wakes one up. *"The old Indian,"* she said.

"Yes. Through him, I learn things. And teach things."

She couldn't have said which was the more heightened sensation for her, the excitement that inhered in this, or her mounting fear. Things were rapidly getting beyond comprehension. *"He's--he's what my people call a wizard. A shaman."*

The Crewman came as close as Anne had ever seen him come to smiling outright, but she realized that part of the impression, for her, was mental, and implanted as such. *"A shaman,"* he said. *"Yes, he is a shaman. But as they would say in your syntax, aren't we all?"*

Anne fell silent, and the Crewman simply watched her. She was forgetting to act, forgetting to make it look like a language-learning game for the camera, but the Crewman took up the slack, speaking now in English.

"I think you have done very well. Do you feel that we have cleared up some of the points that were puzzling you?"

Anne snapped back into the act. "Oh. Yes. Decidedly. You were right, you know, it was a splendid exercise."

"Perhaps," he said, "we may have another sometime."

"Absolutely," she said.

"For now, I must return to my quarters and work on these circuits for the rest of the day." With his willowy hands on the ends of their long forearms, he began gathering up the objects on the table. "I believe the next tech interviews are due in a few days."

"Yes, as I recall," she said. "Two or three days from now, I believe. I'd have to check. Meanwhile, you've given me plenty to think about." Was this a dangerous thing to say? "I'll be ready to write poetry in L-1 yet, one of these days," she added, laughing. She was a better actor than she had thought, after all. At least she hoped she was. "So, I'll see you tomorrow morning."

"Until then," he said. "Or as we would say in L-1--" But what he said to her, in L-1, was: "*Do try not to worry on my account, we will talk again soon.*"

And, clutching his peculiar toys like a child in a strange dream, he stepped through the door into the dimly lit corridor beyond, and was gone from sight.

21

QQ Mart

She was dressed in a fresh, crisp dress that fairly danced with the joyous pattern of the daisies and sunflowers printed on it, wild laughing flowers that to an observer must have given back the golden sunlight in sweeping arcs as she swung up and back, up and back on the swing, watching his lean arms push her up, up in giggling schoolgirl arcs, up into the giddy light like Icarus sporting with the sun. Suddenly she noticed that off to one side her mother was sitting on the luxurious grass, her legs tucked up under her voluminous Mexican skirt, a straw hat cocked to one side on her head, and she was smiling at the two of them. Because it was indeed the two of them now, father and daughter, happy together in the Texas sun, her pigtails tossing like the tails of a kite, his willowy but strong young-man arms guiding the chains of the swing, pushing her up and up in breathtaking cycles, where she delighted in the air rushing warm and delicious and whistling against her face like the sibilant tones of an Indian flute that in some strange way seemed to come back to her from across time, serenading her with a song as timeless as the wind. When she tilted her head backward on the upswing she could see her father upside-down, wearing his gaucho jeans and open-necked shirt, with a lock of his raven hair fallen across his handsome brown face, his dark eyes smiling as he pushed her up and out, over and over, in a never-ending cycle where the distant horizon rose and fell like the sea. Enchanted, she closed her eyes.

And slowly opened them to the first rays of daylight sneaking through the window onto the bed, where the stillness seemed to have settled palpably around her--opened her eyes onto a cheerless little motel room, somewhere on Central Avenue in Albuquerque, New Mexico, in a world where she was not a laughing little girl any more, a world where

154

for a decade and a half the golden sun in its glory had not shone upon her mother in a straw hat and a Mexican skirt, a world where Lucinda Trujillo had grown older without remembering doing so, a world where this dawning day she scarcely knew where she was going to go or what she was going to do.

A world where for about ten hours now, her father had been dead.

It all rushed back in upon her with a force that forbade even tears, a stultifying condensation of bleak reality crusting up around her, a prosaic and tragic denial of the dream, pushing her rudely back into the world, filling her aching temples with a quiet, mind-numbing cruelty of memory that she would have liked to crawl away from, like a turtle withdrawing its head into the viscous and unimaginable folds of darkness beneath its shell. But there was no withdrawing. This was here, this was now. This was real.

And this was unfair, she thought, feeling a flush of anger rush into her cheeks to revivify them. God damned unfair. Why should she be lying here miserable in a strange room, afraid for her life, instead of opening up her shop and greeting her first customers of the day back on Guadalupe Street in Santa Fe?

And why--but no, if she thought about her dad, she was going to cry again, and she didn't want to cry, didn't have time to cry. It wasn't what Carlos "Hap" Trujillo would have wanted, this sitting around weeping, and it did him no good now, did her no good either. She was going to have to get hold of herself and think straight. *That* was what Dad would have wanted to see her do.

For they had had a common enemy. Dad for all of his adult life had understood the viciousness of this enemy; Lucy had not wholly understood it until last night, perhaps still did not wholly understand it. Dad had already fallen to this shared enemy, slain like a nameless soldier on a nameless battlefield, and for all she knew, she was about to fall as well.

But not if she could help it.

She rolled herself out of bed, peeled off her panties and bra, stepped into the rickety metal stall, and took a shower. The water groaned in the ancient pipes like some unhappy beast, but it felt good nonetheless, almost as if it were trying its best to wash off the foulness of her situation. She let the water play over her body until she could feel the muscles in her neck and shoulders beginning to unknot a little. By the time she was out and dressed in one of her extra tops and pairs of jeans and fishing around in her overnight bag for toilet articles, she felt a little better, but she had realized something.

155

She was going to need to go shopping. At one time she would have joked about that--good old Lucy, born to shop, some things never change. But the time to joke was a thousand years ago, when her life was her life. Or when she thought it was.

It wasn't just that she had had to climb back into the same underwear she had worn yesterday, though that displeased her enough. The main problem was that her supplies of toothpaste, mouthwash, and a number of other things were nearly depleted; she had run low on them during that trip to Taos and hadn't gotten around to replenishing them. It was the sort of thing she had never quite disciplined herself to do, and she was annoyed at herself now for not doing it. Her mouth felt scummy, and she realized that she hadn't brushed her teeth the night before. In a way it was almost preposterous, thinking about such minutiae as dental hygiene, when she had lethally serious problems, but she couldn't think straight at all if she didn't feel halfway clean, and she was going to have to maintain considerable presence of mind if she was going to get through this. Going back into the bathroom and squeezing the curled-up toothpaste tube, she succeeded in coaxing out only the tiniest half-dried-up trace of paste onto her brush, which she proceeded to use anyway, filling a glass with water and rinsing her mouth and feeling somewhat refreshed. But that settled it. If she was going to be on the road for a while, she was going to have to buy some things.

She found a plastic bag on the top shelf of the little closet, the sort of bag in which one was supposed to leave dirty laundry to be collected. For her, the bag would serve another purpose. This was indeed *somebody's* dirty laundry, she reflected, placing the volume of Cervantes in the bag and closing it. Pulling her purse strap onto her shoulder and tucking the plastic bag under one arm, she headed for the door. She wasn't sure she wanted to risk taking the Cervantes volume with her, but she was far less sure she wanted to leave it here.

Out in the little courtyard, the day was still not quite born, and the scene lay in tranquil shadows broken only in part as the sun edged over the adobe wall enclosing the little court. Near her feet, a lizard traversed the scruffy yellow grass in nervous little darts, running and stopping and running again. Lucy watched it for a moment, somehow enjoying its irrelevance. Sighing, she looked around. Her car slept nearby, and it gave her a poignant sort of twinge to see it, because it was her only link, really, with what had been her normal life. But the more she drove around with her license plates in plain sight, the bigger the chance she would be taking, and for now she was going to walk. On the way here last night, she had seen a large discount store somewhere up on

Central, a place called QQ Mart, and she thought she remembered a sign in the window saying "Open 24 Hours."

There was something a little eerie about being out on the street this early in the morning. It was after seven, and a good many cars were on the streets, but the city still had the feeling of not being completely awake. Crossing the side streets, she walked along, clutching her plastic bag, and saw only occasional shopkeepers sweeping the sidewalks in front of their doors, or ragtag little groups of boys laughing together or cavorting on brightly painted skateboards. What day of the week was it? Monday, she thought. Wasn't that right? She had had the shop open Saturday, had been off yesterday--

God save us all, could that be only yesterday?

She could see the sign further up the avenue: QQ Mart. And indeed she must have been right; it was open, a few people were coming and going. By the time she got there herself and pushed through the door, she realized with some surprise that she was so out of shape she was tired from the walk, which could only have been three quarters of a mile or so from the motel. This wouldn't do, to be so tired this early; it might well turn out to be a very long day. How could she already feel so worn out?

Well, for one thing, she was hungry, and the sight of a little snackbar inside the store, to her left at the front, picked her spirits up a little. She could smell greasy food cooking, and it didn't smell half bad. There wouldn't even be anybody in line ahead of her.

She went through the line, picked up a plastic tray and plastic fork and knife and spoon, and ordered two breakfast burritos and a large cup of coffee. Sitting in a booth, she doused the burritos in salsa and ate them with such alacrity that she was downright surprised at herself. It was astonishing, how much difference a little food could make. As there were still only a few other people about, she went back through the line and bought a third burrito and returned to the booth and ate this one rather more slowly, washing it down with coffee and feeling a little guilty now. She was going to have to watch her money better than this. But she had been starved, and, up on her feet again and heading into the rest of the store to do the necessary shopping, she realized that she felt distinctly clearer in the head.

More people were coming into the store now, but it still wasn't crowded, so she was able to get through the aisles with some ease. She pretty well filled up the bottom of a pushcart with things she needed: half a dozen cheap but serviceable pairs of panties, an extra bra, a large tube of toothpaste, a new toothbrush, a little bottle of mouthwash, some generic vitamin pills, a bottle of aspirin tablets, a roll-on deodorant, other toiletries she had noticed she was short on. Also, some "car food," as Dad

157

had called such things years ago--little packages of cheese crackers, peanuts, corn chips, strips of beef jerky, a box of vanilla wafers, and cans of generic soda that probably tasted pretty gross but just might make the difference somewhere down the road. Keeping a rough total running in her head, she thought she had somewhere around seventy or eighty dollars' worth of stuff. And barely that much cash. It was time to haul out the old credit card, and to hell with fretting about running up her account--she figured she'd be damned lucky ever to get her life nearly enough back together again to have to worry about it. She proceeded to the checkout.

At the register, a young Hispanic girl, possibly only fifteen or sixteen to look at her, smiled and began ringing up the purchases. When she was done, Lucy handed her her Visa card, and the girl started going through the routine. Suddenly, standing there with two or three other shoppers lining up behind her, Lucy was taken with a bizarre sense of unreality, a sort of contrary conviction that none of this could be happening, none of it could be real. It was ludicrous--her place, on a Monday morning, was behind her cozy little desk in Mesa Bookshop in Santa Fe, with the minds of the past clustered around her head in a million pages of dusty wisdom. Her place, on a Monday morning, was most decidedly not in line at a QQ Mart on Central Avenue in Albuquerque with a shopping cart full of things that bespoke a desperate survivalist mentality rather than anything a woman with a sound mind should be entertaining. And when thoughts of her father began creeping in around the edges of this insane scenario--

"Yes. Thank you." While Lucy had been woolgathering, the girl at the register had been on the store phone, and Lucy, mentally scrambling back over a run of nearly lost impressions now, thought the girl had been reciting numbers into the phone. But then she was handing Lucy back her Visa card and having her sign the charge slip and bundling the purchase up into a large shopping bag with two fat turquoise Q's on the side, dropping the charge slip in with everything else. "*Muchas gracias,*" she said, smiling. "*Vuelva por favor, y tenga buen día.*"

"*Igualmente,*" Lucy said, and left the store. Back out on the sidewalk, where there were more people around now, she felt a little encumbered with the bulky bag in one hand and the Cervantes volume in its own plastic bag wedged under the other arm, and with her purse hanging on her shoulder. She wished she could have brought the car after all, but knew she had been right not to. She started walking.

By the time she was back in her motel room, unloading the things she had bought and packing them into the canvas overnight bag, it was after nine-thirty. Checkout time, if she was leaving this morning and moving on, which she figured she had better do, wasn't till eleven, so she had some more time. She wouldn't wait till eleven, though; she probably ought to be back on the road before then.

Going where? "I knew it was just a matter of time before you asked me that," she said, trying to chuckle to herself. It came out sounding pretty flat. Where indeed? Now that she was heading south maybe she should just *keep* heading south. What was south of here? Socorro, Truth or Consequences, Las Cruces. El Paso.

Mexico.

Stuffing *Don Quixote de la Mancha,* still wrapped in its plastic bag, into a corner of the canvas bag with her clothes and toiletries and "car food," she thought: yeah. *Claro que sí.* Mexico. The thought must have been lurking there on some unconscious level all along. What else could she do, but head for the border and keep hoping that in some miraculous way things would change, that everything would be all right again? Someone would come up to her and say: come on back home now, Lucy, it's okay, it was all a mistake, the game is over, you can come out now. But there wasn't the proverbial snowball's chance in hell of that, and she knew it. It was all that she did know. She certainly had no way to know what lay ahead for her. Maybe she could *never* go back to Santa Fe, back to her shop and her house. How could she ever find out if it was safe to go back? What was she supposed to do, call the police, tell them someone was stalking her, ask them to protect her? She might be naïve about all these things, but she understood perfectly well that the people who had killed her father would come after her too now, and with the full and cheerful coöperation of the police. She could just hear her shadowy pursuers, whoever they were, justifying it: yes, Commissioner Jones, we can use all the help we can get from you local law enforcement agencies, because, you see, she's a fugitive wanted on serious federal charges, so if you should happen to spot her. . . .

Sitting on the edge of the bed in the little room, Lucy wondered what her chances were of making it to the Mexican border.

Well. She slapped her hands on her knees and pushed herself up, as if acting resolute could help. Maybe it could. In any case it was a little after ten o'clock, and she ought to be going. Gathering up her now bulkier overnight bag and her purse, she stepped outside, locked the door, opened the car, and started to put her things in the back seat, but thought better of it. She had taken a chance, last night when she arrived here, leaving the book in the car for even a few minutes while she checked in, and she was unwilling to take that kind of chance any more. Walking toward the motel office, she kept the overnight bag with her.

Paradoxically, while it was this book, and what it concealed, that had put her in her current terrible position, these things might also just be the most precious possessions she had ever held in her hands.

Maybe there were people in Mexico she could show the foil to, people whom she could make understand what it meant, people beyond the reach of the forces that threatened her here. It was a slim chance, perhaps, but she had to cling to something, some thought that held out a little hope to her.

In the office, she chatted for a moment with Mrs. Morales and her husband, signed the charge slip to pay for her room, returned the key, and said goodbye. Something about the little Morales family made her indeterminately sad, as if they represented everything wholesome and healthy and sane that she was cut off from now, perhaps forever. She hated to leave the quiet little couple, in a way, but she really needed to be moving on.

And out in the little courtyard, on her way back to her car, she began wondering about something. Belatedly. Something that sent a horrendous little jab of fear prickling up her spine.

Just now, when she had signed the Visa slip to charge her room, she had done so with a comfortable sense of safety in the knowledge that Mr. and Mrs. Morales would simply mail the slip in to get their money, a process that had to wait on the postal system, guaranteeing that Lucy would be well away before anyone in the computer network of the banking world knew that she had used her card. And essentially the same thing applied at QQ Mart, where in fact they probably sent them in at the end of the week or something, whole bundles of them at a time.

Except there was a little problem, wasn't there? She hadn't thought it through at the time, but now she realized, with near certainty anyway, what it was that had happened at the checkout at QQ Mart, and the realization made her nearly stumble as she approached her car door. This just might be the end of everything for her.

QQ Mart, like so many stores, would probably have a "floor limit," a limit on how much a customer could just walk in and charge without anyone's checking. Something like fifty dollars, most likely. And that was what the phone call and the litany of numbers had been all about. Her purchase had been over the limit, and the girl had called to check on the status of her account. With her card number.

And if the number had gone into the computer--

How long had it been now--she had gone through the checkout about two hours ago. A little over two hours, maybe. Could they? *Could* they know where she was, from that? Dear sweet Jesus, please say no, please say they can't.

160

But you know, she bet they could.

"God in heaven." She fumbled at the lock to her car door with hands that felt cold and uncoöperative, as if they belonged to someone else, some other woman who didn't share her urgency. At length she got the car open and tossed the overnight bag across onto the seat on the passenger side, and was bending over, about to get in, when a shadow fell across her.

Straightening up, she found herself squinting into the sun, then peering into the face of a rather tall man who somehow looked vaguely familiar. His facial expression was not in the least menacing, but what he said to her, in greeting, was striking.

"Frailty," he said, smiling ironically, "thy name is woman."

22

Company Drops In

It was kind of crazy, driving all the way up to the Three Rivers petroglyph site just to see Eric, since he would be busy working and would be back in Alamogordo that evening anyway. It was already nearly three o'clock in the afternoon. They would have to drive separate cars back, of course, not that that mattered much, because even if they had been able to come back in the same car, they wouldn't have dared talk about anything important. For that matter, they couldn't safely talk even out in the open, on the hill at Three Rivers, about the things she really wanted to discuss. But thanks to the Crewman's indicating that he would need to work on his demonstration circuits for the rest of the day, she did have the afternoon off, after all, and she couldn't see just puttering around at home when Eric was up here. She wanted to see him, even if they couldn't talk freely.

She had always prided herself on being a fairly independent spirit, but at this juncture in her life she didn't mind admitting to herself that Eric's support, even just in the form of friendship, was important to her. Friendship and more, she had a feeling. Something nice could be developing again, after all these years apart. Could be developing, that is, if she lived long enough. Or if he did, now that she was dragging him into this sordid mess that she called her life.

No more of that dismal crap, she told herself, parking the car down in the lot below and starting up the hill on the rocky path that led to the area of the petroglyphs. Eric's car was here, but she couldn't see him yet; he was probably around on the other side, still trying to catalog everything. If only one really *could* catalog everything. She felt a little shiver as a breeze stirred the sand on the path. Although the sun, edging toward the western horizon, was still warming the air, in another two or three hours it would be downright chilly out here. That's the way the desert was. She loved it, but just now she didn't feel that she had much time for normal, healthy ruminations in her life, when there were bound to be serious problems ahead.

What in the world was going to happen now, with the Crewman suddenly remarking that things couldn't go on for much longer as they were? Nothing like this had ever happened before, in her exchanges with him, and she found such a development startling to say the least. The very notion that he would resort to an outright subterfuge to speak more freely with her, using the excuse that they needed to converse extendedly in L-1, gave her a curiously mingled sensation, a sort of thrill, a wistful intrigue almost, laced liberally with fear. This wasn't a children's game they were playing; the people she worked for were folks with a decidedly impaired sense of humor, and they wouldn't hesitate to blow away one Doctor Anne Hawk, without hesitation beforehand or regrets afterward, if they even suspected she was conspiring in any way against their interests. Maybe they already did suspect, after that bizarre business of the previous day, with Sage, and with some sort of thwarted surveillance effort apparently, whatever that was all about. She wondered if she could believe the Indian when he said that whoever had been listening to them out here would be unable to hear anything further, after whatever happened happened, that strange business with the wind. And what if the eavesdroppers did find themselves suddenly unable to eavesdrop-- wasn't that possibly just as bad, since it may have alerted them to the likelihood that some pretty damned unorthodox things were going on, up on the hill? Involuntarily, she scanned the desert now with a hand shading her eyes, but could see nothing. Still, they were out there again somewhere, likely as not.

Scarcely realizing it, she had hiked completely through the rocky area on the near side of the hill and had skirted around to the far side, where she suddenly ran onto Eric, who was squatting in the midst of a group of petroglyph-adorned stones and scribbling in a notebook. He looked up at her approach and grinned. "Anne! I didn't know you were coming up."

"Well," she said, leaning over and kissing his upturned face. "Miracle to tell, I got the afternoon off. So how's it going?"

"Oh, okay," he said, "I'm just finishing up my notes. It's going to take me the rest of the afternoon, I imagine, so I may be dull company."

She poked him in the arm. "You're only moderately dull. Even when you're courting a gaggle of petroglyphs instead of an old girlfriend."

He shrugged. "The two are not mutually exclusive."

"Said just like a true scientist," she said, stepping around behind him and giving his shoulders a little massage. "I'll hang around and watch, if you don't mind."

"I'd mind if you didn't," he said.

So the afternoon shaded off into early evening, with Eric working on his notes and Anne sometimes strolling around the site, sometimes sitting on a rock and gazing out into the desert in one direction or another, wondering if someone was indeed out there spying on them, and half expecting to see Sage again. Half hoping to. And half dreading to. Once or twice she thought she did see someone out walking on the desert plain, maybe even more than one person, far off across the way. And around four o'clock she thought she saw what might be a car moving, and possibly stopping, a long ways off to the northwest, where if she remembered correctly some road--Route 380, it might have been--came across from northwest to southeast, joining Route 54, the road from Alamogordo to Three Rivers, a good many miles north of the petroglyph site. What she saw was only a dim point of light in the distance, too far away to make anything out of it, but it almost had to be a car. No big deal; there were roads out there, after all, and although there certainly wasn't much traffic on them, there was bound to be a car along from time to time. But for some unfathomable reason this glimmer of light gave her a sort of pang, as if she ought to know who was in the car, ought to be concerned about who it was, or as if at any rate it all had something to do with her.

And a little later she thought she caught a glimpse of reflected sunlight on metal closer by, only a quarter of a mile or so out in the chaparral toward the west, but if so, it quickly disappeared. Snooping sons of bitches were probably out there again with one of those--what did you call them? Rifle mikes. Well, let them. They weren't going to hear anything, because there wasn't going to be anything to hear.

By sundown Eric was gathering his cameras and notebooks and getting ready to leave. They sat on low rocks for a few minutes on the near side of the hill and had a drink of water from Eric's canteen. "See you this evening?" Anne asked.

"Absolutely," he said. "When we get back to Alamogordo, I've really got to spend some time in my motel room typing these notes and scanning the rest of these sketches into my computer, so I may be a little while. I want to get it all done so the rest of my time down here will be ours. We can still have dinner tonight if you don't mind eating kind of late."

"Whatever works. I just want to see you." Looking around and catching his eye as if to say *Careful, they may be listening,* she took a stick and wrote in the dirt at their feet: *NEED TO TALK.* Looking at the message, he nodded, taking her hand, and she quickly scratched the words out, scattering the dirt. "We'd better get doing," she said.

On the way back she drove behind him, watching in the rear view mirror to see if anybody in turn was following her, but she couldn't be sure. If it had been a little darker she might have been able to tell, but as it was, it was just dark enough to make it hard to see back there but not quite dark enough for headlights. Almost certainly both her car and Eric's were bugged, which in the present situation was pretty funny; what did they think, that she and Eric would talk to themselves? Not that she didn't feel a little like talking to herself, at this point.

All the way back down to Alamogordo she forced herself to think about the old days up in New Haven, when life was simple and all she had had to worry about was getting her doctorate from Yale. By the time they had passed through Tularosa she did turn her headlights on, and saw Eric turn his on, and saw someone far behind her turn theirs on too. She herded her thoughts back to Connecticut, those old times of graduate courses and comprehensive exams and dissertation writing and dinners and drinks, and wondered if it had just been a case of the people being right but the time being wrong. Dear Eric. She remembered, again, building the snowman with him that winter, the two of them laughing and beating their gloved hands together and stamping their feet to keep warm. But the lights of Alamogordo brought the present back to her.

When they reached her house, Eric stopped for a moment and got out and kissed her, and they talked a little about nothing in particular, and he waved goodbye and drove off, heading west into town. She went into her house, closed and locked the door, and already missed him.

So this was the independent woman of the world, she thought wryly. Well, now, there sure as hell wasn't anything wrong with the way her feelings for Eric were reasserting themselves after all this time. Sure, she had made her way in the world all by herself, but that didn't mean she wanted to be alone forever. Whatever "forever" meant now. She had always assumed it meant a reasonably long time, but now she could scarcely take such things for granted. Wouldn't it be ironic, she thought: Eric and I just get back together, and--

But again, why dwell on the more dismal possibilities?

She went into the kitchen, filled the watering can from the sink, unlocked the back door and stepped out into the crisp evening air and watered the plants on the back railing, and stepped back in and closed the door. Amazing, she thought, how a lot of normal little concerns go on as usual, even when all the normalcy in life seems ready to vanish forever.

It was after seven now, and she was hungry, so made herself a sandwich in spite of the likelihood that she and Eric would be having dinner later on; she'd be hungry again by then. Sitting on the sofa in the living room and propping her feet up on the coffee table, she ate the sandwich and drank a can of diet soda and watched a half-hour news program on TV, and finally took the remote control in hand and switched the set off and just sat listening to the silence.

Or to what should have been just silence, but wasn't quite.

Somewhere, somewhere toward the back of the house, there had been a sound.

Or she thought there had, something that the television prattle had blanketed over, something that stopped stirring when the television went silent. As if not wanting to be heard but not quite stopping in time.

Suddenly her bowels felt like a bag of ice.

She sat very, very still, listening, not even wanting to put the remote control down, not wanting to breathe.

Nothing, nothing, she must have been imagining--

But no. Softly, furtively, a little crinkle of sound emanated from somewhere back there. Her bedroom?

Had she locked the windows back there?

What about the back door? When she came back in after watering the plants on the back porch, had she locked the door? She agonized over this point to no effect; she simply couldn't remember.

Dear God, don't let there be anyone in the house.

Slowly, softly, she drew a breath in and held it, and listened.

And, unmistakably now, another unplaceable little rustle of sound came from somewhere in the back of the house. The kitchen, or the bedroom, or somewhere.

And in a kind of quiet panic, as if her fear had nearly paralyzed her body but left her mind aflame with speculation, she began to review the possibilities.

Eric. Eric sneaking in earlier than she expected, to surprise her. But no, it wouldn't quite be his style, not under the circumstances, when he would have to know that she was already pretty jumpy. So, if not Eric--

A burglar. Someone skulking about back there with every willingness to kill her if need be, or maim her, or rape her, or all of the above. But another explanation rose slowly in her mind now, the gray, grainy scenes forming in her head like an old black-and-white movie.

In her mind's eye she saw a vague picture of a huddled conference in someone's office, a secret place like so many secret places she had known over the years, a place without windows. Someone was saying: Dr. Hawk has outlived her usefulness, she's come to be a security

166

risk just like George Quintana. We'll get what we finally want from the Crewman now anyway, with or without her help, now that he's building demonstration circuits for us, circuits that we can learn to build and use without her. No more translations needed from the esteemed and scholarly Dr. Hawk, and we ought to lose no time in taking care of what has to be done. Quickly, quietly. Just a nocturnal visit to her house, and presto, no problem. Simple and clean.

And a tear that felt feverishly hot welled up in one eye and traced a course down her cheek. God help her, she wasn't ready to die.

She sat frozen completely motionless, letting her breath out slowly, quietly, and listening.

And there it was again, an unidentifiable whisper of insidious sound.

Right here in the house with her.

She struggled through layers of terror to find the strength to stir, and slowly, quietly got up off the sofa, finding her legs shaky underneath her when she stood on them.

Thank heaven she had wall-to-wall carpeting underfoot anyway, to muffle her steps. She crept over to the kiva, her snug little corner fireplace that had comforted her on many a lonely evening but offered little comfort now. She closed her grip around a heavy andiron. It felt cold against her palm. She slowly lifted it, desperate to make no sound, and finally held it in the air before her. She had her back to the door that led to the hallway in the back part of the house, and suddenly had a conviction that someone was already standing there watching her.

It took more courage than she had ever in her life tried to summon, to turn around and look.

She saw no one.

But, expelling a breath of relief and then straining to listen again, she still *heard* someone, something.

Sneaking, unnameable little sounds. Undeniable. Real. There was someone in the house.

She looked at the front door, which she was sure she had locked after coming in. It seemed certain to her that if she tried to unlock the door, open it, unclasp the screen door, and make a run for it, she'd never make it, they'd be upon her in a second. Whatever happened, had to happen right here, right now.

And, by God, she wasn't going to make it easy for them.

Clasping the heavy andiron, she took a couple of uncertain steps toward the door that led into the hall, and stopped and listened. Nothing now. Somehow, that was worse--they had heard her moving around, they were waiting for her. She just knew it.

167

Taking a deep breath and biting down on her lip to keep from sobbing, she stepped into the hall. There was no light on in here, but the light from the living room filtered through to illumine her path, faintly but adequately. There were of course no lights on in the back anywhere. She moved silently down the hall and stood just outside her open bedroom door, listening.

Nothing.

She stepped into the bedroom.

Nothing, nobody in here. There was nowhere in here for anybody to hide.

Except, of course, under the bed.

Or in the closet.

She had visions of stepping across the room, opening the closet door, seeing nothing but clothing on hangers, pushing the hangers aside, and looking into the shadows there to see a merciless face leaning out to her. . . .

Holding the andiron in both hands to keep them from shaking, she stood absolutely still, not even breathing now. Listening.

And the odd, fleeting hint of sound came again.

But not from in here. From the kitchen, she was almost certain this time.

She softly retraced her steps, edging back out into the hall, where in the pale diffusion of light from the living room she could still see nothing but the usual contours of the house: door jambs, corners, brown plastic molding along the tops of the walls, a hall light not turned on. Nothing out of the ordinary, except for the outrage that she felt at knowing that she had an intruder in her kitchen, and knowing that that intruder could only mean her harm. In her own house!

She stood for a long time just short of the doorway into the kitchen, which yawned out of a throat of darkness in there--in there where she very distinctly now heard another muffled little stirring of sound.

It was now or never, before she lost her nerve altogether.

Gripping the andiron tighter than ever in her right hand, she reached with her left hand around the door jamb, into the dark, found the light switch, and flipped it on. And in the same instant, with an inarticulate yell that she wouldn't have thought herself capable of, she lunged into the room with the andiron raised over her head, ready to strike.

And she met her intruder face to face.

It wasn't a burglar holding a bag of silverware. It wasn't a government official calmly leveling a revolver at her head.

It wasn't even human.

168

Emerging, like a cocoon, from what looked like a sort of cowl made apparently of aluminum foil, it put up a hand momentarily to shield its eyes from the sudden light that had invaded the corner where it crouched in the midst of a clutter of strange-looking bric-a-brac. It looked up at her with no particular expression, and nodded to her.

It was the Crewman.

## 23

Doing Lunch

Lucy stood transfixed, her car door still open as if to admit her. The stranger held his hand out in front of him, and for a moment of insane *naïveté* she half thought he wanted to shake hands with her. But, pointing into the front seat of her car, he said: "I'll take that bag."

Wondering if he could hear her heart beating, she looked him square in the face. "Who the hell are *you?*"

He spoke softly, in a mock-confidential sort of way. "You can call me Roger. You should feel privileged; I don't go around telling everybody my name. Now, I'll take that bag." Pointing again with his right hand, he planted his left on his hip, swinging his jacket a little open, and she could see that he was wearing a shoulder holster.

It felt like the lowest point in her entire life, dragged tauntingly out as if in slow motion, the terrible few seconds it took her to lean into the car, stretch across the driver's seat and the gear shift, clutch the straps of the canvas bag, pull it across and out of the car, and hand it to him. All the while, her mind seemed to lock up on one fixation, one point: that this was not the way it was supposed to be.

She had had the feeling once before, at least, in a big way, back in college, when her mother had died. She remembered thinking: no, we were supposed to take a trip to Oklahoma City next summer, I had things picked out to give you next Christmas, we had things to talk about, things to do, it isn't supposed to *be* this way. She thought that that must be the thought that runs through some people's heads when they're having a heart attack: no, not like this, don't you understand, I had something else in mind altogether.

And now, standing in a little motel courtyard in Albuquerque, she certainly *had* had something else in mind altogether. It couldn't be ending like this, not when she had envisioned it so differently, not when she had made her plans so bravely and in such good conscience, not when she had seen herself spending the rest of the day driving south with every determination to get away--not when in her mind's eye she was supposed to be in Las Cruces this evening and El Paso tonight, and across the border into Ciudad Juárez. She would have had to be careful, watch for the state police, worry about being spotted, but God damn it, she was supposed to have had a *chance.*

And it couldn't end like this, when the simple act of handing this canvas bag to this man was a negation of everything her father had ever stood for.

With one last inward show of hope, she let herself wonder if maybe she could get away with ignorance, with feigned misunderstanding, with thinking that his intentions were of another kind. Anything was worth a try.

"Look, mister, whoever you are, if it's my money--"

He snorted and stepped around her and placed the canvas bag on the hood of the car. "Don't be coy with me, little girl," he said. "I think you know damn well what I want. And it's right here in this bag, or I'm much mistaken. What do you say we have a look? If it isn't here, well, then we'll have to talk."

He rummaged through the contents, found the little plastic bag, and took out the book. "Aha. And now I will unclasp a secret book, and to your quick-conceiving discontents I'll read you matter deep and dangerous."

She stared at him, incredulous. "What?"

He shrugged, and offered a faint smile. "Oh, it's from *King Henry the Fourth.* One of Shakespeare's historical plays."

"I know it's one of--that's not what--I mean, I don't know what you--" The conversation had turned so absurd that all she seemed to be able to do was splutter.

"Ah, so you know the Bard," he said. "Commendable."

"I have a degree in English literature, as a matter of fact," she said. "But what in God's name does that have to do with--"

Holding a finger to his lips to stop her like someone silencing a chatterer in a library, he started flipping through the pages of the book, pausing over them, feeling them. Out of the corner of her eye, she noticed that Mr. and Mrs. Morales were standing in the door of their little office, watching all this. God, what must they think? That she was some sort of--

"Mm. Yes. I do believe we have something here." He was fingering a page that he evidently suspected to be double in thickness or

171

weight. He took out a pocket knife, snicked open a small blade, and began running it around the edge of the page, which indeed was doubled, opening up now like an envelope. "Ah," he said. "In nature's infinite book of secrecy a little I can read." He separated the pages all the way around but held the book aside so that only he could look between them. He seemed quite satisfied. "Oh. *Antony and Cleopatra*. But perhaps you know that. Have you ever had the pleasure?" For a bleary moment she thought he meant had she read the play, but then he motioned for her to look into the book too.

There, innocently enough, rested a bright little strip of metal foil about the size of an ordinary bookmark.

He only let her look at it for a few seconds before snapping the book shut again, but at the sight of the thing a confluence of emotions rippled through her with such force and such confusion that she thought for a moment she was going to faint. So, then. That was it. That unassuming little object, a piece of another world. A relic so coveted by these people that her father had died for it. Had died, for Christ's sake, just so that the government, for its own reasons and in its own way, could keep its filthy secrets. And for this--the secrecy, not the relic itself-- she was going to die too.

"How?" she said, hating her voice for sounding quavery. "How did you know where I was?"

"Oh that," the man who called himself Roger said. "Piece of cake, my dear."

"Don't you dare call me 'my dear,' you son of a bitch. It was you people who killed my dad." She blinked away a tear that was threatening to overflow; damned if she was going to cry for this scumbag. Then it came back to her, what she had already been worrying about before he showed up. "It was my credit card, wasn't it? And you're going to kill me."

"Let's not talk about sordid things," he said. "And let's not incline toward rancor. Not when we're going to be traveling companions. Because we are, you know. You were headed downstate, and by the most amazing coincidence, so am I." He pointed toward the entrance to the little court, where just inside, on the drive, a policeman in uniform was standing and watching them now. Roger motioned for the officer to go, and he did. "To answer your question, yes, when QQ Mart, God bless 'em, called in your credit card number, we had the location of the store right away. It was just an hour's drive down here for me, from Santa Fe, and while I was on the way down we told the local police to have a look at the motels up and down the avenue till they spotted your license plate and gave us a call back. I had them watch on the street out there till I arrived. Law enforcement is a wonderful thing sometimes, don't you think? Which reminds me."

He reached into his jacket and came out with a gun in his hand and let the barrel, which was nasty-looking, large beyond belief, drift in her direction. "Mm. Yes. This is a .44 magnum. It would make a hole in that pretty midriff of yours big enough to slam-dunk a basketball. It isn't that I think you'll give me trouble, you know, running away or anything. It's just that we have a necessary bit of theater to take care of here. Public relations. Tiresome stuff, but one has to make a good impression." He motioned with the .44 for her to accompany him to where Mr. and Mrs. Morales were standing in their doorway. Walking over there with him behind her, she could scarcely bear to look into their faces.

"Ah, I'm sorry for this little unpleasantness," Roger said, holstering the gun. Clearly it had been entirely for show; Lucy reflected grimly that this man did have a certain sense of the dramatic. "I know you people don't like trouble at your motel." He produced a badge in a little leather holder. "I'm a federal officer, and I'm arresting this woman on a number of charges." He held the book up for a second for them to see, then tucked it under his arm. "Drugs," he said. "You know how it is these days."

To Lucy it was impossible to discern any particular emotion in Mr. Morales's face, but Mrs. Morales was looking at Roger (or whatever his name really was) with an expression of unconcealed contempt. Her face seemed to say: this woman hasn't done a thing wrong, it's always Hispanics you people pick on. But if this sentiment got across to Roger, he seemed not to mind.

"Well, sorry again to inconvenience you folks," he said. He motioned for Lucy to accompany him back to her car, which she did. When they got there, he wrapped the Cervantes volume up in the plastic again and stuffed it back into the canvas bag, which he handed to her to carry. "We're going in my car. It's out on the street."

"Where are you taking me?"

"As I *said,*" he replied, in a tone of voice that sounded like something addressed to a child with whom one is nearly out of patience, "downstate. Why? Is there someplace else you wanted to go this morning?"

She drew a deep breath and let it out in a sigh. "Would it matter?"

"Not a whole lot," he said.

# # # #

173

On their way south on Route 25 out of Albuquerque, she sat in the front passenger seat and the canvas bag had the back seat to itself. Roger drove the metallic-gray rental Ford at exactly the speed limit.

"I don't understand," she said, looking straight ahead at the road, "why you didn't just kill me back there and take the book and be done with it."

He glanced sidelong at her. "You keep talking about me killing you. I almost think you *want* me to."

They didn't talk again until they pulled off the highway in Socorro a little after one o'clock and parked next to a diner. He turned to her when the engine was off. "Let's do lunch."

"Oh, cute," she said. "Christ."

"I'm not leaving the bag in the car," he said, "so get it and bring it in."

Inside, they sat at a table in the middle of the room; she placed the canvas bag on the floor by her feet. At other tables nearby, other diners talked and laughed quietly among themselves. Ordinary people on an ordinary day, regular people having lunch, Lucy thought; just like me and Roger. Ho hum, another day. On the jukebox George Jones was singing "Hell Stays Open All Night Long." Roger handed her a battered little menu.

"Order anything you want," he said.

Was this for real? You would have thought they were two junior high school kids out on a first date at the local burger haven, the way he said it. She set the menu down. "I'm really not hungry."

"You'd better eat while you can. I'm not too sure how the rest of the day is going to go."

She wondered just how ominously she should take this.

After a while the waitress, a middle-aged woman in jeans and white tasseled boots and a New Mexico Tech sweatshirt, came to their table. Roger ordered a cheeseburger, french fries, and a root beer. Lucy decided she might as well go along, whether she had the stomach for it or not, and ordered a hot roast beef sandwich and a cup of coffee. She didn't say anything to Roger while they were waiting, and tried not even to look at him. He seemed content just to sit and wait, only glancing at her from time to time. On the jukebox, Patty Loveless was singing about somebody who was a waitress in Beaumont.

When the food came, Lucy did manage to eat most of hers, though her stomach was protesting. She had had time to think, and she was really beginning to chafe now. She watched him eat. He looked amazingly relaxed, making his way through his food as if he were on a routine business lunch. She supposed that that was what it was, to him.

174

Dressed in his western-style clothes, he could be a farm machinery salesman from down the street, nobody would know any different to look at him. Nobody but Lucy. Every time *she* looked at him, her blood came more nearly to a boil with the thought that--

"You bastard," she finally said in a fierce whisper, not able to contain herself any longer. "You had him killed."

"No," he said, "I didn't have him killed. As little as this is going to endear me to you, I must confess: I did it myself. Unfortunately, some things simply have to be done, and very often I have to see to them myself, rather than entrust them to someone else. It's the nature of things."

"I see," she said. "The nature of things."

At this point the waitress was hovering over her with a coffeepot. "Freshen up your coffee, ma'am?"

She pushed her cup closer to the edge of the table. "Yes, please." When the cup was full again, she said, "Thank you," and the waitress went off to another table.

And Lucy, who had just wanted to be sure that the coffee in the cup was plentiful and very hot, dashed it square in Roger's face. Now that she thought about it, a cup of tea would have been the more appropriate choice, but this would do. The hot coffee caught him with his fork halfway to his mouth and, crying out through a mouthful of food, he choked and dropped the fork in his plate, scattering french fries over the table top.

"That's just a little something for my dad," she said, feeling her face hotly flushed, and dimly aware that just about everybody in the room was looking at them.

She felt supremely justified in what she had done, even as small a gesture as it was, compared to the enormity of the man's crimes. It was a personal gesture, and one delivered with an audience, and that was very gratifying to her, just now. But the sensation was short-lived. Half standing, Roger reached over the table and cuffed her across the face so hard that she tipped over backward in her chair and landed crumpled up on the floor, her ears ringing, her face a raw welter of pain. When she put her hand to her mouth and nose, it came away smeared with blood. Somewhere, it seemed like miles away, Travis Tritt was on the jukebox drowning his remorse for some lost love in a bottle of whiskey. Things went kind of gray, then, but she didn't quite pass out.

She realized in the next instant that her eyes were flooded with tears, and she blinked up at Roger through them. He had pushed his chair back and was just standing there looking at her and wiping at his face with a handkerchief. At the next table over, a huge cowboy-type was getting up from his table and tossing his napkin onto his plate, and staring at Roger the way someone might look at a stinkbug on the sidewalk. Roger was pretty tall, but this man was a good foot taller, and probably outweighed him by a hundred pounds of brown muscle. The waitress just stood and gawked, evidently expecting mayhem on a scale larger than this diner was accustomed to witnessing.

"Mister," he said, like a line in a bad movie, "I don't know where you come from, but we don't treat our women like that around here."

He was reaching for Roger, and in another second would have had him by the scruff of the neck. Roger, however, had the .44 out and pointed at him.

"Don't even think about it, Tex," he said. "You just take care of your problems and let me take care of mine, what do you say? Though this be madness, yet there is method in't."

"What in the *hell* are you talking about?" the cowboy wanted to know.

"Polonius," Roger said, as if that explained everything. "Like I said, the lady is my problem. You'll excuse us, please."

Lucy was getting up off the floor, dabbing at her nose with her sleeve and watching all this with a sense of unreality. Roger holstered the .44, reached in his pocket and tossed some money on the table, fetched Lucy by the upper arm, grabbed the canvas bag, and headed for the door, leaving the cowboy standing there saying something like, "If that ain't the damnedest--"

Outside on the sidewalk, Roger turned her loose with a push.

"Okay. Look. I'm not so thin-skinned that I can't take a little horseshit from time to time. So you're pissed about your father. Fine. I can understand that. But let me tell you something, you little bitch. The reason I *didn't* just kill you back there at the motel and take the book, is that I've got other business to see to, when we get downstate, and I figured I might as well take care of all of it at the same time, so bringing you along was the best way. Any more nonsense from you, though, and the simple fact is that I'm going to shoot you and dump you at the side of the road and let the desert turn you into lizard shit. Now get in the car. And here." He handed her the handkerchief with which he had been mopping her second cup of coffee off his face. "Wipe your nose."

24

A Conference

Anne Hawk was so flabbergasted that she had to lean on the door jamb, half in and half out of the kitchen. The sight of the Crewman, the colossal surprise of his presence, literally took her breath away. He blinked slowly at her once, twice, then said: "I am sorry if I frightened you, Anne. There was no other way."

Anne rubbed her eyes, as if this impossible vision might go away. She didn't think she wanted it to go away, but she wasn't sure. She wasn't sure of much of anything right now.

"How the hell did you get here?" she finally managed to ask. It was the first time she had ever sworn at him, if this counted as swearing at him. She certainly wasn't angry with him, just astonished and bewildered.

"I must confess," he said, waving a willowy hand at the strange paraphernalia around him, "I have been less than honest. In fact, I have been duplicitous, and duplicitous in more than just our conversation of this morning. It is a habit, I am sad to say, that I have learned chiefly from the actions of your government."

Anne laughed outright. "*Touché*. Where better to learn it? But explain." It suddenly hit her. "My God, when they find out that you're-- but how in the world did you get out of there?"

The Crewman sat down at the kitchen table, pushed aside some of the little metal objects on the tabletop, and motioned for her to sit across from him. When she had settled herself, he went on.

"I have never been a prisoner, Anne. Not really. Time does not mean to me what it means to you. I could have done this any time. You see these devices." She stared at them. Some of them resembled what he had called demonstration circuits that morning, others were different, but they all seemed to consist mostly of oddly configured circuitboard designs clustered with little mirrors, dishes, and less explicable appendages. "These things are responsible. I had to give your superiors to understand that I was simply building circuits with which to teach the next round of theory. They scarcely would have stood still for my doing what I really intended doing."

"Which is--damn," she said, "you're talking about--what do they call it in science fiction stories? Teleportation? Is that what these things do? They got you here, transmitted you? Teleported you?"

Again, he blinked slowly. "And teleported themselves. You could call it that. That's basically what these things do. Some of them. They manipulate phases of matter and energy. Some of the other devices here, however, perform--for now let us just say other functions. You will see."

She felt a little like a Neanderthal attending a symposium on particle physics. "And that's part of the new phase of theory? You're going to teach *them* how to do that?"

"At one time I was considering it," he said. "I have long since had second thoughts."

But there was still a very scary question that had not been answered. "You didn't say anything when I asked what's going to happen when they find out you're gone. Jesus. Oh, Christ, what am I saying, they must already know! They watch your living quarters constantly."

"They will eventually know, but not just yet. What they are watching on their monitor now is a videotape of me working on circuits. I made a tape for that purpose, simply taping myself while indeed working on circuits. I do not believe they know that I made such a tape. In requesting the recorder, I employed the excuse that it was necessary for testing the system of mirrors associated with the new circuits."

"And you patched the videotape into their--hot damn, you are clever. Makes me proud to know you. Not that I wasn't, already. But sooner or later--"

"Yes," he said. "They will find out, but perhaps not for several hours."

"Oh!" The new realization had hit Anne in the head like a brick, and she felt absolutely stupid for taking this long to have it occur to her. "Oh, shit! Excuse my language."

"Such colorful expressions are not unknown to me," the Crewman said.

"They're hearing this!" she whispered, knowing as soon as she did it that it was useless to whisper; the audio surveillance of her house was bound to be supersensitive, and was in any event something she had always taken for granted, trying not to think about it, and not ever giving anybody anything juicy to hear. "They'll be--"

"Please rest your mind, Anne," the Crewman said. "You people would say, 'Give me a little credit,' I believe the expression is. I have taken care of the 'bug,' as you call them. It was easy to detect and disable. That is what I was doing when still in my metal-foil cover; it was just a question of reaching out of the cover with one arm, after reintegration, and scanning the room--my intuition was correct that the kitchen would be the right room, but I could have found it anywhere--and then intercepting the signal with a wave pattern absorption from that." He pointed to a little device on the floor in the corner, something that looked a bit like a cluster of tiny hectic-looking umbrellas fused into a sort of bizarre metal flower. "All they will hear now is dead air. My hope is that they assume you have simply fallen asleep, hence the silence. Since the teleportation circuitry has functioned as intended, I am trusting that my other devices are working as well. This, despite my having made them from inferior metals. As I believe you know, your metallurgists have still not succeeded in alloying or reproducing any of *our* metals."

"I know," she said. "But now what are we going to--"

The doorbell was ringing.

"Oh, God," she said, reaching across the table and taking the Crewman's dry, leathery little hand. "God in heaven. What if it's them?"

"I do not believe they would ring the doorbell," he said.

"I hope to Christ not," she said, and went down the hall and across the living room to answer the door. She thought she knew, on reflection, who it must be, and experienced a relief beyond anything in her recollection when she turned out to be right.

"Eric," she said, and whisked him inside off the porch and closed and locked the door again. She kissed him, held him for a moment, then pushed herself back to look him full in the face. "Wait till you see the surprise I have for *you*. C'mon. Hurry up."

She led him back down the hall and into the kitchen, and just stood and enjoyed the pageantry of expressions that crossed his face: shock, incredulity, amazement, fascination. She had been with the Crewman for so many years now that she could hardly remember, or imagine, what it must be like for a human being to see him for the first time. Eric's face at first was nearly the color of chalk, and she saw him start to speak, then swallow, then start to speak again, and finally just keep silent, while some color slowly crept back into his face.

"This is my friend Eric Hayes. Eric, meet the Crewman."

It was the first time, in all these years, she had actually introduced her alien friend to anyone, in any respectable sense of the term. Usually the government types that dealt with him just barged in, stared at him for a while as if he were an exhibit in a freak show, and started dealing with him with no amenities. If she had anything to say about it, those assholes were never going to get their hands on her friend again.

But *would* she have anything to say about it? Would she even live out the night, if they found out what had happened?

"He, ah, teleported himself here," she told Eric. "A little trick I don't think anybody has ever suspected he could pull off."

Eric just nodded, and didn't seem to be able to take his eyes off the little creature who sat at the kitchen table. At length he went over and sat down at the table himself, as did Anne.

Suddenly she was taken with the conviction that there was no more time to lose.

"What are we going to do now?" She just threw the question out on the air, addressed equally to Eric and to the Crewman, and to herself for that matter. She had the feeling that they might probably just as well spend the evening picking out coffins.

Eric finally got his voice back, and addressed the Crewman. "You, ah--" Anne felt a little embarrassed for Eric, but a little amused as well, because she knew how he must feel. The first time one spoke to an alien would likely be something remembered forever, and it wasn't easy to do. "You must have had a plan in mind yourself," he said, "coming here."

"Yes," the Crewman said. This, Anne reflected, was the first time Eric had heard him speak, and she saw him start a little. There was something about the reedy little alien voice that would strike any sensitive person that way at first. "Yes, I have a sort of plan. As I am sure you will readily agree, we cannot remain here for long."

"I'll say," Anne said, and suddenly had yet another unsettling realization. "Eric, he disabled the bug they monitor my house with, so that they'll just get dead air. But if they were watching when you came to the door, they're going to wonder why they haven't heard us talking."

Eric considered this for a moment and shrugged, a little hint of a smile creeping into his face. "Maybe they'll think we're--"

"Eric!" she said, not able to keep from grinning, herself. "We have company."

The Crewman's face was inscrutable as always, and he said: "*W'hle-'ng-fta-m'ft, r'sfweh-na.*"

Anne felt the smile widen on her face, and glanced sidelong at Eric. "It's untranslatable," she said. But the Crewman followed it up with a jolt of mental impression that enhanced the meaning, and in the "something like" mode in which translation of L-1 always had to function, the meaning was something like: I share an understanding of the joy that your thoughts of lovemaking bring. But it was a little explosion of harmoniousness whose real nature went far beyond that, deep in the nervous system, and Anne could see that Eric had received it too, wordlessly, and with no need for words. His face was like that of a child seeing some incomprehensible wonder for the first time.

"But I digress," the Crewman said. "Those whom you fear could come down upon us at any time. You are in danger. Even I am in danger. There is a place we must go. A very special place in the desert. I will be, to use your term, teleporting myself and the equipment there. The place is a number of miles away, just about at the limit of possibility for these simple devices. And, unfortunately, the scope of my circuitry is limited; I cannot teleport you two there as well. You will have to get there your own way. As quickly as possible."

"Where is this place?" Anne asked.

"It is near the place you call Three Rivers, where you recently were. About two miles to the west of the hill, out in the desert plain, there is a large--" He paused. "A large arroyo. That is the Spanish word, is it not? A long, dry riverbed with high walls of sand. This is where we must all go."

"Why?" Anne asked. "Why there?"

"It is a very special place," the Crewman said again. "A place where we may hope to find--resolution."

"I don't understand," Anne said, "but if you say so, I believe you."

The Crewman nodded, and got up from the table and began arranging his devices around and inside the metal-foil pod or cowl from which he had been emerging when Anne discovered him earlier. "I wish to lose as little time as possible. While I am able to breathe your unadjusted atmosphere for a few days with no ill effects, I will eventually experience some discomfort from it. I am not so young as I once was, you know." He paused, and in the interval Anne felt that inimitable little tingle of alien humor in her mind, and wondered if Eric felt it too. "I will allow the bugging device to operate again now," the Crewman said. "This may be to our advantage, if those who are listening can hear you moving around and talking. They may think that everything is normal. Be careful what you say."

He took up the little device in the corner and did something to it. Anne understood that from that moment on, everything they said would be overheard.

But there wasn't anything else to say. The Crewman slipped inside the pod. A peculiar medley of faint sounds arose, and the pod and surrounding objects grew grainy-looking, then simply vanished.

It was very quiet then.

181

"I'll be God damned," Eric said.

"Don't tell me," Anne said, pointing to the walls as if to say they had ears. "I bet you've never done it *that* way before."

# # # #

When they were headed out of town in Eric's car, he suddenly turned to her. "Isn't that Fall Festival still going on, down in Las Cruces?"

She wondered if this was just some empty talk he was providing for the benefit of the bug that must be here too. "Yes," she said. "I think so. I think it runs right through to the end of the month. Why?"

"I was just wondering," he said, then winked at her, not smiling. "I thought we might get down there to see it sometime, before it's over."

But she could tell he had something more in mind. She wasn't about to ask what. He pulled the car over at a little carry-out store on the edge of town, got out, stepped up to the pay phone at the edge of the parking area, and seemed to be making several calls. Then he went into the store, stayed only a couple of minutes, and came out with a little paper bag. When he got back in the car, he handed the bag to her. She still resisted asking him anything, and they drove off to the north, up Route 54.

"Did you have any dinner?" he asked.

"Just a snack," she said.

"Ah. I didn't get around to eating anything myself. I picked up a couple of sandwiches and some potato chips and Coke back there."

"Another great American meal in the making," she said, laughing, though she scarcely knew whether she felt like laughing or crying or shouting or what. She had more time to think now, and she was beginning to realize that she was scared.

At one point Eric reached across, opened the glove compartment, fumbled around for a minute, and brought out a flare gun. "Mm," he said, evidently glad to verify that it was there, and tucked it into his jacket pocket. Then while they nibbled at the sandwiches he started talking in a rambling way about his work with the petroglyphs, his sabbatical from the college, and other things, no doubt for the entertainment of the inevitable listeners.

And he drove on into the desert night, through Tularosa, toward Three Rivers.

Anne wondered whether anyone knew yet that the Crewman was missing.

Whatever the hell was happening, she thought, it was going to have to turn out to be a very interesting night.

She hoped they all survived it.

25

The Coyote

Route 380 across the middle of New Mexico was a lonely road, stretching through infinite expanses of sage-dotted desert under a turquoise sky that was painted with a great billow of cotton-white cloud to the north. They had met practically no other cars all afternoon, and that seemed to suit the man who called himself Roger just fine. He drove with an expressionless concentration on the road, scarcely bothering to glance at her. She just sat with her thoughts, her anger, her fears, and watched the road slip beneath the car like an endless ribbon of reflected sunlight. Her head hurt, and she thought she had a little trickle of blood starting again from her nose, but she didn't want even to put her hand up to her face, for fear of extracting some remark from the strange and frightful man who drove the car. She also resisted the temptation to look at her watch, because she feared that he would make some caustic remark--"Am I keeping you? Is there something else you needed to be doing?"--and she didn't want to exchange any conversation with him at all, if she could help it. It must have been at least three o'clock when he finally broke the silence.

"Did you really think you were going to get away with it?"

The remark, on reflection, stunned her. "Get away with it? *Me* get away with it? Get away with what? Seems to me *you're* the one who's getting away with something."

"Huh," he snorted. "You know goddamn well what I'm talking about. I'm talking about you running. Running away with a highly classified piece of stolen government property. Did you really think you'd get away?"

She mulled this over. "Frankly, yes, I did think I'd get away."

He laughed, a short, barklike, unpleasant sound. "Then you underestimate us just a bit, wouldn't you say? Let me tell you something." He appeared to be collecting his thoughts. "I shouldn't tell you this, but I will, because it won't make any difference now. We've gone to great trouble to keep the Roswell matter secret. More trouble than you could ever imagine. This has been no ordinary coverup. This has been a coördinated work of art. A masterful project stretching over half a century." He seemed to settle into his posture at the wheel, as if making ready for an extended tale-telling.

"It started with President Truman. He agreed readily enough that the event must be kept from becoming common knowledge, though he didn't expect it to remain classified forever. My predecessors had trouble, though, even back then. Do you remember the name James Forrestal?"

She shrugged. "Vaguely."

"He was Secretary of the Navy from May 1944 to July 1947, and then he became the first Secretary of Defense, under Truman, and resigned after two years, under pressure. Secretary Forrestal knew all about Roswell. Shortly after his resignation, he was admitted to the Naval Hospital at Bethesda, suffering from severe depression. He had been collecting notes to write his memoirs at the time, and there was reason to believe he was planning to reveal classified information about the Roswell incident. However, he ended up committing suicide first."

"Suicide," Lucy said.

"He jumped from a sixteenth-floor kitchen window, at the hospital."

"Jumped. Right."

"After that, things went fairly smoothly, on into the Eisenhower years. Ike knew all about Roswell. Knew, and understood the importance of keeping it classified. The next trouble we had was with John Kennedy."

Lucy's stomach felt as if it wanted to turn over. "Are you telling me--"

"The Kennedy mentality was a problem. You know, the image of the straightforward and popular President, close to the people and all that horseshit. When he learned the basic facts about Roswell, he made it very clear, internally, that he thought the American people had a right to know, and that he was of a mind to declassify everything. We couldn't let him do that."

"So your people--"

"You have to understand that when I say 'we' in this case I mean my predecessors. I wasn't in government service yet. I was eighteen years old. Let's just say that our people were content, all things

184

considered, with the way things turned out in Dallas in November of 1963," Roger said.

"Jesus," Lucy said. It came out in a whisper.

"Then you may recall that Jimmy Carter during his campaign made some remarks to the effect that when he was elected President, he wanted to declassify all UFO-related documents. After his election we persuaded him that that wouldn't be a terribly smart thing to do. So you see, Lucy, from this perspective it's bound to strike me as a little odd that you thought *you* could get away with running around the New Mexico desert with a piece of alien debris."

"Right," Lucy said. "Silly old me."

They lapsed into silence. After a while, the landscape turned from sandy to rocky, and on both sides of the road vistas of brown lava stretched away to the horizon; they were driving through the Malpais Lava Flow, and for several miles it felt and looked like being on the moon. Ordinarily she would have found this scene bleakly beautiful, but in her present mood she found it only bleak.

It was at least the right mood in which to ask: "Who the hell *are* you people, the CIA or what?"

Roger chuckled, without smiling. "The CIA? Christ, little girl, you watch too much television. The organizations in government that really work are structures that most people don't know exist, structures that a lot of people in *government* don't know exist, or hear only vague rumors of. Even in Washington most people have neither the clearance nor the need to know. And if they don't have those two things, they don't find out."

The question she was going to ask, she had once asked her mother, twenty years ago, walking in the park in Wichita Falls: *What's the big deal, Mom, about a piece of--* But of course she remembered, too, what her mom had been saying, about Dad's experience when he'd been stationed at Roswell: *He saw them bringing in a little man.* Seventeen-year-old Lucy had asked: *A midget?* And her mother had said: *No, dear. A little creature something like a man.* And in answer to her question concerning what the big deal was, about a piece of foil: *It's a big deal because the government is keeping it all secret and they can't afford to have anything like that sitting around, because it's evidence that they've been lying to everyone.* Presumably the man beside her had no idea that she knew this much. What would he say if she asked:

"So why is a piece of foil all that important? You're telling me it'd be the end of the world as we know it, or some such God damn thing, if everybody knew you people had some alien debris?"

185

He waiting a good while before letting a long breath out and answering succinctly: "It isn't that simple."

"Anyway, it's all just a game to you," she said. "Move a pawn here, move a pawn there--"

"Lady," he said, "a game can be damned serious. Ask any chess master."

He volunteered no further remarks, and they rode on through the midst of the barren and lonely lava fields in silence. One thing was very clear to Lucy, a cold realization that she felt settle in the pit of her stomach like a stone: that she was history. Unwritten history at that. She most certainly didn't have--what were the two things he said?--the clearance and the need to know. He wouldn't be telling her the things he had told her, if he had the least intention of letting her live.

An earlier realization came back to her too, and she turned toward him. "You came into the bookshop the other day, didn't you?"

"That I did."

"You even bought something. I can almost remember what it was."

"It was a paperback copy of *Titus Andronicus*," he said.

"I see." She turned back to face the oncoming road. "Makes me wonder," she said.

"Wonder what?"

She cast a glance at him. "How a man can read Shakespeare and be intelligent and well educated and still be such an asshole."

"Ah, as Marcus Antonius says, this was the most unkindest cut of all."

"Save it," she said. "I'm not impressed."

They rode on through the wilderness of lava, not speaking.

She had noticed, some time before, that on the floor in the space between the driver's seat and the passenger seat Roger kept an object that looked like some kind of communication device; it appeared to be enclosed in a case of some hard black plastic and was about the size of a bowling ball, but cube-shaped, and had a TV or computer screen, a number of switches and controls, a tiny keyboard, and a telephone-type receiver on the side, together with what looked like some sort of power supply or battery pack strapped to it. And about the time they were emerging from the lava flow into ordinary desert terrain again, a little orange light beside the receiver came alive, with a faint buzzing sound, and Roger hoisted the whole device onto his lap and picked up the receiver.

"Yes."

He listened for several seconds. "All right, Blake. I'm not surprised, considering how you've been pissing away every chance you've had to do something right. No sign of him at all?" Pause. "What about Hawk and the boyfriend?" Pause. "All right. Maintain the audio surveillance at the hill as long as they're there, and you pull in the rest of your men and get on back to Alamogordo. I'm taking personal charge of the search and setting a meeting up for tonight. Nine o'clock. You know where. Bring your ass, because you're going to get it chewed in spectacular fashion."

He hung the receiver back in its cradle, and was lifting the whole unit, in one hand like a bowling ball, back up over the steering wheel to set it back down, when something happened.

Out in front of them, only a few yards away, a coyote ran into the road.

He was directly in front of the car, and not making much haste to get out of the way. Roger had apparently looked down for a minute while fumbling with the communication unit, and looked up and saw the coyote only when it was nearly too late to react at all. His reaction could only have been automatic.

He slammed the brakes on, hard.

The rear of the car slewed wildly around to the right, and the vehicle skidded sideways in its forward momentum and screeched to a stop. It all happened so fast that Lucy had to reconstruct it in her mind later. Roger's seatbelt would have kept his head from hitting the steering wheel in any event, but he had been holding the communication unit between the steering wheel and his head, and when he lurched forward she grabbed the unit and slammed him in the head with it, hard. Her mind registered a sickening crunch that might have been the unit's casing or Roger's skull, or both. The instrument panel was spraypainted with blood, and Roger hung forward in his seatbelt like a red-faced rag doll in a sling. The car's engine had died. No cars were coming from either direction. Silence settled in like a shroud.

Lucy's seatbelt had held, so she was unhurt but she felt dazed, and it took her a few moments to realize what she had to do.

She reached across Roger's inert form, unlocked his door, and pushed it open. When she moved the communication unit onto the floor, Roger's head lolled a little farther forward, his mouth and nose drooling a sticky little web of blood down his front. She pulled his seatbelt up and off. After considerable puffing and straining, she managed to push him out the door onto the road, where he fell like a pile of dirty laundry. She climbed over into the driver's seat and tried to start the car.

It wouldn't start.

187

She tried again. She cranked it and cranked it, but no luck. God! She thought this kind of thing only happened in the movies. And in her mind's eye she had a terrible vision of Roger, lying out there on the road, Roger opening his eyes, Roger getting up. . . . But when she looked, he hadn't moved.

She got out of the car, stepping over Roger and leaving the door hanging open. Leaning back in, she pushed the seat forward and reached in the back and retrieved the canvas bag. On an impulse she took the communication unit off the floor in front where she had dropped it. Moving some things around to make a little room, she stuffed the unit into the canvas bag. She gave Roger, bloody-faced and crumpled and unmoving, only a glance before hoisting the bag onto her shoulder and running.

She had gotten only a few yards down the road in the direction they had been going, before realizing that if he was alive back there and came to, the first thing he would expect her to do would be to stay on the road, and she was damned if she was going to let him get his hands on her a second time.

She plunged off the road to the right and started running through the chaparral. Even here, traces of the nearby lava fields lingered as occasional extrusions or scatterings of brownish-gray porous stone, very dangerous--a twisted ankle out here, right now, and it could be all over for her. Dodging among the stones, she ran on, with limitless vistas of baked-yellow desert plain all around her and a vast dome of deep blue sky above her and the sun beginning to wester. From what she knew of the road and from the position of the sun above and slightly to her right, she figured she was running roughly south, maybe a little south-southwest. If it mattered.

After a time she had to fetch up somewhere out on the sandy plain and catch her breath, and standing still, she noticed something that she had not seen while running.

There was a coyote far out in front of her, trotting along in the same direction she was going, maybe a hundred yards off.

She tried to harvest any memories she might have about coyotes. Were they vicious? Rabid? Likely to attack humans? She didn't know, didn't know, couldn't remember anything about them.

But there was certainly something remarkable about this particular coyote. He was just a moving speck among the sagebrush and creosote bushes, far out there in the chaparral, but she saw what she saw.

The coyote stopped, turned around and looked at her, ran on for a few paces, and stopped and turned around to look at her again.

It was very much as if he wanted her to follow him.

That was crazy, of course.

Nevertheless, when she had caught her breath somewhat, she hauled the bag more firmly onto her shoulder by the strap and started running again--in the direction of the coyote. Her thoughts kept flashing back to the scene at the car--to Roger, injured and bloody but perhaps still alive, perhaps about to come around, sure to come after her when he did--and she picked up her pace, loping across the sand with a desperation she had never felt in her life, an urgency to get far, far away, yet a tormented sense of moving too slowly, like the lethargic paralysis of a nightmare, where you have to run faster, faster, but you can't do it to save your life. She wasn't in as good a physical shape as she would have wished, and before long she was going to have to stop again, but not now, it couldn't be now, she had to wait till she was well away from the road. She ran on, her lungs aching, her free arm going up to clutch her ribcage. Somewhere far up ahead, the coyote trotted on, turning from time to time to look at her with its inscrutable wedge of face.

She wouldn't stop, not yet. After a while, when she turned around to look behind her, trying to see the car back there, she could sometimes see a distant point of reflected sunlight and sometimes not, depending on the terrain, which was uneven to the point of being treacherous. She couldn't very well watch where she was running and keep looking back too, but she thought that she had gotten a considerable distance from the road, maybe far enough away so that if he woke up now he wouldn't be sure right away which direction she had taken.

Or had she left tracks? Dear God, what if he came after her now? In very little time she would be reduced to utter exhaustion, and if he was coming, back there somewhere, he would be upon her, and no helping it. She had to keep moving.

Far ahead, the coyote paused, turned to look at her again, and went running on.

She followed him. It was insane, but she felt somehow that she *should* follow him.

A terrible thought came to her. If Roger did wake up and did figure out which way she had gone, could he *drive* across this terrain? It was rock-strewn and bumpy, but a person might just be able to manage it. A determined person. A person with a mission. Damn, she should have taken his keys--but it wouldn't have mattered, he would know how to start the car without them. The thought of a gray Ford bumping along the ground behind her, coming closer every second, filled her with such terror that she sucked painful air into her lungs and ran even faster.

But after maybe half an hour she simply couldn't move any more, and stopped, and let the bag drop with a thud in the sand, and collapsed beside it. Her lungs were exploding, and she felt nauseous. She dimly noticed that out on the plain, just about at the limit of vision, the coyote stopped. Let him, let him stop or go on or whatever, she couldn't help what happened. She had to rest. By the time she had caught her breath and remembered to look at her watch, it was nearly half past five. The sun would have finished setting before long, and the desert plain would get chilly; she hoped the jacket she had on would be warm enough. Five-thirty; what time had the accident happened back there on the road? Around four? In any event, she must at the very least have gotten far enough away by now that he wouldn't be able to see her from the road, if he was conscious. She realized that she should have checked his pulse, before running away, to see if maybe he was dead.

She realized something else too, with a sickening sense of possibly having made a truly fatal blunder. Never mind his car keys--she should have taken his gun. Damn!

Standing up, she looked back in the direction of the road, but could see only an unbroken vastness of desert.

Out in the distance, the coyote had curled up and sat down, like a dog, and appeared to be watching her.

She dug a can of soda out of the canvas bag, popped the top, and took a swallow, finding that she was so parched that the carbonated liquid burned her throat on its way down. But God, it tasted good, better than anything she'd ever tasted in her life. The nausea she thought she had felt before had mostly subsided, but she had to drink the soda slowly nonetheless, and finished it and tucked the empty can into the canvas bag before getting up, hauling the bag back onto her shoulder, and starting off again, walking this time. She just couldn't run any more.

Across the way, the coyote, looking back at her once again, got up and began walking away too.

What followed was a seemingly endless dream of walking, walking, walking through the sameness of mile after monotonous mile of sagebrush and sand. At times she felt as if the sandy plain beneath her feet were a great inclined ramp tilted upward, so that every step was a transgression against gravity, but at other times the ramp seemed to tilt downward, precipitating her into a giddy, stumbling, headlong fall through dreamscapes of sage and sand where occasional cacti nudged their comic heads up as if in defiance of the elements. She walked without being entirely conscious that she was doing so, and with only a vague tendency to notice that out ahead of her the coyote walked too, turning from time to time to beckon her, or so it seemed. She followed, plodding on through the sand without any notion of where she was going, or why.

Her face seemed to burn beneath a pasty coating of dust and sweat. Even now, late in October, the sands, though cooling, retained a residuum of warmth from the day's onslaught of the desert sun; she could feel the remaining heat radiating up into her face, if this was not just the flush of her agitation. Late October, the autumn of the year, and the autumn of my life, too, perhaps, she thought. She was uncertain whether to welcome the sunset or dread the coming dark.

At one point she paused and listened, thinking she had heard something far off toward the east, a sound like the faint grumble of a car starting and driving off. After a few minutes she heard it again, or something like it, and thought she could make out a faint haze of dust in the direction of the sound, but she couldn't be sure, because the daylight was going.

For one heart-stopping moment she entertained the notion that maybe the sound of the car had been *behind* her. She looked back, but could see nothing but gently undulating miles of yellow-brown chaparral stretching away in the fading light like a great dry ocean.

By the time it was indeed getting dark she saw, ahead some few miles perhaps--distance in the desert was always hard to judge--a low rocky hill or group of hills off to the left, humped above the desert like some great dormant creature stirring itself to see who was coming. What was it Roger had said, talking to whoever he was talking to? *Maintain the audio surveillance at the hill.* . . . What did that mean? Maybe that there would be people out here. *Those* people. And who were "Hawk and the boyfriend"? In any case she would have to watch herself. Maybe she should stop here and wait and try to think what to do.

But out ahead of her, at a shorter distance now because he had let her catch up somewhat, the coyote had stopped at the mouth of an arroyo and was watching her. He moved forward a pace or two, into the arroyo, and stopped and turned to gaze at her again. From here, she could almost see his eyes, and however crazy it might be, she felt sure now that he wanted her to follow him, had wanted her to all along, with a kind of calculating sense of urging her on behind him, drawing her across the desert.

All the way from the road, where he had run in front of the car.

Before going on, she set the canvas bag down and looked at her watch again. It was almost half past seven. She did some rough calculation, considering her usual walking pace, and figured she might have come something like ten or twelve miles. She didn't think she had ever walked, all at one time, twelve miles in her life. Somehow the thought kindled a little ember of pride inside her, a refreshing alternative to the fears that threatened to keep nibbling around the edges of her mind if she let them. But she couldn't afford to get too confident, considering the trouble it had gotten her into this morning, back in Albuquerque. Shouldering the bag again, she hobbled the remaining distance to the arroyo, watching the coyote recede into its walled depths ahead of her.

When she entered the arroyo herself, she began to have the strangest feeling.

"This is a special place," she said aloud.

Why she had said that, she had no notion. But the feeling persisted as she walked on, seeing the dirt walls of the arroyo rise canyonlike on both sides of her until they formed a dark, narrow passage ahead, a well of blackness that only lightened a little when the moon crept up to send an exploratory hint of bony light feeling its way down the sandy walls like tentative fingers. Somewhere ahead of her, she thought she glimpsed the coyote, padding on deeper into the arroyo.

It seemed incredible to her, how far into the desert plain this dry riverbed cut its path, twisting, fragmenting, branching. At times she was conscious only of how much her feet hurt, and would lose her sense of where the main course of the riverbed ran, and would wander into blind cul-de-sacs walled with root-twisted sand, and have to back out again and get her bearings. But always, far ahead in the shadows, the coyote dimly moved through the arroyo, seeming to pause to let her follow him.

At length she came to a sort of concourse where branchings of the arroyo became so numerous that no particular direction felt like the right one, a place where, punctuating the high walls, forks of the riverbed radiated off into unthinkable distance like spokes of a great wheel. Here she stopped, because she could see the coyote no more, and had no idea where to go. She dropped the canvas bag to the sand and sat down beside it and watched the chalky moon nibble its way along the top of one of the arroyo walls like some benign grazing beast. Silence welled up around her like an ocean of shadows, and she sat and waited.

At least it was peaceful here. It might not even be a bad place to die.

She rummaged in the canvas bag and brought out a package of dried beef strips and a package of crackers and another can of soda, and had her dinner. It was perhaps the loneliest dinner she had ever eaten. She wasn't as hungry as she would have thought, but she ate anyway, thinking that whatever happened, she was going to need her strength. Assuming nobody followed her and found her, she was no doubt going to be spending the rest of the night here.

And then what? She couldn't imagine. Today had been a day she wouldn't have been able to imagine yesterday, and at this point she couldn't envision a tomorrow of any kind at all.

Wiping at her face with her hand, she suddenly felt very grimy after her trek across the sands, and thought a change into fresh clothes would make her feel better. She slipped out of her shoes, peeled off her pants and socks and top, and took off her panties and bra. For a few moments, she stood there nude under a black desert sky encrusted with cold stars, and felt oddly--*fulfilled.* At first she had thought that a bath would have been nice, in addition to clean clothes, as she could smell dusty sweat drying on her body, but that didn't bother her now--in a way, it was ennobling. It was natural, it was wholesome. It was good. Somehow she felt more a *woman* now than she had at any time in her life, in this primal awareness of her sweating naked body out here under the dome of desert sky, her skin caressed by the cool night air and by a wan wash of ivory moonlight that came by stealth into the arroyo. Her sweat was honest sweat, the frank, unapologetic smell of a person running from evil.

Running toward freedom.

The wind rose on the plain above the arroyo in a faint soughing, like someone whispering nameless fingers of air over the windy stops of a flute. Playing *her,* making a sublime kind of love to her. The night, the icy stars, the desert made love to her, to the flute-tones of the wind. It was like her own thought, set to ancient music: running to freedom. She had bared her mind to the desert just as surely as she had bared her body. This was indeed a special place, a magical place, and right now, tonight, she belonged here.

Somewhere in the darkness a night owl hoo-hooed, then all was silent reverie again.

At length she pulled clean clothes out of the bag and put them on. Stretching out on the sand with the canvas bag as a pillow, her knees up at an angle, her face toward the stars that frosted the sky, she thought about Roger, about whoever these other people were, the surveillance people or whatever. Despite everything, she almost laughed out loud, the thought struck her with such force: little boys. Little boys with their pathetic little-boy games. Even the highest people in government-secrecy circles, just pouty-faced, snot-nosed little boys with infantile enthusiasms they had never outgrown, strident little brats who had never emotionally progressed much beyond the saliva-spewing *vrrrroom-vrrrroom* of toy cars and the sweaty head-banging acquisitiveness of the sandbox. Power-mad children and their cowshit imbecile games. *A game can be damned serious,* he had said: *ask any chess master.* Well, Mister Roger, at any age, truculent little boys and their little-boy war games can be damned contemptible. Just ask any woman.

Even a lonely, scared woman. Because now that the epiphany of standing nude under the stars had passed, it was going to be lonely out here tonight, lonely and scary.

From somewhere she seemed to hear a faint burring sound, like an angry insect, and it took her a few seconds to realize that it was coming from inside the canvas bag. She fished through the odd assortment of cellophane wrappers and dirty clothes near the top of the bag and pulled out Roger's rather badly cracked communication unit, whose call indicator was blinking and buzzing. Walking over and placing the unit on a stone at the base of the arroyo wall nearest her, she picked up another good-sized stone and smashed it down on the unit. It took two times for the blinking and buzzing to stop.

"I'm sorry," she said to the dead unit, and to the air around her. "Mr. Roger is busy bleeding on the highway and can't come to the phone right now. If you'll leave a brief message, he'll get back to you as soon as possible." Idly, she wondered why someone was calling her erstwhile traveling companion. Then again, maybe it was better not to know.

The thought had barely formed, when something happened, off to her left, maybe twenty feet away, between her improvised bed in the middle of the sandy arroyo floor and the near-vertical wall to the left.

She wasn't sure what her senses were telling her.

It was as if the sand whispered and stirred ever so slightly, almost as if in anticipation of some disturbance rather than in reaction to it, since so far as she could see, nothing was happening to disturb it. But then in the next instant something was happening, after all. Her mind couldn't seem to grasp exactly what it was. In the uncertain light it was as if the air currents over there, above the subtly shifting sand, were thickening, growing somehow more palpable than the surrounding dark. The impression suddenly became irresistibly strong that *something was gathering itself together, moving, taking form, in the space before her.*

By the time she started making sense out of the impression, the feeling of gathering, of motion, had passed. She rubbed her eyes and peered across the wanly moonlit space, to see a nondescript configuration of what looked like metal, something like a pod of aluminum foil with other silvery things clustered close to it.

And something, something small and agile, was crawling out of the pod and raising its impossible little self to a standing posture in the moonlight.

It stood perhaps four feet tall, a willowy figure either attired in a leathery, clinging suit of some sort, or possessing thin, leathery skin. Its bulbous head, rather too large for its body, nodded on a fragile-looking stalk of neck, and it blinked two large dark almond-shaped eyes at her and held up a thin little hand, which had four fingers and no thumb.

She distinctly felt the hair prickle up on the back of her neck.

The creature spoke to her, then, in a voice whose spectral and unplaceable tones made her catch her breath, yet somehow calmed her too, as if, in the very archetypes of its eerie timbre and rhythm, it spoke some long-awaited comfort to the cells deep within her being, connecting to her, touching her bones, her soul, with gentle fingers of sound.

"Don't be afraid," the voice said, and she suddenly knew, with a strange certainty, that her father had once looked into this same face. When she burst into tears at this realization, the little creature took slow, spidery steps across the sand to close the distance between them, and took her hand.

26

Flute Song

Eric's car bumped its way onto the turnoff that led to the parking area for the petroglyph site, the headlights cutting through the night like scissor blades separating sage from sage, chamisa from chamisa. For some time he had been driving, Anne noticed, with one eye on the rear view mirror, and she knew they were thinking the same thing: back there in the dark on the main road a surveillance team would be shadowing them, both to stay in range of the car and, in all probability, to set up a rifle mike to try to listen in on them yet again, once they were out of the car. But evidently Eric had been mulling that scenario over, and had come to the same conclusion she had, because even though they had no intention of climbing the path to the hill as before, he pulled into the parking area and shut the engine off, motioning for her to lose no time in getting out of the car.

Once they were out, she didn't have to wonder what they were going to do. Clearly Eric had parked here to make the surveillance team assume, incorrectly, when it arrived behind them, that they had gone on up the hill. But two things about this bothered Anne.

One was: weren't the operatives following them going to be asking themselves why Anne and Eric were back up here, when they had only left the site a little over three hours ago? Nobody could be *that* damned much in love with petroglyphs. They were sure to wonder. Maybe that was good--it might give them things to think about: the *wrong* things. But they were going to get suspicious before long anyway, because they weren't going to be hearing anything from the hill. Nobody was going to be up there.

The second question Anne's mind was nagging her with: if that team is coming along behind us, aren't we going to have to haul some

196

fairly serious ass to get out of sight before they get here? But she could tell Eric had been pondering that one too, because he was pulling her along by the arm, and they were sprinting away, back across the main road, away from the site. On the other side of the road they plunged into the westward chaparral and started across the desert at a run.

Just in time, too. Far off to their left, a car had come up, slowed nearly to a stop, killed the lights, and turned off the road into the same westward chaparral a couple of hundred yards south of them. Whoever was driving had no doubt spotted Eric's car parked over at the base of the hill and, sure enough, they were going to set up an audio surveillance of the petroglyph site, here on the plain west of the hill, and were trying to get off the road far enough short of the site not to attract notice.

Trouble was, it was getting damned crowded out here, for a desert.

Nudging Eric, Anne pointed toward the car, which was trundling a dusty path through the sagebrush off across the way, roughly paralleling their own track. Eric nodded, and both of them ducked low and concentrated on moving forward with as low a profile as possible. The ground was somewhat uneven, and off where the car was headed there was a kind of ridge jutting off the desert floor, so if things worked the way Anne hoped they would--

And they did: the car eased around behind the ridge, looking, in the pale moonlight, for all the world like a disgruntled armadillo scuttling away in a drowse of unsettled dust. At least this put the ridge in between, and she and Eric straightened back up and ran flat out, while they could. They both knew that whoever was in the car wouldn't want to stay there, behind the ridge, for long; they would be anxious to get out and set up surveillance. Anne and Eric had managed to run another hundred feet or so by the time she spotted two distant figures emerging from the dusky cover of the ridge. One was carrying something shaped like a rifle. She pulled at Eric's arm, and they both dropped behind a cluster of chamisa and waited, catching their breath.

God, Anne thought--what if they see the dust we've stirred up? She looked behind, but couldn't imagine how much of a dust cloud might be visible from over by the ridge. There *would* have to be a big bright gibbous moon! She would have given anything she owned, just now, for a cover of darkness. Whatever dust was floating in the moonlight, she and Eric could do absolutely nothing to keep the people across the way from seeing it, and that was a terrible feeling. It was just a surveillance team over there--she hoped--but that was bad enough. They didn't need the company of any government types right now.

And for the first time, with this reflection, she realized that she had fully accepted the idea that she was no longer a government type herself.

Across by the ridge, the two figures had dropped out of sight.

Eric shook her arm and pointed out ahead, and they took off at a fast walk, trying to keep low and not make any noise or raise any more dust than they could help. To the right, the ground dropped off a little, then rose again, and they followed this lower contour, hoping that it would keep them out of sight. The Crewman had said that the place to which they were headed, a large arroyo, was about two miles west, and Anne figured it would take at least half an hour--*if* they could find it at all.

After a few minutes they felt justified in straightening up and running full tilt. As they darted through the sand and the brush, Anne stole an occasional glance at Eric's face in the milky moonlight, and wondered how he must be feeling about all this. At least *she* had had years to get used to the whole idea of the Crewman, the whole idea of frightful levels of government secrecy and the outrageous extent to which her superiors would go to maintain it. To Eric, all of this was a stark new reality, and his whole world must have changed radically in the past two days. But his face revealed only an earnest desire to move forward and do whatever it was they had to do.

After a while they stopped and sat in the cool sand for a few minutes to catch their breath again. Anne's lungs and ribcage ached, and she gathered that Eric was finding himself pretty thoroughly winded too. The hill was still in sight behind them, because it would stand visible above the level of the desert for many miles around, and it made it seem as if they hadn't come very far for their effort, but at least the ridge where they had seen the car was now lost to view. Out ahead of them, perhaps a hundred feet away, a large crow swooped in a graceful arc in the moonlight and came to a stop in the scraggly upper branches of a mesquite bush. They watched it for a moment, then by wordless consent got to their feet and started forward again, at a trot.

Off across the sandy plain, the crow roused itself and fluttered off toward the west.

The trot turned into a brisk walk, but they didn't stop to rest for another twenty minutes, and when they did, they noticed that the crow, which had been up ahead of them somewhere all the while, stopped too, not quite so far from them this time. After a moment it took to the air with a raucous *caw-caw*, wheeled, and settled back down again. Anne could have sworn that it was looking back at them with a kind of impatience, as if it wanted them to get going again.

As if it wanted them to follow.

They did start off again, and the crow did too, flying in slow, leisurely patterns and never letting them fall very far behind. Sage-dotted sand led on to more sage-dotted sand, and Anne found herself wondering if maybe they had gotten off course and missed their goal altogether. If so, they could conceivably walk for countless miles out here, surrounded by desert expanses that all looked alike.

But at length they came upon the shadow-filled mouth of a large arroyo, where the sides, fairly low at first, gradually angled themselves into tall canyonlike walls of sand and bushy outcroppings and twisted roots of mesquite and cedar. The crow entered the arroyo, and Anne and Eric, running across the remaining distance, followed, but saw no trace of the crow in the shadowy realm inside the arroyo walls, where only scattered shards of moonlight penetrated.

They followed the dry riverbed for what seemed like an interminable distance, not speaking, not knowing what to say. From time to time they wandered into dead-end little blinds or cul-de-sacs etched into one arroyo wall or the other, and had to back out again and find the main track. Once, when they did this, Anne thought she glimpsed the crow again, up ahead in the darkness somewhere, black against black, fluttering around a corner, but she couldn't be sure. They kept to the main rivercourse as well as they could, but the arroyo increasingly branched in wild and jagged bifurcations, making it difficult to know which path to take. Anne was quickly losing her sense of direction here, and thought, from the look on his face when an occasional access of moonlight played across it, that Eric was too. She realized at some point that she had taken his hand, or he had taken hers, and had no idea how long ago or far back it was that they had done so.

At length they came into a sort of sandy concourse, from which various branchings of the arroyo seemed to radiate farther off into the night like roads to unthinkable places. But the place where they stood was unthinkable enough, because they weren't alone.

Not that it surprised Anne to see the Crewman here, since he had said he would transport himself to this spot. What did surprise her was that he had company.

She and Eric walked a few more paces into the little opening. In its center lay a lumpy canvas bag. Beside it, crosslegged in the sand, sat not only the Crewman but a woman with black medium-length hair and dark Hispanic eyes, a woman who appeared roughly the same age as Anne. Off to one side, fugitive wisps of moonlight reflected off a scattering of metal objects, the Crewman's paraphernalia. Some other pieces of it lay on the sand near where the Crewman sat. It appeared that he and the woman beside him had been talking, more like two prospectors meeting in the desert to chat and compare notes, than two beings from different solar systems.

What in the world was going on?

Anne and Eric came across and stood for a moment looking at the two, then sat down in the sand beside them. The woman was dressed in clothing that looked clean, slacks and a plain brown top, but her face was smeared with what was apparently dust and perspiration, possibly mingled with dried blood. She looked physically exhausted, yet there was something in her facial expression that seemed to transcend this exhaustion in a bemused kind of way. She managed a smile.

"My name is Lucy Trujillo."

Eric got half up and leaned over and shook her hand. "I'm Eric Hayes. This is Dr. Anne Hawk."

"I know," Lucy Trujillo said.

# # # #

In the dimly illumined little sandy space, Anne told her story.

Lucy told hers.

The Crewman sat in silence. As did Eric; but unlike the Crewman, Eric's face registered increasing levels of shock as Lucy's story unfolded. Anne supposed her own face did too, but she wasn't entirely surprised by Lucy's tale of horror; it was very much like her employers-- her former employers--to do such things as this woman was relating.

By the time they were done with their stories, it was around ten o'clock; Eric had stood up and held his arm up in the moonlight to read his watch, and seemed to be particularly concerned, all of a sudden, with the time, as if there were something he needed to do.

"They should be here by now," he said.

This took Anne back a couple of paces. "*Who* should be here?"

Some terrible, cobwebbed corner of her mind began entertaining the thought that he meant government operatives.

Which could mean, of course, that he was one of them, had been one of them all along.

Dear God in heaven, she thought, don't let that be true.

If there is any mercy in the universe, please don't let that be true.

From far off in the night, up on the plain outside the arroyo, a sound came grumbling down the winding way of the rivercourse. The sound of a car.

Anne looked into Eric's face, but had only a second to try to read his expression there, because he was up on his feet, fumbling a hand into his jacket pocket and bringing out the flare gun. He pointed it straight up, fired it, and for a few seconds an umbrella of jittery light filled the

200

sky above their heads. Eric sat back down. "That should pretty well show them where we are," he said.

"Show *who*, Eric?" Anne asked. She wasn't at all sure she really wanted to hear his answer. But in that answer, she was instantly ashamed of her suspicions of him.

"I have this friend named Bob Cruz. He's a big TV news anchor in Albuquerque. His station is a CBS affiliate. He did some coverage on my work a couple of years ago when my students and I were doing research out at Chaco Canyon. Bob and his people have been down in Las Cruces this week covering the Fall Festival. He had asked me a couple of weeks ago if I could meet him there for a drink, since I was coming out here anyway on sabbatical, but I never got around to going." He took Anne's hand, seeming to sense that he had given her quite a start. "When we stopped on the way up here I called his hotel in Las Cruces and told him that the news story of all time was waiting for him here. Pulitzer Prize material. I figured if he left right away he'd be about an hour and a half behind us, coming up from Las Cruces. I couldn't tell you about it before. Do you think I did right?"

She squeezed his hand. "Absolutely."

"Well, it's going to be pretty tough driving in here, so I hope their news van is a four-by-four."

It was, apparently. As the sounds of the engine grew closer, wavering little stabs of headlights began crisscrossing the arroyo walls, until finally the van jolted into the opening and stopped, headlights flooding the space with a dusty illumination. The doors came open. A man and a woman emerged from the front seat, another man and another woman from the back. The people from the back were both carrying news cameras, and the woman from the front was carrying a portable floodlight. The remaining man, a jumble of boxes and wires under one arm, stepped across the intervening distance and started to shake Eric's hand.

"Eri--"

He froze.

His eyes were glued to the little creature who sat between Lucy Trujillo and Anne Hawk on the sand beside the canvas bag.

Anne knew how he must feel.

For a full minute the man didn't move a muscle. Didn't even blink. Anne didn't think he was even breathing. He seemed to retain some vestige of newsgathering instinct, though, because after a few moments he made a little circling motion at his side, with the hand he had been extending to Eric, signalling for the cameras to roll. He was evidently too shaken to notice that they were already rolling, both of them.

Anne decided it was time. This had to go right, had to make sense. She stood up, careful not to block either camera's view of the Crewman, and looked into the camera that the woman from the back seat was pointing in her direction. Bob Cruz was hastily untangling wire and shoving a microphone closer to her face.

"My name is Anne Hawk. Until tonight, I worked for an agency of the United States Government so secret that very few people outside its confines even know it exists. Its function has been to keep secret the fact that an alien spacecraft, struck by lightning, crash-landed, during the Fourth of July weekend of 1947, in the desert between Roswell and Corona, New Mexico, about sixty miles northeast of where we are standing right now. Popular rumors have circulated for years, about such a crash. Those rumors are essentially true. Among the crew members aboard the spacecraft there was one survivor, whom the government has kept under wraps for fifty years, and who survives to this day. I am the linguist who has worked with him for the past twelve years. This is that survivor."

She turned toward the Crewman, and the cameras and lights followed her gesture.

The Crewman blinked into the lights, his head slightly nodding. "I am honored," he said, his reedy little voice causing a ripple of shock to spread through the newcomers.

"I'll be God damned and horsewhipped and split open and fucking hung out to dry," Eric's friend Bob Cruz said in a hoarse whisper. *"Dios mío, ¿quién lo hubiera creído?"*

But now something else was happening, something with which Anne was not altogether unfamiliar. A low surge of unplaceable sound was welling up around them, first so faint as scarcely to be audible, then gradually more noticeable, until it rode the air as a subliminal sort of hum underneath the normal sounds.

It was sibilant, like a low sighing of the wind. Or like--

Off near one of the arroyo walls, in the periphery of the lights, a coyote darted along and stopped to look at the people. But the newspeople's eyes were fastened upon the Crewman.

Anne started to continue. "Since July 1947--"

"Stop!"

From behind the van, a man had strode into the edge of the light, and stood between the front of the van and the rear guard of the news crew. The woman with the camera turned and trained it upon him. He was disheveled, dirty, and barely seemed able to stand. His face was caked with blood, and blood had run all down the front of his jacket and pants. He was carrying a gun in his hand.

"Turn those cameras off," he said. The cameras, however, kept rolling.

"Oh, shit," Anne said to Eric. "It's Roger Wynn."

"Who?"

"Roger Wynn. How the hell did he--"

"Well. Well, well," the newcomer said, for the moment ignoring the camera crew and stepping around them to come closer to Anne and Eric. The woman with the camera followed him around. "I saw your flare. Quite a little party we've got going here. Are any of you people really stupid enough to think you're going to get away with this?"

"As I started to say," Anne resumed, "since July 1947 the government has engaged in the most ambitious coverup in the history of the world. It has employed lies, threats--"

"One more word," Roger Wynn said, "just one word, and I'll cut you in half."

No one had been looking at the coyote, where it squatted on its haunches near the arroyo wall. Anne could have sworn she *had* glanced there, just a few seconds before, seeing nothing but a coyote. Now it was Sage sitting there. And the low hum in the air still murmured on, a wind down the dusky throat of the arroyo, a wind from across unknown reaches of desert, a plaintive wind that more and more took on the quality of the husky sighing of flutes. Somehow it didn't surprise Anne that Sage was here. He had been out here all along. He had led them here.

But at this point the Hispanic woman sitting beside the Crewman got to her feet and stepped in front of the cameras.

"This man," she said, pointing to Roger Wynn, "this man and his government people murdered my father yesterday in a nursing home in Wichita Falls, Texas. My father's name was Carlos Trujillo. He was in Roswell in 1947. He knew about the flying saucer. He had a piece of it. This piece." She stooped and retrieved a plastic wrapper from the canvas bag, pulled out a large book, opened it, and took out a small strip of metal foil. "They killed him trying to get it back and keep it all quiet."

"I'll tell you the same thing I told this other traitorous bitch," Roger Wynn said, his voice low, level, frightfully devoid of emotion. He might have been ordering a pizza. "One more word, and I'll cut you in half where you stand."

Off in the shadow of the arroyo wall, Sage was getting to his feet, pushing himself up, *drawing* himself up into a stance that looked almost regal, his white hair floating around his head like an ethereal crown.

"No," the old Indian said quietly, addressing himself to Roger Wynn. "No sir, you will not."

As if in corroboration, the low hum in the air, a sighing chorus of windy flute-sounds, swelled a little in volume and became unmistakably musical now, redolent of tones strange and ancient and unplaceable. Anne saw that the news crew had noticed it too.

Roger just stared at the Indian for a moment, apparently incredulous. "And who invited *you* to the party, Geronimo? Ah, but I know who you are. You've given me a world of grief, old man, but you're not going to give me any more of it." He took a step toward the Indian.

Out of the corner of her eye Anne noticed that the Crewman had picked up one of his peculiar metal devices, one with a kind of lens in front like a camera, and seemed to be training it on Roger Wynn. The news crew had one camera on Wynn and one on the Crewman.

Roger snorted, "I've had just about enough." Taking the first step toward the old man, he kicked up a little whirl of sand. He walked toward the Indian, raising the gun as he advanced. The Indian stood his ground. On the ground behind Roger, the dust began to settle. For some reason, every tiny detail of this scene etched itself into Anne's mind in sharp, bright relief.

Then it happened.

Behind Roger, the dust that had settled began to unsettle, drifting back up into the air. Lowering his gun, Roger moved backwards, and the dust that he had scuffed up settled into its original place. "Fun-eh toub-ah ts'uj da'h vai," Roger said, and Anne was probably the only one who was equipped to realize right away that what they were all hearing was an English sentence phonetically backwards.

But now: Roger, saying "I've had just about enough," took a step toward the old Indian, kicking up a little swirl of sand and raising the gun as he advanced. The Indian stood his ground. Behind Roger, the dust began to settle. Then it began to unsettle, drifting back up into the air. Roger stepped backwards, lowering his gun, and the dust settled into its original place as Roger said, "Fun-eh toub-ah ts'uj da'h vai." And Roger, saying, "I've had just about enough," took a step toward the Indian, kicking up the sand and raising his gun as he advanced. The Indian stood his ground. Behind Roger, the dust began to settle. Then it began to unsettle, drifting back up into the air. Roger stepped back, lowering his gun and saying "Fun-eh toub-ah ts'uj da'h vai" as the dust settled into its original place.

At this point the Crewman lowered his device.

Roger stood frozen to the spot, open-mouthed like a fish. For a long while, no one moved or spoke. Besides the low windy music that ululated and hummed in the night air, the only sound was the whirring of cameras.

"Jesus," Eric whispered to Anne. "God Almighty. Can he *do* that?"

Anne, still stunned, put her hands to her face, massaging her temples. "If he did it, it means he can."

Roger was still glaring at the Indian, and hadn't spared even a glance at the Crewman or anyone else. It soon became evident that not having seen the Crewman's actions, he attributed everything to Sage.

"You're messing with my mind, old man. I don't know how you do it, but like I said, I've had enough." He raised his gun, leveling it at the Indian's face.

The Indian, who wore a little leather bag around his neck, grasped the bag in one hand and lifted the other hand in the air, gesturing toward Roger, muttering, shaping his hand into a kind of claw as if to close it around Roger's throat or heart, though Roger was several feet away. The Indian's eyes fairly glowed.

Anne saw Roger's finger actually tighten on the trigger. No doubt he planned on killing them all if he had to.

But something was happening to him.

Anne glanced sidelong at the Crewman, who this time, however, wasn't doing anything, so far as she could tell. Roger, motionless where he stood, had let his mouth gape open, and had started sucking air down his throat in abortive croaks that could only mean that he was having trouble breathing. His face, ashen now beneath its smearing of bloody dirt, was a rictus of pain and terror. He dropped the gun. The hand that had held it, trembling wildly, went to his chest, and he continued gasping for breath. At length his chest hitched convulsively, and he choked up a mouthful of blood and fell heavily on the sand, rolling onto his back, twitching his hands, opening and closing his mouth but making no articulate sound. Gradually, the twitching in his hands diminished and his mouth was still.

Anne stepped across the sand and knelt over him. She had a sense that others, behind her, were doing the same. Sage had dropped his hands to his sides, and stood motionless, watching Anne check Roger's pulse.

"Is he--" Eric started to ask.

"No," Anne said. "No, he's still alive." The man's face in the artificial light was chalky, deathlike, terrible to see.

"All right," a voice called from behind the crowd that had gathered over Roger. "Move away from him. All of you. What the hell's going on here?"

Anne straightened up and looked past the news crew (cameras still rolling) to see two men standing near the van. One of them was carrying what she hoped was only a rifle mike, and not a rifle. She had forgotten about the surveillance people back at the hill.

"I said, move away from him." The two men advanced. The one who spoke, an incongruously rather scholarly-looking man, looked familiar to Anne; she had met him at some time or other, and thought his name might be Blake. The other man, carrying the rifle mike, was someone she had never seen, so far as she could recall.

Anne, Eric, Lucy Trujillo, and the newspeople stood watching the newest arrivals. The Crewman stood off to one side. Roger Wynn lay where he had fallen, his chest heaving slightly, erratically, from time to time. The oddly musical hum in the air drifted up and down, now softer, now more insistent, now softer.

"Surveillance people probably wouldn't be armed," Anne whispered in Eric's ear. But the man who she thought was called Blake seemed pretty well to be taking charge, armed or not.

"Okay, all you people listen up. I am an agent of the United States Government. A number of federal crimes and serious breaches of security have taken place here tonight. Turn those cameras off."

The cameras kept rolling.

"I *said*--all right. You're all under arrest."

This announcement seemed to stun the whole group. Nobody spoke, nobody moved, for a long while. It was like a still photo embedded in a movie, a frozen moment in time.

At length the man operating one of the news cameras snickered. The woman carrying the floodlight looked at him incredulously, then began to grin.

Anne glanced at Eric, and he made a sound like stifled laughter, and finally laughed outright.

Then she started laughing too. Lucy Trujillo, covering her mouth at first, started laughing. Soon the whole news crew, all four of them, were laughing. From the corner of her eye, Anne could see the Crewman just standing and looking, eyes big and dark like an owl's, and something about this made her laugh even harder.

"You think this is *funny*--" Blake started to say, but Eric took a swing and decked him. Blake hit the ground like a bag of rocks, and didn't move. This was a side to Eric that Anne had never seen. Under the circumstances, she rather liked it.

"That felt good," Eric said, turning to the other surveillance man. "I think I'd like to do it some more. You want to play?"

206

The man, surrounded by derisive faces, said nothing, but his eyes said no. In any case, Lucy had poked Anne in the arm and handed her the .44 magnum that Roger Wynn had dropped. She took it and stepped up beside Eric and trained the gun on the remaining man, who made a conciliatory motion in the air with his hands. "Okay, lady. Hey, Christ, c'mon, it isn't worth it."

Obviously he thought she was going to shoot him. She loved it.

She noticed that Lucy was bending over Roger, on the sand, and she handed the gun to Eric. "Watch this asshole, will you?" That story about killing the father in the nursing home had stayed with her, even as accustomed as she had become, over the years, to rumors of such things, and she wanted to hear what Lucy was saying.

As she was stepping over there, motioning for somebody on the news crew to follow her with a camera and mike, the sensation of unplaceable sound, always seeming to ride the air just below notice, gradually began swelling into a chorus of windy tonality that made the newspeople look at each other in new astonishment. The sound was like what Anne and Eric had heard that time up on the hill, but a hundred times more--more *something*, more imbued with some mingling of qualities that seemed to play hide-and-seek with the mind when the mind tried to pin it down. It was mellow, it was lilting, it was pensive, it was lusty, it was playful, and it was impossible--a sound that came from nowhere, and everywhere, a sound that could not be, but was. It was like the sustained pedal-tones of some unthinkable organ in a cavern of dreams, like the concerted sighing of some nameless band of windblown flutes, as if a host of Kokopellis had stepped out of the very stones to fill the night with sound.

The whole desert breathed with it.

For a moment, the effect took Anne's own breath away, making her forget what she was doing. The music seemed to touch something so deep inside her being, so profound a part of her, that she felt drawn into it, made part of it. It was only with considerable effort that she redirected her attention to Lucy, who was still bending over Roger down there on the sandy floor of the arroyo. She knelt beside Lucy, and listened.

Lucy, appearing to find pathos even in this man, had cupped her hands and mounded the sand up beneath his head, making a kind of pillow. Roger, drawing what sounded like very painful breaths, looked up at her.

"Like Macbeth," he managed to say, "I have supp'd full with horrors."

Lucy dabbed at the corner of the man's mouth with her sleeve, wiping away a spume of blood. "Yes," she said, "I think you have."

He tried to say something else but choked, bringing up another bubbly froth of red. Lucy wiped his mouth again, and leaned closer to his face. Anne was vaguely aware that behind her somewhere, the cameras were still rolling.

The musical tones in the air rose to a new chorus of flute-notes, and they seemed to affect Roger where he lay. "I--oh, Jesus God, I can't stand it, I can't stand it. It sounds so sad."

"No," Lucy said, "it sounds joyous, wonderful. You hear in it what you are."

They fell silent, as the sibilant tones capered and swirled on the dry desert air. Finally Lucy spoke again.

"I want to say something else to you," she said. Roger, wincing as his chest hitched from time to time in some internal upheaval, was listening. "Do you have a family?" she asked.

"No," he said, coughing, rolling his head a little to the side.

"I just wondered," she said.

Roger had a more protracted fit of coughing, and she waited for it to subside.

"You know," she said, "my father was a good man. I wasn't the best daughter in the world, but I loved him. My mother loved him too. He wasn't perfect. He drank, he wasn't always the best father or the best husband in the world either, but we still loved him. His life had a meaning. You think he was just another dumb spic with a liver full of holes and a wandering mind, rotting away in a rest home, but let me tell you something."

Her voice started to break up here, and she paused before going on.

"He was a better man than you. Maybe he wasn't very educated, maybe he couldn't quote Shakespeare, maybe he never had a nice job or drove fancy cars, but he did more in an average hour of his life to be human than you've done since the day you were born. When he died, there were people who cared. There were people who cried. People will miss him. There's nobody for you. I just wanted you to think about that."

And to judge from the stricken expression in his muddled and wandering eyes, he *was* thinking about it, when his head lolled to one side and she got up and left him for dead.

27

Reverberations:
The Way it Should Have Ended

Contrary to Roger Wynn's predictions, they did get away with it.

Within a few minutes of Wynn's collapse, everyone except Sage--Lucy Trujillo, Anne Hawk, Eric Hayes, the Crewman, Bob Cruz, and the other three members of the news team--had piled into the news van, which bumped and jolted its way back out of the arroyo and back across the chaparral country to the road, heading, then, home to Albuquerque as fast as Bob Cruz could drive. The van, fortunately, was roomy inside, but it was still crowded under the circumstances. (There would even have been a prisoner, Blake's fellow surveillance man, to take along, had Eric not solved that problem by simply cracking the fellow a lusty blow on the head and leaving him beside Blake in the sand. He gave Blake an extra knock in the head too, just to insure a good night's sleep for all. Anne suspected him of positively enjoying this sort of thing.) Nearly everyone in the van had a lapful of camera or other hardware of one sort or another, and the Crewman, to everyone's amusement and delight, made the trip sitting on Anne Hawk's lap.

Sage stayed behind. He was at home, right where he stood, in the arroyo, in the moonlight, with a susurrant murmur of vaguely musical wind playing about him like earth-spirits.

Wynn, mortally stricken, had died about 10:45 P.M. Anne, Eric, and the others were all headed across the open plain, toward the road, by eleven. It turned out that a little after one in the morning, someone back down at Holloman Air Force Base discovered, quite by accident, that the video monitors in the Crewman's quarters were only playing an elaborate videotape of the Crewman working on circuitry. The whole installation went on alert at 1:13 A.M. At that time some diligent soul pointed out that Blake and his cohort hadn't reported back from their surveillance site, and this took on a new significance because of the Crewman's disappearance. By 2:30 A.M. the whole area around the petroglyph site at Three Rivers was swarming with military and government people, all heavily armed.

By the time they searched the hill and surrounding area and branched out to the arroyo (where they knew Varelli had died) and found Roger Wynn dead and the two other men unconscious--both had skull fractures, it turned out--the time was nearly four in the morning: about the same time the news van was rolling into the station in Albuquerque with footage that was about to make history, not to mention a few of those Pulitzer Prizes to which Eric, true to his word, had alluded.

The government tried, in a frantic and vicious last-ditch campaign, to head off what was happening, but it was too late. Within minutes of the news team's arrival back in Albuquerque, the whole story had gone to the network and the wire services. Newspapers scrambled to run special editions, and at six o'clock that morning pictures of the Crewman, of Anne, of Lucy, and of the armed and threat-dealing Roger Wynn were on the streets of every major city in the United States. Special issues of *Time* and *Newsweek* were already rolling. By mid-morning, full details of the story would be all over the world.

About the time the newspapers were hitting the streets with their curious gallery of photographs, government and military people invaded Bob Cruz's television studios, took the Crewman back into custody, and arrested everyone in sight: Lucy, Eric, Anne, Bob Cruz, his entire staff, the station manager, and a group of nuns who were coming through on a visit to see how a television station starts its operation on a typical morning. About an hour later, around seven o'clock, the President ordered them all released, and by this time had not only declassified all Roswell-related documents but ordered them published. By 10:30 that unforgettable morning, the President himself was in Albuquerque, standing in Bob Cruz's newsroom amid a cluster of armed and dark-bespectacled bodyguards and announcing to the world that several special prosecutors were being appointed.

The proverbial shit had hit the fan.

The proverbial heads were starting to roll.

The Congressional investigations and hearings would go on for many years to come.

# # # #

About a month after their experience at the arroyo, Lucy gave a little party at her house for Anne, Eric, and the news crew from Albuquerque. Bob Cruz came, but the others were off on assignment. As a surprise, Eric, during a quick trip back down to Three Rivers for a news special, had taken the time to sniff around in the desert, and had

210

been able to find Sage and persuade him to come back to Santa Fe with him. (Sage had apparently never ridden in an automobile before.) Now everyone was gathered around two bottles of wine, one white, one red, and an assortment of finger-food. Sage sat a little apart and seemed disinclined to partake of food or drink, but his face was placid, and his eyes were following the proceedings closely.

"How's it going at your bookshop?" Eric asked Lucy.

"Well, things are getting back to normal, but they made quite a mess of things there--and here," she said, indicating the room around them. "They just about tore this place to shreds looking for you-know-what." She pointed to a nearby wall, where a small strip of metal foil resided in a picture frame. "That's what I get, I guess, for being a showoff and having the only piece of alien debris in the neighborhood."

"Not the only one."

Everyone turned to look at Sage, who was lifting the leather medicine bag from around his neck and fingering it open. He fished around in it for a moment and came up with a little strip of silvery foil, which he held up for all to see.

"I'll be damned," Eric said, laughing. "How did you--"

"When great silver bird spill her insides and fall to earth, pick this up," Sage said. He curled his fist around the foil and struck his chest a blow. "Big power."

"You'd better believe it," Anne said, looking around at the rest of them. "The most powerful thing a medicine bag could hold."

"How did it happen?" Lucy asked. "I mean, our all coming together like that, almost like it was--"

"Planned?" Anne supplied. "It *was* planned."

Lucy shook her head. "I just don't understand. How much of it was Sage, and how much of it was the Crewman?"

Anne seemed to struggle with this. "I don't completely understand it either. In any case, I don't think you can entirely separate the two influences. They had a bond between them. They still have a bond between them." She looked at Sage again. "How much of it *was* your own magic?"

Putting the foil back into the medicine bag and slipping the leather thong back around his neck, the Indian was silent for a moment, then shrugged. "There is magic in all things."

Everyone was quiet then for a while. Lucy finally broke the silence. "Where is the Crewman now?"

"Oh, they've flown him back to Washington for a couple of days, Congressional hearings or something, but he's supposed to be back later in the week," Anne said.

211

Bob Cruz poured himself a little more wine. "Did you see the *Washington Post* this morning? The Pentagon is howling bloody murder about it, but the craft itself and the rest of the debris are being turned over to the Smithsonian. There's not much left of the bodies of our little friend's fellow crew members, but the remains, such as they are, will be available for private teams of scientists to examine now."

"It's about time," Eric said. "Have you all looked at the film footage of that routine the Crewman did, rewinding Roger Wynn in real time like a videotape?"

Everyone had seen it.

"Well," Anne said, "the human community isn't going to get its hands on that one for a while. The Crewman has dismantled those devices, and the matter-teleportation stuff. He tells me he just doesn't think we're ready."

"He's got *that* right," Eric said.

Anne finished off a sandwich and took a sip of wine. "I have a couple of announcements."

"Let me guess," Bob Cruz said, grinning. "They've given you your security clearance back and you're returning to government service."

"Yeah, right. Gimme a break," she said, tossing a peanut at him. "First announcement. Besides the book I'm writing on the grammar and syntax of L-1, I'm going to have plenty to do in the coming months. The University of New Mexico is planning to create a Center for Extraterrestrial Studies. I will be the director, and at first, until we can train some other people, I will teach just about all of the courses. We don't have all the details worked out yet, but I'll be offering language courses on L-1, for sure. We expect to get graduate students from a variety of fields: psychology, sociology, anthropology, comparative linguistics, information theory, semiotics, you name it."

"Is the Crewman going to be involved in the programs?" Bob Cruz asked.

"Some," Anne said. "Even without the teleportation devices and the time-rewind stuff, he's evidently got a number of things he wants to teach the circuit theory people, so there may even be a technical wing to the Center. The government will still be participating, but it's all going to be open to private research interests now too. Anyway, the Crewman will be around for a while. You should see the living quarters the University is already preparing for him. I'm not sure, though, how long we'll have him. He seems to have intimations of going back home before too long. Of course the way he measures time isn't the way we do, so I don't know--"

Cruz stopped nibbling his sandwich. "You mean they're coming for him? Coming back?"

"Apparently so, at some point," Anne said.

Everyone was quiet again. Finally Lucy said, "You promised us two announcements." She said this with a smile, as if she knew perfectly well what the other announcement was.

"I did indeed," Anne said, taking Eric's hand. "Eric and I are going to be married."

A little ripple of applause went around; even Sage nodded, and something like a ghost of a smile crossed his wizened face.

"I thought about asking the Crewman to be my best man," Eric said, "but I'm not sure the rule books would allow it."

Bob Cruz laughed and finished his wine. "I think humankind is going to have to write some new rule books."

# # # #

Shortly after his appearance at Lucy's house, Sage just vanished back into the desert.

A few years later, another of his "great silver birds" landed a little west of Belen, New Mexico. Within a few hours the Crewman had indeed left to go back home, home to the second planet in a planetary system revolving around what human astronomers know as a faint star in the constellation of Orion.

# # # #

Lucy Trujillo lived to be a very old woman, running her bookshop on Guadalupe Street in Santa Fe. She never married again. Her love was her books, her desert nights, her memories.

# # # #

Anne and Eric grew old together loving the desert too, and each other. Sometimes of an evening they would drive out into the desert and stand looking over its vastness, its serenity, like two old explorers surveying the spoils of their journeys. The sandy plains would seem to breathe forth a sage-scented breath redolent of unplaceable music, then, a dry sound vaguely like the husky sighing of some scattered multitude of nameless flutes whose elusive tones capered on the mesa tops and played among the chamisa and the mesquite bushes and fled laughing down lost shadowy reaches of arroyos in the desert night. Anne and Eric, content, would turn to go home, but would pause once more to hear what may have been the enchanted music of Kokopelli and the desert and the icy stars, or may have been just the wind.

## 28

Reverberations: The Way it Ended

They were all determined to see to it that contrary to the predictions of the fallen Roger Wynn, they *were* going to get away with it.

Everyone piled into the news van: Lucy Trujillo, Anne Hawk, Eric Hayes, the Crewman, Bob Cruz and the three other members of his news team. Everyone except Sage, who raised a hand to them in the jittery headlights as the van began to bump and jolt its way back out of the arroyo, then back across the chaparral country to the road, to head home to Albuquerque as fast as Bob Cruz could drive. One of his news crew in the front passenger seat worked on a script for the story, holding a flashlight in her mouth and scribbling in a notepad.

The back of the van was roomy inside under ordinary circumstances, but these were not ordinary circumstances, and nearly everyone had to sit with a lapful of camera or other hardware of one sort or another, and the Crewman, to everyone's amusement and delight, made the trip sitting on Anne Hawk's lap. It was just as well that they hadn't taken a prisoner, as they could have done: Blake's fellow surveillance man, whom Eric had simply leveled with a lusty blow to the head, leaving him beside Blake in the sand. Eric had given Blake an extra knock on the head too, just to insure a good night's sleep for all. Anne suspected Eric of positively enjoying this sort of thing.

Sage stayed behind. He was at home, right where he stood, in the arroyo, in the desert moonlight, with a surreal murmur of vaguely musical wind playing about him like a passing presence of earth-spirits in the night.

Lucy had left Wynn lying unmoving in the sandy bottom of the arroyo about 10:45 P.M., and they were all heading across the open plain, toward the road, by eleven. By a little after one in the morning someone back down at the secret bunker at Holloman Air Force Base would discover, quite by accident, that the video monitors in the Crewman's quarters were only playing an elaborate videotape of the Crewman working on circuitry, and the whole installation would go on alert at 1:13 A.M.

Sage, standing miles away in the moonlit arroyo, knew perfectly well that the area would soon be crawling with military people. He also knew that he would stay right where he was, or nearby, and that the military people would never see him there.

It was the privilege of a shapeshifter to go unseen.

Sure enough, when the secret installation went on alert, some diligent soul pointed out that a surveillance team had been working the Three Rivers area, and it was not long before the whole countryside around the petroglyph site was swarming with military and government people, all heavily armed. Jeeps and trucks cut swaths through the dusty chaparral, and helicopters roared overhead with searchlights that carved conical tornadoes of swirling dust in the night air.

By the time the military searched the hill and surrounding area and branched out to the arroyo, where they found Roger Wynn and the two other men lying in the sand, the news van was rolling up to the station in Albuquerque just before dawn, with footage that seemed certain to make the history books and to provide some of those Pulitzer Prizes to which Eric, true to his word about the importance of the events, had alluded. By the time the film footage of the Crewman, of Anne, of Lucy, and of the armed and threat-dealing Roger Wynn were on the air, special editions of newspapers would surely be rolling, special issues of *Time* and *Newsweek* would surely be hitting the stands in every community in the United States, and it would be too damned late for the government, try whatever frantic and desperate and vicious last-ditch garbage they might--too late for them to keep the secret. The Roswell coverup would be over. By mid-morning, full details of the story from Three Rivers would be all over the world.

It was these thoughts that drove an exhausted but excited little band of adventurers up the steps and into the studio, and within minutes Bob Cruz had distributed his staff among the camera and control room positions the best he could and was settling himself at the news anchor desk, getting ready to go on the air. Lucy, Anne, Eric, and the Crewman watched from the sides as the cameras dollied into position and tilted their ponderous heads toward Bob Cruz, who asked: "Everybody ready?"

The from the control room response was quick. "Lisa's got the script in the prompter, and we're ready up here when you are."

"Well all right," Cruz said. "What do you say, let's get that goddamn Godzilla movie off the air and kick some ass."

215

The cameraman was about to give him the high-sign when the studio doors opened from the hall, and a group of nuns came in.

Cruz looked astonished. It took him a moment to regain his composure. "Ah--what can we, ah--?"

One of their number stepped forward, smiling. "Your station manager Mr. Jackson invited us to come by for a tour this morning, to see how a television station starts its operations on a typical day."

Cruz shook his head, laughing lightheartedly. "Well, sisters, I can't promise this is going to be typical. But it is going to be interesting. You're going to see history made here today, unless I'm much mistaken." He looked to the control room window. "Let's do it."

The cameras were rolling.

"We interrupt your early-morning movie for a news announcement of great importance. A few hours ago, in the desert near Three Rivers, New Mexico--"

# # # #

At a top-secret communications monitoring center, far underground at a location unknown to almost everyone not actually working there, a tall and distinguished-looking black man named Louis Gardner stood at his command post, from which there stretched away into the distance, in all directions, rows of monitor positions at which people in headphones watched computer display screens. In the wan light of these screens, the whole scene looked surreal, eerie. Unless one was used to it.

An army major came running up to Gardner.

"Sir, Station 7 at Holloman is on alert. The Crewman is missing."

Gardner eyed him incredulously. "Missing? *Missing?* Shit." He flipped a mike switch and hit the public address system. "All right, listen up, everybody. There's an alert on. Probability is high in New Mexico and adjoining states. Be on your toes. Let's shine, now."

A sort of rippled murmur went through the vast room, but at all the monitor positions, then, heads were bent to the task at hand. Rule number one was: not a syllable of classified information must be allowed to go out on the air. Ever. It was a matter of national security, after all.

# # # #

In the desert near Three Rivers, the military people were finishing their operations. Army-green trucks grumbled their way along the desert plain, choppers buzzed in the air somewhere like great angry insects. Off in the night a coyote stood on the edge of an arroyo wall, watching the scene in the distance, where three men were being carried on stretchers to a waiting vehicle. One of the men was Roger Wynn. It would not ordinarily have been possible to tell, from this far away, by sight alone, but the coyote knew very well that Roger Wynn, though gravely injured, was alive.

An observer near the coyote might have noticed that around the animal's neck hung a small leather pouch. An observer sufficiently familiar with life in the desert might also have recognized it for a Native American medicine bag. If that observer had looked away for a few seconds, into the surrounding night, and then looked back, there would have been no coyote. In its place, the observer would have found Sage, alert, unmoving, his white hair blowing about his ancient head like a wreath of dream.

The old Indian fingered the medicine bag around his neck, worked it slightly open, and pulled out a small strip of metal foil, which he rolled thoughtfully in his fingers. Around him, from the desert plain, the windy suggestion of music rose like the enchanted breath of husky flutes.

# # # #

Some switches were thrown, and up the line certain relays clicked in instant response. Circuits opened; other circuits closed.

An army master sergeant, operating a console near where Louis Gardner was standing, motioned for Gardner to come over and see what was happening.

"Station in Albuquerque, sir. I'm already diverting it to off-air and taping it. Jones is looping the tape back and checking it, but we're sure nothing got out."

"Yeah, well," Gardner said, "it better not have, you know what I'm saying?"

On the sergeant's glowing monitor, a tiny Bob Cruz was talking.

"--government coverup that has been going on for half a century. But this morning in the desert we recorded the following remarkable statements. First, a woman named Lucy Trujillo--"

"Ah, sir," the sergeant said, "viewers've got blank air. We ought to patch something in."

Gardner nodded impatiently, first snapping his fingers to call over a military liaison officer. He pointed to the face on the sergeant's console.

"I want combat-ready military force on this site in three minutes. Kirtland. Priority One."

The liaison officer snapped to. "Yes sir."

On the little monitor screen now, Lucy Trujillo was pointing out a livid and beaten-up-looking Roger Wynn for the cameras. "This man and his government people murdered my father--"

Gardner leaned across the master sergeant's console, selected an icon on the computer screen, and flipped a few switches.

217

"Okay, Lucy, my foxy little lady, you want to be on TV? Well, I'm sorry, we can't quite do that, but we *can* give the people some Lucy."

# # # #

In a bedroom somewhere, a young man and woman were lying in bed watching an early-morning Godzilla movie on television. Suddenly the movie cut off and a face appeared on the screen, talking fast and excitedly.

"We interrupt your early morning movie for a news announcement of great importance. A few hours ago, in the desert near Three Rivers, New Mexico, our news team came upon--"

Then the picture vanished completely, leaving only dead air. The screen remained blank for perhaps a minute, then the picture returned.

It was a rerun of *I Love Lucy*.

"So," the man in the bed said, "what the fuck happened to Godzilla?"

# # # #

Bob Cruz at his news desk was talking a mile a minute.

"--amounts to the most extensive government coverup in the history of humankind. Our historic film footage, of the remarkable alien creature called the Crewman, and of human witnesses who have been profoundly affected by these events, constitutes positive proof that the--"

"Hey Bob." It was someone in the control room. Cruz kept talking. "Bob! Hold up. Something's happened. We're not on."

Cruz frowned. "What the hell do you mean we're not--"

And the studio doors crashed open, scattering the onlooking group of nuns, and a squad of military personnel entered, led by a boyish-looking lieutenant.

"Listen up," the lieutenant said. "My orders are to take you all into custody. Line up along the wall here. Right now." He turned to his men. "Jenkins. McLaughlin. Weinberg. Search the building, bring anybody else you find down here. Doubletime!"

The military people rounded everyone up, pausing only to stare in disbelief at the Crewman. One young soldier said, in a hoarse and audible whisper, to another soldier next to him: "Jesus, what is this, some kind of goddamn freak show?"

The lieutenant clapped his hands for attention. "Can the chatter. Sergeant! Let's move 'em out."

They herded everyone along--Anne, Eric, Lucy, the Crewman, Bob Cruz, all the station personnel, even the fretting and bewildered nuns. For a moment Anne and Eric tried to hold each other, but a soldier pushed them apart. The soldiers moved everyone toward the door. Outside, military vehicles were waiting in the gray light of dawn.

In this cheerless half-light, the Crewman's face was, as always, inscrutable. Lucy's face, Eric's and Anne's faces were masks of disappointment, of fear.

Of doom.

# # # #

Louis Gardner was still at his post, looking fairly pleased with the way things had gone, though the lines around his eyes revealed a residuum of concern. A civilian stepped up to speak with him.

"Sir, shall we inform the President?"

Gardner took a deep breath, and thought for a moment. Then he said: "No. Not now. Everything's under control." He paused, looking off into space. "All's well that ends well."

# # # #

At the edge of the arroyo stood a coyote, its head erect, its eyes dark and intelligent, its neck encircled by a leather thong on which hung a medicine bag.

Suddenly the coyote threw back its head and howled.

# # # #

On the street in Albuquerque, in front of the television station, the Crewman, in line with the others, paused before stepping into the waiting vehicle. Paused, cocked his head, and blinked his large dark eyes once, twice, as if listening. Then he moved on.

# # # #

Untold miles away, in the secret communications center, Louis Gardner, standing at his post with a clipboard in one hand and a ballpoint pen in the other, paused in his deliberations. Paused, cocked his head, listened. Something--he couldn't have said what--something had obtruded upon his consciousness faintly, subtly, for just a moment, then had passed. He shrugged, and drew his attention back to his clipboard.

# # # #

At the arroyo in the New Mexico desert, the coyote was howling, flinging his ululant cry into the bone-white face of the setting moon. The howl echoed down the labyrinthine reaches of the arroyo, whirled around obscure corners, blended itself with flute-notes, cavorted with the sighing wind.

It was a cry of anguish.

But it was also a cry of freedom. And of hope.

About the Author

DONALD R. BURLESON's fiction has appeared in *Twilight Zone*, *The Magazine of Fantasy and Science Fiction*, *2AM*, *Deathrealm*, *Terminal Fright*, *Potpourri*, and many other magazines, as well as in major anthologies including *Post Mortem* (St. Martin's Press/Dell), *MetaHorror* (Dell), *Best New Horror* (Robinson/Carroll & Graf), *Made in Goatswood* (Chaosium), and the Barnes and Noble anthologies *100 Ghastly Little Ghost Stories*, *100 Creepy Little Creature Stories*, *100 Vicious Little Vampire Stories*, *100 Wicked Little Witch Stories*, and *100 Tiny Tales of Terror*. Burleson's collections of short stories include *Lemon Drops and Other Horrors* (Hobgoblin Press), *Four Shadowings* (Necronomicon Press), and *Beyond the Lamplight* (Jack-O'Lantern Press). He and his wife Mollie (herself a fiction writer) met at a horror convention in Providence, Rhode Island in 1979 because of their common interest in New England writer H. P. Lovecraft; they were married in 1982. In July 1996 they moved from Merrimack, New Hampshire to Roswell, New Mexico.

Photo by Mollie L. Burleson